GLASS DOLLS

An addictive crime thriller with a fiendish twist

D.E. WHITE

JOFFE
BOOKS

First published 2020
Joffe Books, London
www.joffebooks.com

**Please join our mailing list for free Kindle books and
new releases.**

www.joffebooks.com

ISBN 978-1-78931-352-9

"Where have all the pretty girls gone?"
In a mind where perfection is everything,
he has his eye on the ultimate prize.

You.

PROLOGUE

I wonder when she knew.

When did she realize she wasn't going to get out alive, that this was her last mistake? Was it when he spoke, or was there some evil in his eyes that made her turn and run, slipping in her polished brown boots, dark hair blowing in the icy wind? Maybe she really didn't know until his hands fastened around her throat. I hope she didn't.

In my imagination, there was blood on the snow and dirt on her face, but she kept on fighting. I know she would have struggled until her last breath, because that's just how she was.

I hope she never knew it was my fault . . .

CHAPTER ONE

His breath was hot and sour on her cheek. She flinched as the chisel touched her arm, cold metal meeting warm skin. The blade slid up to her shoulder.

"You screwed up. I've been watching you for a while now, and I know you aren't who you say you are." He studied her face, his blank brown eyes showing no hint of feeling, no emotion. "So the question is, who the hell are you?"

She said nothing, feeling the chisel run back down her arm, trying to control her shaking body. The wires that bound her hands and feet were tied tightly to a metal beam, which formed part of the warehouse.

He shrugged and went back to his work, while she sagged with relief. Surely by now they would be on their way to rescue her. She had done everything right, followed the protocol. Almost everything.

The *chip* of the stonemason's chisel filled her ears, the smell and taste of dust and marble. And blood. Her face was bleeding from where he'd hit her and her lip cracked. Only the pain from her injuries and the cramping of her muscles, forced and tied into standing position for hours, kept her from dropping into unconsciousness.

After a while he came back, walking carefully around the neat piles of gravestones and memorial plaques, his boots thudding softly on the concrete.

She held her breath. There were no words. It had all been said. This was the endgame. He knew who she was and he knew that she knew.

"You're getting boring," he told her, his voice steady.

He struck swiftly, unexpectedly, with the chisel. She felt it as the weapon struck deep in her abdomen. The agony, the fierce heat searing her lower body made her scream.

She was dimly aware of sirens, shouts and running feet. They were coming, but it was too late. Her blood, dark and sticky, soaked her body, her legs, splashing on the floor.

"Isn't it ironic? I don't want children and you can't have them. Funny how things turn out . . ."

* * *

Dove pushed the nightmare away. The morning light was struggling through the darkness. Without giving herself time to think, she pushed her sweaty sheets away and threw on some clothes.

The rangy grey cat coiled neatly at the end of her bed watched her as she ran out of the room, still shaking, one hand unconsciously pressed over her scar.

The sea was icy, the early morning mist enclosing her body in freezing fingers, but gradually, the rhythm of the waves, the solitude and freedom helped the memories to recede.

Finally she dragged her wetsuit off, towelled her cold, salty body, and re-dressed. Chucking her board on the roof rack, she started the short drive home. Only now, returning from the half-world of tangled dreams and horrors, did she think to check her phone.

No calls, thank God. Her breathing slowed, her heartbeat calmed and the pleasant feeling of tiredness crept into her muscles as she drove the short distance home.

As usual after being out on the waves, her senses were filled with the sea, but her mind was still stubbornly cluttered with ghosts. Her therapist said she was holding on to the past, which seemed so unlikely Dove had almost laughed in her face.

The phone rang as she fumbled with the front door keys, making her jump. Swearing, struggling to answer it and keep hold of everything, she dropped her bag and surfboard on the path. "DC Dove Milson."

"You need to get over here now, we've got a body. The text alert's gone out, but I thought I'd ring you as well. It's a bit of a weird one."

DS Steve Parker was her partner. From what she had seen in the first couple of months working together, he was solid. The new DI, Jon Blackman, had done well, putting them together. Like her, Blackman had recently transferred from another unit. It was strange being a "newbie" again, fighting for inclusion, regarded with suspicion by the close-knit team.

"I haven't got the text yet . . . Anyway, clarify '*weird*' for me, Steve." She made it through the door one-handed, phone wedged between shoulder and ear, nearly falling over the cat.

She chucked her surfboard and wetsuit on the hall floor, making a mental note to rinse it out later. Then grabbed her work bag and retraced her steps to the car, slamming the door behind her. Her long, coarse black hair was still damp and she could taste the salt on her lips, could feel it itching on her skin. No matter, this was what she had been waiting for. Being on call meant she had been checking her phone day and night, waiting for the alert that would bring the Major Crimes Team together.

"Dove, are you still there?"

"Yeah, sorry, on my way. Go on about the scene . . ."

"Gibbons Copse, off the North Shore Road. Victim is female. Probably late teens. A dog walker called it in. She's . . . Fuck, I've never seen anything like this up close,

4

but it reminds me of another case." He paused. "The body is encased in glass. Like a bloody statue but with a human inside it. Ring any bells?"

"Bloody hell! I'll be with you in ten." Dove's heart rate accelerated again, and she ran a shaky hand through her hair. It felt like she had been punched in the gut. *I needed them to be perfect.* His voice rang out inside her head. How was that even possible? Was he coming at her from beyond the grave?

She ordered the memories and the ghosts away. Her first big case with the MCT: she needed to keep her head together, to prove she still had what it took. It was just bloody typical that this clearly wasn't your usual homicide.

North Shore Road was clear and she drove fast through the light drizzle, biting her lip as she always did when she was thinking hard. A quick glance in the driver's mirror showed her dark eyes were bright with anticipation. And fear. Definitely fear, but what were the chances of it happening again? Her lashes were still salty and her thick black rope of hair hung over one shoulder, making her T-shirt damp. Not the best look, but she wasn't wasting any time on this one. At least her trousers were black and could pass for casual office wear at a glance. Why the fuck was she worrying about her clothes? Her brain buzzed with possibilities as she drove, and despite her best efforts, memories slipped tiny fingers of horror around the darkest corners of her mind.

* * *

Dove grabbed her coat, slammed the car door, and walked quickly up the wide track that led to Gibbons Copse. It was a favourite with dog walkers and runners. She and her boyfriend, Quinn, had been up here hiking across the hills a few weeks ago, and it was a picturesque area. But now the scenic innocence of spring growth was tainted by death.

Had he been working with someone who had been overlooked last time? Surely that wasn't possible, and besides, why would they choose to start killing again now?

The body was situated about fifty yards from the road, deep inside the small wood that made up Gibbons Copse. The team were already busy organizing the scene. A redundant ambulance stood at the edge of the road, blue lights flashing through the fog.

She ducked under the tape that sealed off the scene, introducing herself to a uniformed officer as she made her way towards DS Steve Parker.

"She's over there. No attempt to hide her. There is usually a lot of traffic along this path, so we're assuming at the moment the body was dumped late last night or early this morning, or it would have caught someone's eye." Steve looked grim, but managed a quick smile as he passed a coffee cup filled with steaming liquid. "CSM is Jess Meadows. Her team have just started arriving, and the DI is on his way over. He'll be a bit longer because he was up in Kent for a conference."

"Morning, Jess," Dove called over to the petite blonde woman, but her mind was elsewhere. She couldn't take her eyes off the body, her hands shaking even as they wrapped around the warm cup. It had to be a copycat. There was no way it could be anything else . . .

Jess waved a welcome in Dove's direction. She was suited and booted in white plastic, issuing instructions to her team, who moved smoothly into action, each with their own individual job to complete. A couple of officers were carefully stretching a tent over the scene around the glass case, as the light patter of raindrops filtered through the tree cover. Vehicles were parked either at the roadside, or in the case of Jess's van, pulled to the far side of the crime scene, away from any possible evidence.

The body lay at the heart of the copse in a little dell between two towering oaks. Bluebells and milkwort stretched a vibrant carpet across the whole copse, and the vivid greens of spring made a striking backdrop for the victim.

Dove gulped her coffee, pretending she was just letting the team get to work, before she too booted up. It would be professional suicide to let anyone see her freeze up. Jess was already shooting her worried glances.

Forcing her body into motion, one step after another, she approached the scene. Being professional would see her through this. They were all watching her, waiting for her to prove her worth.

Or maybe they weren't, perhaps it was her own paranoia making her feel the burn of so many eyes. Her photographic memory was both a blessing and a curse. Often it felt as though she had a kind of old-fashioned ticker tape streaming through her mind, analysing and comparing as her mind dismissed possibilities. Details of the previous Glass Doll murders were rocketing through her brain, the echoes of his voice locked inside her head forever. But he was dead. It was over.

The victim, clearly visible through the glass casing, looked to be in her late teens. Her blonde hair was arranged into two bunches fastened with pink ribbons, cascading down over her shoulders. She was slim, naked, and her blue eyes were wide and staring. The glass that encased her was fairly thick and highly polished. *Pristine*. The word popped out from memory and she knew that was how he had liked them.

The glass case looked to be joined like two halves of an Easter egg, the seal neat and professional. Again, a hallmark of the previous murders. It must weigh a ton, and yet somehow somebody had got it up the hill. A lone killer, or was this the work of several perpetrators?

"Sick, isn't it? Just like the Hayworth victims, if I remember rightly." Steve was at her shoulder, frowning. His curly brown hair was slick with rain, his hazel eyes sombre above a thin, slightly hooked nose.

Dove pushed her hair back. Damp tendrils had escaped, framing her face. "Do we know who she is yet?"

It felt as if she wasn't really present, just watching herself go through the motions, when all the time her stomach churned with horror. Her worst nightmares had nothing on this.

7

"Still checking. That glass case must weigh a fair bit, and to get it up here from the road would be a long haul . . ." Steve glanced back along the track, echoing her thoughts. "Not sure how we're going to get through that glass without shattering it and wrecking any evidence that might be waiting for us, but that'll be a job for the pathologist to figure out."

Dove was still looking at the girl, doing a quick head-to-toe. She didn't seem to have any obvious injuries on her body. No bruising or blood. No burns to indicate she had been present when the glass was moulded around her body. Dove recalled reading the process from the previous murder cases, and discovered time hadn't made it any less horrific.

"I suppose the pathologist will have to get specialists in. I believe that's how they handled it last time. Can you see anything on her arm?" She crouched and leaned forward, peering through the glass.

"Looks like needle marks and some faint bruising." Steve squinted, adjusting his glasses. "Hard to be sure until we get her out of this thing."

More of Jess's team had arrived and white-suited figures were moving quickly and carefully around the scene. A woman crouched next to Dove, photographing the body, while another took measurements. Three men were spreading out for a fingertip search of the surrounding vegetation.

Dove moved back towards a tree, and Jess joined her, her expression concerned.

"You all right?"

"Of course." She didn't mean to snap, but she was terrified of letting her emotions show. It would ruin everything, and she would be taken off the case before she'd even started. As a close friend, Jess knew about Eden. Dove prayed she wouldn't mention it, not here.

Jess nodded, lips pursed, considering her. Eventually she said, "This scene is going to be a bitch to process. Not only is the body behind glass, but the rain is on its way." She lifted a gloved hand, palm up, and frowned at the massing grey clouds.

"Might be some fingerprints on the glass," Dove suggested. "Any immediate thoughts?" It was always useful to get everyone's first take on a scene and she valued Jess's professional opinion. The woman was meticulous and she never seemed to get flustered.

"I know what everyone's thinking. It stands out a mile that this is another Glass Doll murder, but all that was back in 2014. Peter Hayworth didn't serve much of his sentence, did he, because he had a terminal illness? He died in Wandsworth and there was no family left," Jess said, her blue eyes fixed on Dove's face.

"2016," Dove supplied, pushing down a wave of nausea that threatened to derail her.

"Yeah, I guess everyone who sees this is going to dig Hayworth right back up. We've got ourselves a sick copycat for sure." Steve had re-joined them, and was taking careful notes.

"I'm going to have a quick look around while we wait for the DI, and I want to talk to the dog walker who found our body too. Is that her over there?" Dove could see a woman in running gear sitting on a fallen log, with a red setter leashed next to her and a police officer standing at her side.

"Yes, it is," Steve told her.

She made her way quickly across the wet grass and smiled as she made eye contact with the woman.

As Dove approached, the police officer made hasty introductions. "Victoria, this is DC Milson. She just needs to ask you a few questions. This is Victoria Carter."

"I don't know what else I can tell you." Victoria had short brown hair, half-hidden under a Nike headband. She was tall and athletic, but her face was pale and she shivered despite a thick blanket that was wrapped around her shoulders.

"I know you've already spoken to the police officer, but I hope you don't mind if I ask you to run through this again. Nice dog. What's his name?" Dove rubbed a hand over the dog's head and his tail wagged. Out the corner of her eye, she noted that DI Blackman had finally arrived, and was walking quickly up to the wood.

"Bailey." The woman fussed over the dog, hugging him to her.

Dove was pleased to find that, although she was understandably shaken, Victoria was able to answer questions coherently. Anything she said could be of massive importance to the case. Their priority would be to follow leads and collate evidence to find the perpetrator as quickly as possible. As a significant witness, Victoria could make the difference between a positive or negative result.

"I left home at about six this morning." Her voice had a soft Irish twang. Her hands were shaking as she petted the dog, and she stopped and cleared her throat a couple of times. "I'm sorry. I'm going to see that poor girl in my nightmares. She was just staring . . ."

"Is that your red BMW in the road?"

"Yes. We got here about half six, and I let Bailey straight off, adjusted my watch and started up the track. I actually ran right through the copse to the stile before I realized Bailey wasn't with me. Sometimes he'll go off after rabbits, so I wasn't too bothered. He always catches up. I called, and then waited . . . That was when I heard him barking. I still thought it was a rabbit or something, but I could tell something was wrong. He sounded scared, and he still wouldn't come, so I ran back . . ." Victoria paused to take a deep breath, then she cleared her throat again.

"Take your time," Dove told her, stroking the dog's ears.

"Well, when you look that way, you can't miss it, can you? I saw . . . I saw her right away in the flowers. Bailey was barking and barking. He didn't want me to go near. At first I thought, and I know it sounds crazy, but I thought it wasn't real, like a theatre prop or something. I work in Abberley Road Theatre, so it was just the first thing I thought of."

"And then?"

"I put out a hand to touch the glass, just to check I wasn't going mad. When I realized it was a real dead girl,

I put Bailey on his leash, ran straight back to the road and called 999. I waited in my car until your officers arrived."

"Did you hear or see anything unusual when you arrived today? Any other walkers, runners or vehicles?"

She was shaking her head. "Nothing. It was unusually quiet, but then I put that down to the weather."

"Okay. Which way did you come? Along North Shore Road from where?" Dove asked.

"Abberley. I live near the river in one of the new apartments. Riverside Drive."

In her head, Dove tracked the route the woman must have driven. "Did you notice any traffic pass you when you came off at the traffic lights? Anything going in the opposite direction that you noticed in particular?"

Victoria was trying to be helpful, but Dove could tell she was struggling now. "Sorry, I can't remember anything. Maybe a couple of cars, but I couldn't even tell you what colour they were."

"That's fine. Thank you. I'll leave you with PC Ellis, but if you do remember anything else, here's my card."

Victoria tried to smile, but her face was pinched and drawn. "Thanks. You know what did strike me? That poor girl in there, she looks like a little doll, so perfect and almost still alive . . . That's what will haunt me. I remember reading about Peter Hayworth. There was a documentary, too, quite recently, I saw that . . . She would have been still alive, wouldn't she, when he put her in there?"

CHAPTER TWO

Dove chose not to answer, but thanked her again, turning away to greet the DI. It had been a hallmark of Peter Hayworth's Glass Doll murders, the fact that each victim had been carefully displayed, with no signs of violence to the body. He had encased them in glass and watched their last, terrified breaths. *Perfect.*

"Hey, boss, I'm just going to have another chat with Jess and then get back to the station," Dove said briskly.

"DC Milson, give me a quick update on the scene." He was probably no more than a couple of years older than her, but his sombre, slightly awkward attitude aged him. His dark hair was shaved close to his head, accentuating his facial bone structure, his square chin and his grey eyes.

Dove responded, giving a rundown of the team members present, the activity ongoing. A worm of worry squirmed inside her stomach, as his eyes flickered over her. Hopefully he wasn't going to comment on her clothing.

"At this stage it looks like a pretty identical MO to the Hayworth murders," she concluded.

He nodded slowly, scanning the area. "We'll get the scene processed as soon as possible. I want to know who she is, when she was killed and everything in between. I need DS Parker up here for at least another hour, as we're short-handed, but you can get back to the station as you've already spoken to the witness. Start looking for an ID on our victim; we'll get the briefing done as soon as we can pull everything together." His expression was cool, analysing her responses, as though he was watching for any weakness. "The press are going to be crawling all over this so I want a quick result. For as long as we can, we need to keep a lid on the fact the victim is in a glass case."

Did he know, or was she being paranoid again? This was not a man who would take his team down the pub after a good result, Dove thought, feeling a flicker of nostalgia at the thought of her previous team. But then keeping things professional was another of Dove's recent promises to herself, and maybe distance was best.

* * *

Mindful of the lightning speed of this kind of news, Dove dithered over calling her sister. Officially, she really shouldn't, but the press were sure to find out and, as DI Blackman had said, they would be crawling all over this sensational murder. It was her old battle of family versus job, but she had vowed to put family first.

She would never forgive herself if Ren found out from the news. If she was the one to break it to her, perhaps she might be able to prevent the downward spiral that would surely come. It was a compromise of sorts, she told herself. Professionalism fighting a losing battle with her heart again.

She called her sister as soon as she left the scene. "Ren, are you in the shop today?"

"Of course. Why?"

"We need to talk later. I'll come over. About eight?"

"Shit. I'm not going to like this, am I?" There was fear in Ren's voice, and Dove felt her chest constrict in sympathy. "Is it Eden?"

"No. Sorry, I should have said that straight away. Can't talk now, but I'll see you later."

Dove pulled into the police station, four storeys of grim concrete and lines of squad cars decorating the car park. There would be a briefing as soon as the team had finished with the scene. Already, the machinery had kicked into action, with officers from various specialized teams deployed, and she needed to be part of it, stepping up, proving her worth, however much the case was affecting her.

The office space was buzzing with activity. The house-to-house teams would be busy knocking on doors, while the specialist search team continued their fingertip search of the immediate scene. The information would be fed back to HQ and officers dispatched after the briefing to follow up leads, and hopefully make arrests. This was the Golden Time, the hours immediately after the discovery of a body, and everyone was working at maximum capacity.

Dove took a message from Jess saying she had called the mortuary and made sure the specialist pathologist was booked. She'd made him aware that professional assistance would be needed for the glass casing.

Biting her lip, Dove pulled up notes on HOLMES. The IT system was an absolute blessing and made the investigation of serious incidents, particularly serial murders, far easier. She skimmed information relating to the previous Glass Doll murders, double-checking who the main players had been, although she knew them by heart already — the senior investigating officer, the pathologist, the DCI, all people who might be able to give them a head start in catching the killer this time. The problem, of course, was that the infamous Glass Doll killer had already been caught and convicted, and was now deceased.

She typed the search criteria into the Local Missing Persons Database, studying the possible candidates. Nothing was jumping out. It always astonished her that so many people of all ages went missing and were simply never found. Some wouldn't want to be found, of course, but others had families who were desperate for any news, good or bad. Like Ren and Alex.

A large team had assembled by the time DI Blackman returned from the scene. Some thirty officers called in by the alert were waiting for the official handover and duties to be assigned. Steve and Dove were to carry on searching for the victim's identity. Jess and her team would continue to process the evidence drawn from the scene, feeding back anything that was discovered. Having nothing that could be seen by the naked eye meant they might have to rely on forensic evidence, which could be plentiful — or practically non-existent.

DI Blackman, as the senior investigating officer, took the lead, although Dove could see DCI Franklin in the corner of the room, leaning against the wall, arms folded, sharp blue gaze missing nothing. The DI kept the brief short and sharp, collating and relaying facts, checking that all duties were understood. Each member of the team had a vital role to play. Mistakes happened when people weren't clear on what they needed to do.

DI Blackman wrapped it up after twenty minutes, ordering them back to the station for the changeover brief at eight, after which the night shift would take over. So far, no witnesses apart from the dog walker, Victoria, had come forward. The body in its glass casing was on its way to the mortuary pending the autopsy.

Dove, with the memory of the victim fresh in her mind, plunged back into information gathering. An hour later, one of the enquiry team called in a possible sighting of a dark blue Ford Transit van parked at the side of the road near Gibbons Copse. By six thirty that evening, they'd had two more reported sightings of the van in the area in early morning, plus some CCTV footage of its route. But the footage was grainy and difficult to clean up.

"Looks like just the one person in the front." Steve was screwing his eyes up in an effort to make out the blurred figure. He took his glasses off and gave them a quick wipe. "The number plate is obscured, but I think there's some kind of logo on the side doors?"

Dove thought so too. "Maybe a square and a couple of letters. We're not going to get it better than this. It was cleaned up before it was sent over. Shit! Although if he took the trouble to obscure the number plate, he must have been pretty confident the logo wouldn't matter, or that would have been taped or painted over, surely."

"Not sure how much weight a van like that could take . . . I'll get on to the manufacturers."

"Okay, I'll check for anything stolen that fits the description, and ring round the local dealers," Dove said, still staring at the footage. "With a bit of luck we might get something better, and then we can identify that logo."

Dove wasn't seeing the blue van now, she was visualizing the blank blue stare, the blonde bunches. Who was she and where had she been? Had she known her killer?

DI Blackman, as tall and lean as a long-distance runner, was moving around the room, checking in on everyone, and when he leaned over her work station she caught the smell of his aftershave. It was sharp and peppery, but not unpleasant. He glanced at the computer screen, then told her she would be accompanying him to the autopsy the next morning.

Surprised and gratified, Dove caught a few jealous glances, but mentally congratulated herself for dropping everything and heading straight to the scene. She had inserted herself into the heart of the investigation, and that was exactly where she needed to be.

As the evening drew in, they still didn't have a name for the victim. The on-call team, DI Lincoln and his four officers, listened intently to the changeover brief, ready to delve into the mountains of information that would continue to pour in late into the night.

* * *

Dove drove fast across town, parking opposite the chemist, taking a moment to collect her thoughts. The media had already started making enquiries via the press officer, and it wouldn't be long before news broke that this was another Glass Doll murder. It would only take a witness who talked to her family, or a first responder, trying to lay the trauma of discovery to bed, who confided in a friend. Like Chinese whispers, the threads would spread until the whole thing went viral.

This certainly wasn't protocol, but her heart would never allow her sister to discover the murder any other way. This was personal, adding another layer of complexity to her job and tearing her in two. It was a sickeningly familiar feeling, and made a hundred times worse as her phone screen flashed with texts from her boyfriend and from Jess. Quinn would be supportive, she knew, but also afraid that she might lapse back into her previous workaholic persona. It had nearly cost her their relationship last time.

Ren was waiting by the door, her pretty, round face anxious.

"Let's go out the back."

Although the shop was now closed, luscious scents of coffee, cake and sweets filled the rooms, and the low hum of the radio followed the sisters out into the back premises.

On the desk in her office were two cups of coffee and two slices of her own chocolate mud cake. For some reason the sight brought tears to Dove's eyes. Typical Ren, she thought, smiling a bit stiffly at her sister. Normally Ren was the one she got on best with, and they could talk about anything, but now, what might happen? Now that past nightmares were being relived, who could she rely on to be strong?

"Why didn't you just come round to the house?" Ren asked. "Doesn't matter because I had some extra baking to do for tomorrow, but even so . . . " Her black curls were tied back with a red scarf, and her face was flushed from the heat of the kitchen.

Dove cleared her throat. "Sorry to freak you out on the phone, but I needed to tell you before the media get hold of it." She described the happenings of the day.

"You look like you've been out on the beach. I thought you'd had a day off," was all Ren said at first, taking in her sister's outfit. She sipped her drink carefully, but her body was rigid, shaking slightly with the effort to remain calm.

"Not a proper day off, I was still on call."

"But the dead girl wasn't Eden, was she?" Ren could say her daughter's name now, but her voice was flat with pain.

"No." Dove wanted to say more, but she was aware that whatever she said could never be enough to help her sister, whose eldest daughter was always on her mind. Some wounds never heal. To Ren, who kept a gallery of photos, her daughter would never age. Eden would be eighteen years old forever. Never mind that four years had passed since her death.

"But this is just like him, isn't it? Putting the girls in glass like a fucking sarcophagus, leaving them out for people to find." Ren's anger flared briefly on her face. "Except he never left Eden. He just killed her and abandoned her. Almost all the others, they had a body, but he never told me where he left her, what he did with her . . ." She was crying properly now.

"Oh, Ren, I'm so sorry." Dove moved across to her sister, leaning in to give her an awkward hug. Of the three sisters, Ren was the tactile hugger, whereas Dove often shrank from physical contact, even with her family. "I thought you should know first."

"Do you know who she is, this poor girl?" Ren's voice was unsteady, clogged with tears.

"No, not yet. That's one of the reasons I've got to dash."

"But that bastard *is* dead, isn't he?"

"Yes, you know he is, Ren."

"So who the fuck could be doing this?"

"Oh, Ren, I'm sorry . . ." The frustration at not being able to fix things, to make it right, bubbled in Dove's chest. She drew back, giving her sister's hand a squeeze.

Her sister wiped her face and blew her nose. "I'm fine. Thanks for telling me, but it's just, you know, it's just brought it all back. You know, I didn't think you'd change, but I can see how you shouldn't even be here tonight, and I love you for it. It was a brave move. Can I tell Alex?"

Dove shrugged, blinking back tears again. "Technically no, because I shouldn't have told you. Alex is away with Delta at the swim camp tonight, isn't he?"

Ren nodded. "He's helping out with some of the other parents."

"So wait until the morning. Everyone will find out when the news story breaks tomorrow anyway. There will be a press release going out and it won't matter then. Do you want *me* to tell Alex, or Delta?" Alex was her brother-in-law. He ran a market stall selling antiques down in Church Square. Their remaining daughter, eighteen-year-old Delta, helped out when she wasn't at college.

"No . . . Oh, God, I don't know." Ren wiped her eyes and gulped the last of her coffee. "No, it's okay, I'll do it."

Dove's phone buzzed with a message, and she glanced down automatically, heart beating faster. But it wasn't work-related, it was Quinn asking if she had finished work for the evening. She squeezed her sister's hand across the table, and tapped out a quick text to her boyfriend before she answered her sister. "Got to go now, but ring me in the night if you need me, okay?"

Ren was staring blankly at the wall, and she spoke without turning away, her eyes glassy and unfocused. "Alex said at the time, if we could just have a body. You know, if we get nothing else, he said, we need her body . . . We knew after the first night she wasn't going to come back alive. Not with that bastard out there hunting."

CHAPTER THREE

I've laid my traps, I'm waiting for my prey to take the bait. It's funny: they would say it's the other way around, those bastards who fish for underage sex online. They tell me they love me, that our relationship is "special." They ask for photos, which I have to get clearance to use, because technically one of the rules is not to entice the prey too much.

The photos are from stock, and it made me feel physically sick when I saw them first, but Taj says they're all models, all legal and all consenting, so I suppose it's okay. We go further than anyone else with our traps, and although we pass evidence to the police, they really don't like us. We're dangerous and we put ourselves in danger, so we remain anonymous — shadows lurking among the darker blackness that our prey exists in.

I turn back to my computer, adjusting my security, checking each tab carefully. I'm mid-conversation with a couple of men. I assume they're men to start with, but I've snagged a woman on my fishing line before, which shocked the hell out of me. "Naïve," Taj had said, laughing. He'd told me I'd soon learn that anyone can hide behind the screen.

Taj has no idea that I am already far more aware of the danger than most of us. I spend longer at my computer, I volunteer to do phone calls, to go on meet-ups. I've been patient for a long time, waiting and watching, but now I finally feel like I'm striking back.

My screen flashes with a message, and I click on the green icon.

Hey Baby, I would luv to meet up and then maybe you could pose for some special photos, just for me. I've never seen/met anyone like you.

xxxoxx

I grin to myself, raising my hand to indicate to Taj that I have a possible catch, and he hotfoots it from the office to my workspace.

It's now that the real work begins. My heart rate accelerates in anticipation, and I know I'm addicted. Each one is revenge, bittersweet and bloody.

I live for it.

CHAPTER FOUR

Dove pushed her chair back, eyes sore and head aching. It was two in the morning, and she was back at home, supposedly grabbing a couple of hours' sleep. Actually, unable to even think about rest after her talk with Ren, she was still working. She would be expected to be back in at six thirty for another full briefing. Time was ticking on with frightening speed, with nobody even in the frame yet. But they had to assume the trail was still fresh, and officers from the team would still be sifting through everything from the witness statements to CCTV coverage of the area.

Often, once the news had broken, the phone lines would be busy with potential information. Sightings of the victim before she died, sightings of the killer by those convinced that the slightly odd bloke down their road was the one police should be looking for. At a time when the police force was stretched to the max, a major crime took all the bodies they had.

She wondered what the murderer was doing now. He or she must be revelling in their success. Dove had no doubt that the careful positioning of the body, the picture-perfect location and the professionalism evident in the glasswork meant that the killer was looking for praise. But why go for a copycat crime? Why not do something original?

She yawned, rubbing her tired eyes, stretching her arms above her head, feeling her muscles ache from this morning's workout.

It was good to be back by the coast, and able to swim, surf and run along the rough pebble beaches. She had been convinced she had turned into a city girl, but now it was almost scary how quickly she had reverted. Even Quinn had laughingly told her she was a different woman from the one he'd met six years ago.

Quinn. He was still there, even after everything that had happened. She loved him and he loved her. After the attack, after she was told there could be no children, she'd asked him to move out of her flat. Not because he had done anything wrong, but because she'd needed space to come to terms with her new life, to be alone with her nightmares and ride them out.

They still had rows, still had sex, and still behaved like any other couple, but Dove felt the darkness between them, even if he didn't. He had been so patient, but she felt almost like she didn't deserve him. When she was abducted and attacked, she had been working, and there was nothing she could have done to prevent the blade from slicing through her skin, from taking away a possible future she had hardly considered. But a tiny voice insisted that she'd chosen the path she had taken, had put herself at risk. It wasn't rational, but it was there. Guilt.

Dove glanced back down at the computer, but the words blurred and the page seemed to move before her eyes. Definitely time to call it a night. Was there a connection to Hayworth, or, as Victoria Carter had mentioned, was it just another person who had seen the documentary, trawled online for the gory details? It was a tough scene to recreate, and the victim must have been held somewhere to allow time for the mould and the glass coffin to be created. And then transported. Hayworth had used a bespoke kind of sled . . .

Buzzed again, she fetched fresh coffee and a packet of jelly sweets. She was speed-reading the case files for Peter

Hayworth now. He had been active further south as well, but this was still very much his original patch, so what did that tell them? What were the chances of a copycat killer on this coast? Perhaps he had moved here to imitate his hero in every detail?

Layla, the grey cat, was stretched out on the desk, yellow eyes narrowed, watching Dove as she worked, purring her approval. According to Quinn, the adoption of Layla right after she moved in had proven Dove was turning into a crazy cat lady. She had retorted that there was nothing wrong with that. There were worse things to be.

Dove grabbed a pen and paper, and made a quick note to check Hayworth's old haunts, including his home address and grave site. She felt her stomach tense at the thought of the autopsy tomorrow, the nauseating clinical smell of the mortuary, and the pain she always felt at not being able to bring the victim any comfort.

It was a strange way to feel, but Quinn sympathized, telling her it was human nature to want to help, they just did it in different ways. His job as a paramedic meant that he often fought to preserve life, whereas she worked hard to identify the perpetrators of violent crime.

She felt the need to push herself, to show she was working hard, inserting herself into every area where she might gain knowledge. Being present at the autopsy would certainly help her case. As long as she managed not to vomit.

The examination of the body would throw up extra information, and the glass case hopefully more still. Fingerprints could be run through the database, the victim's dental records could be traced. It was annoying that they still didn't have a name for her. Why had nobody reported her missing? Not friends, not family, employers, neighbours . . .

There was also the niggling doubt that Dove's personal link with the previous Glass Doll murders, coupled with her recent history, might be enough for the DI to consider taking her off the case.

This was too close to home, and her old anxieties, battened down tightly after moving and landing a new job, bubbled to the surface. She had transferred from the Divisional Source Unit, based at Nantich Valley, to start over, and she needed the hang on to that. She was no longer working with *grasses* or *snouts* or *informants*, the unsavoury slang names for her sources that left a bitter taste on the tongue. Now she was with a solid team focused on solving a murder case. It was a big change.

But several members of her old team had sent texts tonight, asking if she was okay. She took care to respond quickly to their messages, thanking them for their concern, but reassuring them she was fine. Gossip spread quickly, and although her move had taken her into the neighbouring county, the blue light community was a small one.

Her phone rang and she smiled as she answered. "Hi, Jess."

"I knew you'd be awake."

"What are you thinking?" Their relationship had always been easy. Jess was a straight-talking, petite woman, with a sharp Brummie accent and an acid sense of humour. She and Dove had clicked instantly when they met on a training course, and although their packed schedules meant they rarely met up socially, it was a solid friendship.

"Not much since I sunk a few glasses of wine, but I've got to admit it looks like we've got a copycat. How are you holding up?"

Dove frowned into the phone. "All right. I told Ren."

There was no pause. "I would have done the same, love," Jess said.

Dove let out a long breath of relief. "That makes me feel so much better."

"We'll know more after the autopsy, but if you need me, chick, just call. Any time, okay?"

"How are the kids?"

"Sleeping, I hope, at this time of night." Her voice changed. "And if you're having the nightmares again, remember what I said, you still have options. You can take control, if that's what you and Quinn choose to do, but don't let anyone pressure you."

Jess and her partner, after several heartbreaking unsuccessful attempts at IVF, had finally adopted two girls. Dove, seeing how happy her friend was, gradually realized the same might be possible for her. Some day, in the future.

"Thanks, Jess. Is Dion working?"

"Of course. You don't think I'd be up drinking alone like some sad cow if he was home, do you?" Jess was laughing. "Actually, I've only just finished sorting out the washing."

"The glamour, my friend."

"Yeah. The glamour and the shit!"

Dove smiled as she turned back to her computer after the call. She shoved another handful of sweets into her mouth, tasting the sickly sweetness on her tongue, scrolling down through her files.

Eden had been a much-loved member of the family, with so much to live for, and Hayworth had coldly terminated her life. He had admitted he enjoyed the killings. She sifted through the interviews, and found the one she hated most, forcing herself to concentrate as his voice filled the room.

Dove had been working as an elite source handler when Eden was abducted and murdered. By living with her phone day and night, inserting herself carefully into the lives of her sources, she had been one of the most successful on her unit. But it had meant she had no life outside of work, and constantly felt she was treading the line between success and failure, when failure meant lives lost.

CHIS, or Covert Human Intelligence Sources, were tricky beasts, and being a handler was tough. But the very fact she was working in the police force had made both her sisters, not to mention Dove's parents, feel like she should be able to find Eden, to give them all the details they craved. Again and again, she had explained that it wasn't her area, not even her borough, but they hadn't stopped putting on the pressure. The phone calls, the tears, the intensity still made her break out in a sweat when she recalled it. The worst thing had been that she couldn't do a single thing to save Eden. To her, and them, that was failure.

She understood why her family felt the way they did, of course, but her relationship with Gaia, her younger sister, still hadn't completely recovered. It was Gaia who had cruelly uttered the words she heard in her nightmares.

"Isn't it ironic? I don't want children and you can't have them. Funny how things turn out . . ."

Gaia had always been her opposite, and a career criminal until her late twenties. Now she operated just within the right side of the law, while her sibling was a law enforcer. Their laid-back hippie dad, Starr, thought it was hilarious, but Dove failed to see the funny side.

She'd pushed her family away, allowing Eden's killer back in. His words had been so often quoted in the press, and they made her shiver with rage and horror at his Messiah-like opinion of himself.

"All the girls have to be perfect. Not just pretty but free from flaws and pristine. This girl in your photograph was not perfect. I thought she was but then . . ."

"Why wasn't she perfect?"

"It's so hard to find perfection. Where have all the pretty girls gone? You know, the ones without flaws."

"Did you kill Eden Matthews?"

"I did. I terminated her life and left her where she died. You might find her still floating, I suppose . . . Oh no, wait. It wasn't her who went in the river, it was the other girl, Alice. Can I see the pictures again?"

Hayworth's voice had been high for a man, and when he spoke, it was as though considering each word, with an undertone of bored amusement. He'd had an extremely high IQ. An Oxford graduate, who worked as an art dealer for several years, before slowly cutting off all contact with his family and friends, he'd apparently lost himself in academia. All the statements from those who'd considered themselves close to him saw him as a gentle, cultured academic who preferred his own company. Slightly eccentric maybe, but certainly not a serial killer.

Another text from Jess made her phone buzz, asking her to call back if she needed to. Checking up on her again. She sent a thumbs up emoji, and put the phone back on the table.

27

Dove wandered into the kitchen and popped the top on a can of energy drink. The sharpness and fizz made her eyes water. Her terrace house was at the end of the row, backing onto fields, right on the outskirts of town. It was ideal for her. She had been almost glad in the end to give up her flat in the city centre. Not far to move geographically, but for her, she had come a long way in the space of a couple of months.

She breathed in deeply, as the therapist had taught her, and let a long breath out, blowing her demons out through the kitchen into the night. Sometimes it worked, sometimes it didn't.

Living close to her siblings was something she had resisted since she was a teenager, but now, despite everything, she loved having them near. Their unconventional childhood, being raised in a commune, had ensured all three women shared a bond that nobody else could. The memories of that carefree, hippie existence linked them as surely as their DNA.

Lost in the past, she jumped as the next text came in.

2 hours to go & I'm fucked. Hope u not still working babe x

Quinn was on a night shift, which suited her perfectly as he couldn't check in too often and discover she was still up at the computer instead of sleeping. She was desperate to talk to him, but equally desperate to prove she could do this, walk the tightrope of career and relationships. Everyone else seemed to manage it, so why did she find it so hard?

Back at her computer, she pulled up the news sites. The murder had been reported, but so far there were no specific details, simply that a female victim had been discovered in Gibbons Copse, with the usual reassurance that the MCT were working with the local force in the investigation.

DI Blackman would be working all night. She could tell he was that kind of person, and that he also had something to prove. She went back into the room off the kitchen that she had designated as her office, clicking through the files again, skimming the documents, concentrating on Hayworth's initial interviews now. There was nothing to suggest he had had an accomplice. He was a sociopath who had been convinced he was creating masterpieces out of the bodies of young girls.

Again and again, the words *perfect* and *pristine* came up in his replies to the police interviewers. All the victims had been physically different, but all fit the killer's idea of what he had wanted "his girls" to look like.

Dove sighed. Eden *had* been perfect. She fitted the profile of petite and pretty, but he still hadn't given her a glass burial. When pressed, Hayworth had admitted that there were two other girls he had murdered but not turned into glass statues, and he gave the same justification for all — he had been mistaken, and perfection was everything, so they had been disposed of.

He had refused to say where his burial ground was, even when grieving relatives, including Ren and her family, had begged him.

Who would seek to emulate a psychopath? Only someone who thought as he did, felt as he did. A dedicated follower stepping carefully, meticulously in Hayworth's bloody footprints.

CHAPTER FIVE

Dove woke as the sunlight streamed through her office window. Her head was tilted sideways, her neck agony when she moved. She blinked, hazy and confused. She was still fully clothed, half-lying, half-sitting at her desk.

"Bloody hell!" Dove glanced at her watch, and then relaxed. Just past five. Plenty of time. She rubbed her gritty eyes, wincing as she moved and her muscles cramped.

When she stepped out of the shower, her phone was ringing. Fumbling with towel and wet hair, she grabbed it.

"Hi, boss."

"DC Milson, just confirming the autopsy will be at seven and the briefing back at the station at eight, so get down to the mortuary first, and I'll meet you there. We've managed to get an expert in to help us cut the glass. The pathologist will be Dr Harry Iziah, as requested. Obviously, with the tight timescale we will only be able to stay for the initial proceedings."

"Yes, boss."

"We also have a name. The night shift have pulled up one Agnes Nilsson. She was a backpacker. Nineteen years old, from Gothenburg. Her parents reported her missing last Friday, when she failed to check in for a regular Facetime session. According to them, she was staying in Paris for a month. I'll see you at the mortuary."

She was about to say *Yes, boss* again when he put the phone down. Paris was a world away from Lymington-on-Sea and quaint Abberley with its cobblestone churches. Or maybe not. The airport wasn't far, nor was the station.

Dove pulled her hair back into a tight plait and stepped into the spring chill. Mindful of her casual attire the previous day, she was wearing a grey suit. Her road was busy at this time of morning, buzzing with commuters hurrying to the train station, but she managed to get on the road into town with minimal hassle.

Parking in the vast concrete multistorey, Dove joined Jess and her other colleagues at the mortuary, shivering in the chilly corridor that led to the labs.

DI Blackman introduced everyone and suggested they crack on. This morning he wore wire-rimmed glasses which added to his studious image, his grey eyes icy as he smiled at Dove. "I hope you managed to get some sleep?"

Taken aback by his coldness, Dove really hoped her visit to Ren hadn't been a mistake. "Some. I just want to get on with the investigation, boss."

Jess shot her a look, blue eyes sharp and concerned, but she said nothing else.

Dove moved towards the stairs and the others followed her obediently, donning plastic once again. The pathologist, Dr Harry Iziah, the exhibits officer and the specialist there to remove the glass casing were joined by the photographer. Two other assistants were also wearing scrubs, emphasizing the clinical environment.

A screen above her showed CCTV recording every move that was made, a time and date stamped in the bottom right-hand corner. Dove leaned forward, studying the glass case. Laid out in the mortuary it looked enormous, but in reality it was probably no more than six feet long and two feet wide.

Dr Iziah, a small, round man with a neat moustache, clicked on a Dictaphone and made a quick note of all present before the specialist, wielding a large handheld grinder, stepped forward. With the glass case securely clamped, he began to cut through it. It was a tough job, and soon he was covered in sweat, not only from effort but fear. One wrong move and he would shatter the glass, losing any vital evidence trapped inside.

Dove found herself holding her breath, crossing her fingers as the grinder screeched through the glass an inch at a time. With each pause, the assistants hastened forward to check the glass for cracks, carefully sweeping the ground-up glass into evidence bags for analysis.

After half an hour, the thick moulding finally broke with a crack, revealing the body. In some ways, it would have been easier to cut downwards into segments to see if they could lift the glass away from the body that way, but the professional had insisted the best way was to follow the original join. Now, with the casing split neatly in two, the real work could begin.

The pathologist examined the girl. Dove, impatient and aware they were on a tight schedule, turned to DI Blackman. "What do you think?"

He was frowning. "It looks a lot like the Hayworth murders at first glance. I see traces of needle marks on her left arm, which I believe were noted at the scene. There are several, and look recent . . ."

"So the killer could also have used a sedative to control her, perhaps? Or maybe she was a user anyway," Dove suggested. "How soon will we get the bloods back from the lab? Tomorrow?"

Dr Iziah looked at one of the assistants, who shook her head. "They're backed up like crazy and dealing with four major cases at the moment. Probably the preliminaries will be in tomorrow lunchtime if we get cracking."

He nodded, carefully examining the body, his voice soft. "Gone are the days of having a lab on site. Everything has to go to Central now, unfortunately. Budget cuts are hitting us from all sides. I blame the government."

"They know it's going to be a priority, but so are the other cases," Jess added. "Obviously there are similarities to the Hayworth case, but we don't want to be blinded by them, which may well be what the killer wants. This is a new case, with a new victim." As Crime Scene Manager she needed to be present every step of the way, ensuring continuity and smooth passage for any evidence, and for the body itself.

But was she talking to the room at large with this statement, or was this aimed right at her, Dove wondered, catching her friend's eye and shaking her head slightly.

The pathologist spent the next twenty minutes working his way around the body, occasionally calling out information to be recorded by his assistants. There was purple lividity on the girl's back when they carefully rolled her, suggesting she had lain in that position for some time after death.

"Any estimation on time of death?" Dove asked.

The pathologist shook his head. "From the body temperature, I can make a very rough guess. Cause of death is asphyxiation, which, as you will know, messes with the body temperature, not to mention the heat in this damn glass coffin."

Dove winced, trying not to imagine the horrors this girl had suffered prior to her death. Had the killer cherry-picked his victim, or was Agnes, like Eden, simply in the wrong place at the wrong time?

The pathologist continued. "Basically, it looks like she suffocated inside that case, from the evidence present on her body. We'll know from the tox screening what kind of drugs she was taking, or was administered."

"Shit. I hope she was unconscious by then and didn't know what was happening," Dove said, the terrors of the past and present meeting in a solid mass of sick emotion right in her gut.

Hayworth had described in detail how he carefully prepared his murder scenes, revelling in the moment of death. Dove's heart rate was rising and her palms were sticky with sweat, despite the coolness of the room.

It was the stuff of nightmares. She could easily imagine waking inside a glass case, struggling to breathe, realizing that you were trapped, with a monster gloating over you, feeding on your last moments.

CHAPTER SIX

The rules are simple. We never go alone to a meet, and we always get video evidence.

I wait with Elijah, next to the old bus station. It's derelict now, and this end of town is filled with scruffy houses, illegal bars and drug dealers. We're an hour early, but that's part of the plan. We're always early, because the chances are, especially in a rendezvous point like this, that the prey is sitting in his car, watching and waiting too.

Often they are so nervous, they abort at the last minute, which pisses me off, because we put a lot of work into each case. This time, Elijah adjusts his phone, and I slip off my coat and sit on the seat in the old bus shelter. I can see the tall spire of Abberley Road Theatre from here, the lights glittering in the darkness. It's easy access to the road, and to Cove Roundabout, where you can turn off onto the M25.

We're assuming, as he offered to pick me up in his car, and suggested we meet here, that he intends to take me away here and now. Some of them don't. They fuss and chat for ages and then maybe walk away very fast, shouting that they can't do this and they're sorry.

We get them anyway. Just because they couldn't do it this time, doesn't mean that they won't be more confident next time. And next time could be for real.

It's cold for April, and I shiver in my school uniform. The skirt is navy, pleated, appropriately short, and the tie is knotted loosely over a white shirt. My long dark hair is pulled into a high ponytail, and I'm not wearing much make-up. Certainly far less than if I was a real schoolgirl. But then if I was a real schoolgirl, I hope I wouldn't have fallen for this man's lies.

"He just texted to say he's around the corner," Elijah tells me, from the darkness behind the shelter.

"Did you reply?"

"Yeah. You're super excited to be a model for the evening and you're waiting for him. But is he sure he's okay with you being thirteen?"

"What did he say?"

Elijah grins. "'A hundred per cent, baby.'"

"Bastard. Okay, I'm sorted." Next to me on the peeling bench is a pink rucksack with glitter stickers and fluffy pompoms on the zips. It contains four large rocks, illegal pepper spray we order from the US and a rape alarm.

I'm shivering again, but this time it's nerves instead of cold that brings goosebumps to my bare skin. Excitement flutters in my belly, and I stretch my long legs out as a car moves slowly down the road towards us, headlights dipping to just sidelights.

I can see the outline of the driver, hear the click as Elijah uses the larger camera to capture the vehicle. Mentally, I run though my safety checklist. Is he alone? This is always a potential hazard. Taj has told us all over and over again about the time he had to do a runner from a gang of blokes thinking they were meeting up with an eleven-year-old boy. He escaped with a broken arm and a few more scars to add to his collection.

I only have to think about that story to remind myself why I'm here, why we all do what we do, why we go further than anyone else to get what we need.

He leaves the engine running, sitting for a moment, watching me. I wave, and slide off the seat, but I don't approach the car.

The trap is set.

"Are you Lisa?"

I'm not, but it'll do. I have lots of names, depending on who I'm talking to. I nod, fiddling with my bag, mock-shy but really taking long deep breaths, tensing my muscles.

The man isn't getting out of the car yet, which needs to be remedied. Footage of prey sat in vehicles is rubbish. I try a smile, shielding my eyes against the headlights, even though they aren't bright.

"Are you Matthew?"

"Yes," he sits for a moment longer, engine still running, but when it becomes obvious I'm not going to approach, he opens the car door. It's a Nissan Micra, about fifteen years old from the number plate. How naff.

It's always at this moment that I have a split second of panic, and Eden pops back into my head. I remind myself that Elijah is near enough, and Taj, Bollo and Ellie are just at the end of the road in our vehicle. We don't always have the numbers to go with back-up, so tonight I feel safer than usual.

Matthew walks towards me, smiling. He's a tall man, broad-shouldered, and wearing a well-cut suit. Clean-shaven with shiny shoes, and a nice smile. He doesn't look like the type of man to drive a Nissan Micra. Maybe it belongs to his wife.

"I brought a bag of outfits, just like you said. Are we going to your studio?" I make my voice breathy with just a little flutter of nerves and fiddle with my ponytail.

"Yes. I told you, it's only just up the road in Gravestown. Up close, you're even more stunning." He's gaining confidence. "I felt we had a connection from the moment we started talking. What time do your parents expect you home?"

I giggle. "My dad'll go mad if I'm back any later than eleven, and I have school tomorrow." Time to drop in some bait. "Don't you think I'm really tall for thirteen? I'm the second tallest in my class." If this man really knew kids and teens he wouldn't have fallen for my act, but these people see what they want to see.

"You're gorgeous." He comes close, sliding a hand down my bare arm. "You're going to burn the camera up."

"I never thought I'd be a model," I say, smiling into his eyes. On my arm, his palm is slightly wet. Urgh.

He slips his hand down my waist, and I force myself not to flinch away. Instead, I smile and dip my gaze to his polished black shoes. He's far bolder than they normally are, so clearly this isn't his first time picking up a kid. Again, if he stopped to think, it's very unlikely that *any genuine thirteen-year-old would let a man touch them as he just touched me. "Shall we get going, then?"*

I pause, turning as though to pick my bag up, and he adds, "You didn't tell anyone about me, did you?"

"Of course not. My parents think I'm at Sophie's and her mum is out at work until nine. They'll never check."

"I'll have you home before eleven, baby," he promises.

CHAPTER SEVEN

DI Blackman walked out with Dove to the car park.

"I'll see you back at HQ for the briefing, DC Milson. Oh, and I need to have a private word with you later, too. Nothing to worry about," he added, before heading towards his own vehicle.

Dove walked to her car, biting a fingernail. Shit! Did he know she'd spoken to Ren? The idea that she might have screwed up so soon made her slam her car door shut with unnecessary violence.

As predicted, word was out, and the case had caught the attention of the press and was trending on social media. Journalists were camped outside the gates of the police station, and the press officer was under pressure to produce a statement. The DI and Dove had maintained strict poker faces and muttered, "No comment," as they passed through the gates. A media strategy had already been decided and some of the office assigned to deal with it.

The rest of the MCT was already assembled, the night shift red-eyed and haggard, the day shift clutching notepads, iPads and packets of biscuits. Coffee cups and paperwork scattered the table and Steve passed Dove a fresh cup as she slipped into the seat next to him.

"You look like you've been up all night," he commented. She nodded. "Same. But I got out early to catch a few waves."

Dove grinned at him. "Slacker." Their shared love of the sea had boosted their friendship within the two months they had worked together. That and the fact Steve's partner also worked for the ambulance service.

DI Blackman stood at the head of the table, his quick eyes roving over his team. He began the briefing, flicking through various images on the screen behind him as he spoke.

"Agnes Nilsson is our victim, a nineteen-year-old backpacker from Gothenburg. Her parents reported her missing when she failed to check in via Facetime on Friday night. They thought she was in Paris. She wasn't due to visit the UK until next week. We don't have her phone, clothes or any personal items. Her parents arrive this morning to formally identify the body and the autopsy is currently underway."

"Did she maybe have a boyfriend?" DC Clerkson suggested, slightly nervously. She was a fresh-faced new recruit and eager to contribute.

"Nobody has reported her missing in this country, but we are checking the youth hostels and hotels in this area. After the press conference, we should get a lot more information as her photograph is circulated. We have been looking through the CCTV footage out towards the motorway, but so far no joy on any better footage of our navy transit van. The manufacturers have confirmed that it would be possible to adapt a van of this make and model to take the weight of our glass coffin." The DI paused to click on another video. "This piece of footage is from a personal security camera. It's used by one of the homeowners living opposite the traffic lights, and shows the van turning onto North Shore Road at 3.41 a.m. A witness says he was driving home from a late shift and passed the van parked at the side of the road at around four thirty, but can't be sure of the colour. The final piece of CCTV shows the van returning via the same route at 4.57."

"Which means he must have driven it back into town. Perhaps he uses the van for his day job or it had to be back in a depot?" Steve suggested.

"We're not eliminating anything at this stage. Moving on, as you are all aware, this seems an identical crime to those committed by Peter Hayworth in 2016. He committed four murders, and obviously we want to nip this in the bud, in case our copycat has any ideas of making his name as a serial killer."

Dove tapped notes into her iPad, adding question marks and crossing off theories as information was passed on. Beside her, Steve scribbled on his notepad, doodling complex patterns when he wasn't writing. He had told her it helped him think, when she'd teased him about it.

Blackman summed up: "We are still working our way around the door-to-door checks at the Abberley end of North Shore Road, and checking personal security cameras. There are a couple of farms accessible from Gibbons Copse, but marks at the scene, plus our van sightings, indicate that, as with the Hayworth murders, the body was unloaded and a sled used to transport it up to its final location."

"Whoever did that must be bloody strong, or had an accomplice," DS Lindsey Allerton said with feeling. "Even with some kind of pulley system rigged up in the van, plus a sled. The glass was so thick there is no way one person could unload and position it up there." She glared around the room, her short, brown curls framing her square face. Behind her glasses, her eyes were unusual and very beautiful — one clear blue, the other dark green.

"Agreed. Let's try and keep an open mind on this one. We could be looking for a male, female or even a group working together. I don't want us blinkered by the Hayworth similarities. Get to it, and keep me in the loop."

As the team dispersed to various locations, the DI beckoned Dove into his glass-walled office. She noticed with a slight intake of breath that the DCI, Kevin Franklin, was also present.

"Good luck with that," Steve told her, heading back to the main bank of computers. "I'll wait for you over here, out of sight."

"Wimp." She rolled her eyes at his retreating figure, but she was worried.

Alone with the senior officers, Dove resisted the urge to bite her fingernails. It was a schoolgirl habit she had never managed to kick.

"DC Milson, it has been brought to my attention that you have a personal connection to the Hayworth case." The DCI wasn't smiling, but his expression softened slightly as he spoke. Across his forehead ran a long, jagged scar, standing out livid and shocking against his pale skin.

"My niece was one of Hayworth's victims," Dove said, and was pleased to hear her voice come out calm and level. There was a chance he might decide to take her off this case, so she needed to make sure no emotion showed in her face. DI Blackman sat opposite, but the DCI remained standing.

"I'm sorry," DCI Franklin said, and both men waited politely for her to continue.

"It was a while ago. Obviously it affected me, and my family, but we know that Hayworth is dead, so there is no crossover. This might show similarities to the previous murders, but it's a totally new perpetrator. It won't interfere with this case." It was tough, because she didn't know either of them yet, didn't have the bond you get from working as a team on tough cases, from sharing successes and failures, but she spoke from the heart.

DI Blackman leaned forward across the desk. "I need to be sure of that. Obviously, as Hayworth is deceased, and there was no doubt he was the perpetrator of the previous crimes, I won't be taking you off this case at the moment. But I am aware of the circumstances of your transfer from the Source Unit, and I want you to know you can come to me if you need to talk."

This was a bit touchy-feely for her, but he seemed genuine, his eyes resting on hers, unblinking, as though he was seeing into her soul. Her past was scoring a direct hit now. She deliberately relaxed her clenched fists in her lap, and met his gaze. "Thanks, boss, but I'm fine. I just want us to catch this bastard."

"Okay." He was watching her closely, his grey eyes searching her face. "I want you and I to talk to the victim's family when they arrive this afternoon. Meanwhile, see if you and DS Parker can trace the victim's route from France. The parents said Agnes had bought a Eurostar ticket for her original journey, so find out how she got here early, and ideally why."

"Yes, boss." She was surprised, pleased even, having expected the job of talking to the victim's family to be allotted to a more experienced member of the team.

"Because your family has been through this, you bring a unique perspective to the case. So as long as you can handle it, I want to try and involve you as much as possible. Afterwards we'll introduce DS Karen Smith and DC Simon Everley as their designated Family Liaison Officers, and you can pair up with DS Parker again."

She nodded at them both, feeling a flash of relief when the DCI told her, with a smile, to get out and on with her job.

Back at her computer, she checked her phone and discovered another six missed calls from her younger sister, Gaia, two from Ren, and one from her dad, Starr.

Steve was busy checking CCTV from the town centre, and raised an eyebrow at her.

"It's fine. We're on travel duty, and the DI said when the parents arrive, I need to go down for the interview."

"Teacher's pet already and you've only been here a couple of months." Steve was grinning, teasing her.

She rolled her eyes. "I think it's more like he's keeping an eye on me. We need to have a chat, because I've got something I need to tell you."

They walked outside, keeping away from the smokers who lined the outside wall and shelter at the rear of the building.

"What's up, then?"

She told him, as quickly and succinctly as she could, watching his expression soften into concern and pity.

"Are you sure you even want to be on this case, even if they haven't pulled you?" Steve asked.

"Yes. I have ghosts to lay to rest and a career to rebuild. I just wanted to let you know, but it isn't common knowledge and I'd prefer to keep it that way for as long as possible."

"Sure. Thanks for telling me, and if you need to talk, just say the word. Or, you know, if you need to get out on the beach, I find that's a good way to clear everything out."

"Well, now you know why the DI wants me to be a bit more involved than I guess a newbie would normally be. Anyway, let's just get back to work," she said. "Thanks for the offer, though," she added, smiling at him. He was a good bloke, and easy to work with.

DS Allerton and her partner, DC Shipton, were coming down the stairs as they ascended. Dove was sure she could feel the frost between the two pairs. The other woman didn't seem to like her at all. Maybe she too thought Dove had been shown favouritism. Or did she know about Dove's past? Everyone was damaged to a certain extent. Burnout had been common in the Source Unit, but she was trying to be careful, shedding as much baggage as she could, a little at a time.

She put office jealousy to the back of her mind and concentrated on the computer screen.

"Did anything come through from Immigration yet? Oh, and we need to pull any CCTV from ferry terminals, airports, and obviously the train stations, but maybe wait until we get confirmation from Border Control on her entrance into the UK. That will cut down our search area."

"Yeah, fine. I've got the address of the hostel she was staying in when she was in Paris, so I'll get on to them." Steve swigged from a half-empty energy drink and picked up the phone.

"I wonder why she lied to her parents about where she was?" Dove pondered. "You'd think even if she decided to come to the UK early, she would have mentioned it. Or, on the other hand, I suppose, why would they lie if she did tell them . . ."

* * *

Two hours later, she went outside with a fresh cup of coffee and stood in the sunlight, watching the rain clouds dispersing over the sea, feeling the spring warmth relax her tense shoulder muscles.

She called her younger sister, waiting for the outburst. "Gaia? Sorry I didn't have time to call you, but Ren did say she—"

Her sibling, true to form, cut her off. "Shut up for a minute! I've just seen pictures on Twitter of that murder victim, the Glass Doll copycat girl."

"Fuck, sorry."

"Yeah, that's what I thought. A bit close to home, the whole thing, isn't it? Nice of you to give me the heads up. I thought now you're not working with grasses anymore, you might have got it together."

"Sorry. We haven't put any pictures out, only a statement without her name, but you know how easy it is to pull social media profiles," Dove said. She could picture her sister, impatiently tapping her long, red nails on the table, phone clamped to her ear. Gaia always dressed in black, with full make-up, long legs encased in shiny black leggings. Dove's younger sister was tough as shit and glamorous with it. She didn't care who she upset, and never had done.

"Either someone is super quick off the start blocks, or your actual killer has put the word out, because everyone knows who she is. That's not important, though . . . Dove, I actually *know* her!" Gaia snapped.

"What do you mean?" Her fingers clenched around the phone so hard they hurt, and she felt her heartbeat accelerate.

"She's worked in my fucking club for the past three weeks."

44

CHAPTER EIGHT

"Shit."

"Exactly what I thought, and before you ask, I've not being having any trouble at the club." Gaia's voice was harsh, with an undercurrent of tension.

Dove felt her own temper rise. "All right, don't jump down my throat. I'm just trying to get my head around my murder victim being one of your employees."

"Me too. Believe me, this is not going to be good news for my business."

"I don't imagine it came as good news for her parents, either." Dove bit back her anger at her sister's usual single-mindedness. "Are you at the club now, or at home?"

"Club. I haven't said anything to the staff yet, but everyone's going to have seen this on social media. Fuck!"

The club was Gaia's pride and joy, and she had made a lot of money out of her business venture. If such a place could be called classy, Gaia's was it. The front entrance was white and silver, with a marble-tiled interior. The podiums and poles would be empty at this hour, but a few front-of-house staff would be polishing glasses in the three bars, tidying up the posh snacks and restocking champagne into the coolers.

No doubt they were also checking their Twitter feeds and whispering about Agnes Nilsson.

Dove thought quickly. "All right, I'll call my boss, and then ring you back and let you know what's going to happen."

DI Blackman wasn't answering his phone, so Dove left a voicemail. She was torn between wanting to grab Steve and head down to the club herself, and knowing that that would be professional suicide. She could just see the prosecution having a field day with the fact that a significant witness was the sister of one of the investigating officers. No, it was time to delegate on this one.

DCs Marsh and Amin were more than capable, and she briefed them quickly, dispatching them before ringing her sister back.

"Why can't you come?" Gaia demanded. "I don't want any bloody uniforms down my club. They piss me off with their stupid questions, and if anyone sees the police down here, they'll assume the worst."

"They won't be uniform, not that it should matter. But it's because I can't mix my personal life with my professional one. It might screw up the whole case, and I want to catch this bastard, okay?" Dove told her firmly.

"Whatever." Gaia sounded sulky.

Dove killed the call and bit her nails.

"Problem? Because we need to head out. I've got a couple of addresses where our victim might have stayed." Steve was carrying a file and his iPad.

She told him and was pleased Steve was in total agreement with her decision to keep away from her sister.

"Leave it to the others and we can pick up the report when we get back in. Now, we've got four backpacking hostels, and I've spoken to staff on the phone at each one. They get a lot of customers at this time of year, but these all think they might have recognized Agnes's picture, even if she didn't stay with them."

They drove in silence, Steve watching the traffic and Dove replaying her conversation with Gaia in her head. She always felt wrong-footed by her younger sister, awkward and unsettled. Guilt niggled that perhaps she should have told *both* her sisters what had happened before it was made public.

Dove watched the traffic at the roundabout as Steve indicated right. Gaia's strip club sat in the opposite direction, among a busy group of bars, clubs and restaurants. She was sure she'd made the right call, but cringed at the thought of her sister being rude to her colleagues.

* * *

"This is Beach Place Hostel. A classy joint by the looks of it," Steve said, eyebrows raised. "It specializes in backpackers and students, according to the website." They parked up, and entered through the grimy glass doors. A washed-out blue sign directed them to the reception area.

As they walked down the dimly lit corridor, Dove dodged a pile of faded brown laundry bags. Agnes had been here three weeks, working in a strip club. Clearly, the strip club was probably not something to mention to your parents, but why hide the fact she was in the UK?

Deep in thought, she nearly fell over an old woman running a vacuum cleaner across the strips of blue carpet that barely covered the brown lino.

"Sorry!"

The woman scowled and moved the vacuum cord as Dove and Steve walked past. She put a hand out to catch Dove's arm, studying her face intently before speaking.

"Have you come about that girl?"

Her grip was surprisingly strong, despite her frail appearance. Dove gently detached herself from the claw-like hand. "Which girl?"

"Agnes, of course. You're Gaia's sister, aren't you? You two could be twins." She laughed, displaying a full set of stained brown teeth. "She talks about you all the time, how you're a copper. Funny, isn't it?"

Dove, taken aback, stared at the woman. "How do you know that?"

"I'm Janet, babes, I clean at the club. Afternoons at the club, mornings at the hostel. So it *is* about Agnes, then?"

Dove glanced at Steve, and he shrugged. Sometimes you struck lucky in this game, and if you did, you jumped on it.

Steve smiled at the sharp-eyed woman. "Is there somewhere we could have a quick chat? We do need to find Alan Mason, too. He spoke to our officers yesterday, and we're here to follow up on the information received. I believe he's the owner?"

Janet ticked her points off on her wrinkled, twisted fingers. "One, that lazy cow on reception is on the phone to her boyfriend. Two, the boss is down the pub for his lunch break for another forty minutes. Come on, we can talk in the break room down here. Agnes used to chat to me, you know, when she was at the club."

She led them to the end of the corridor and flung open a door. The break room was a bedroom without the bed. The walls and ceiling stained nicotine brown and two beat-up old sofas sat under the window.

"That poor girl. I heard a bit of gossip this morning saying the coppers had found a body, and then some kids at the bus stop were talking about her. Agnes. They were shocked, and it takes a lot to shock kids nowadays."

Dove opened the window as far as it would go, trying to keep her breathing shallow. The cracked ceiling fan was covered in dust and the air was stale and fetid. "When did you last see Agnes?"

Janet lit a cigarette, taking a drag before she answered. "Last week, I think. She came in early on the Thursday night and I was still running the vacuum around. I don't talk to many of the girls, because I knock off before most them get into work, but she was always early, making herself a drink, chattering away about her travels. A lot of them are so up their own arses, they don't even bother with a hallo or goodbye, but she was a good'un." Janet's cheerful smile faded. "I hate to think she's lying in some mortuary now."

Treading carefully, although she didn't see how talking to Janet could be construed by the DI as anything but professional, Dove asked a few more questions, establishing that Agnes had walked in off the street asking for a job, that she had been a good worker and had got on well with Gaia and the other girls.

"Do you know where Agnes was staying?" Dove asked.

The other woman shook her head. "Probably on someone's sofa, or a tent in the garden, if she was a backpacker. They all do it."

"But you don't know whose?"

"No. Gaia'll give you her application form. That'll have her address on, won't it?"

"Probably. Our colleagues are at the club now. Did Agnes ever talk to you about boyfriends?" Steve asked.

Janet sighed. "I reckon she had a lot of men on the go. They all do and they're not careful. It's all online nowadays, isn't it? You don't just pick a bloke up in a pub or club, you go and meet a total stranger. Agnes did mention a bloke called Marc, but I think he was someone she'd had a fling with in Paris. She'd just come from over there, did you know?"

Dove nodded. "Was she worried or upset about anyone or anything in particular?"

Janet shook her head. "Last time I saw her she was fine, love. Her usual happy self. Now you go and get the bastard who killed her. I want to see his ugly face in prison." She stood up, rubbing her lower back, reaching for another trolley containing piles of worn towels and packets of toilet roll. "I can't think of anything else, but if I do remember something useful . . ."

"You can call me direct." Dove handed her a card. "Thanks, Janet, you've been really helpful."

Alan Mason, the hostel manager, was back from his lunch break, but it soon became clear he was more interested in being part of the action than sharing any real information.

"Do you actually recognize this girl?" Steve said, showing him the photograph. "Because you told our colleagues yesterday that you did, which is why we're here."

Alan sat back. "Well, I thought I did, and even now she might have been in with one of the other guests last week. Her face is sort of familiar . . . Can't say from where, though."

"CCTV?" Dove was getting annoyed. What a timewaster.

He winked at her, then gave her what he probably thought was a charming smile. "I've checked and she isn't on any of it. You're welcome to have a look yourselves. Or if your colleague wants to look at the tape, I can get us a drink and . . ." He opened a cupboard and began to take out glasses.

"Alan, have you ever been to California Dreams?" Dove asked him, inspiration saving her from the cheesy chat-up line. Steve was having trouble keeping a straight face and she gave him a quick jab in the ribs.

The manager spun round, fear flashing in his eyes. The glass dropped from his hand and shattered on the floor.

CHAPTER NINE

While Steve drove them to the next hostel, Dove called the DI to update him.

He was pleased with their progress. "I got your message regarding your sister's club. We'll see what comes back from that, and meanwhile you two crack on with the hostels. If she was staying with a friend, why hasn't the friend come forward? Likewise, the boyfriend, Marc. We'll see if her parents can shed any light on him when they arrive."

"Yes, boss." Dove checked her messages briefly and then turned to Steve. "Next on the list is Mayfield Apartments."

"Yes. Worth keeping Alan Mason on the list, I think, as he had obviously seen Agnes at the club."

"Agreed. We'll check him out on the CCTV footage, and follow up on when he got home to his wife."

"I bet his wife's the kind who won't be happy her man's been watching half-naked girls all night," Steve said with a grin.

As they drove towards the coastline, Dove's mind drifted. She was desperate to hear what had happened with Gaia, but extremely glad she hadn't smashed protocol by tearing over to the club herself.

She could just see Gaia marching out from the back offices in her black stilettos, just as she had the last time

Dove had ventured into the club. Her short black hair was cut into ruffled layers. Although her hair was totally opposite to Dove's long unruly waves, as Janet had pointed out, the sisters could easily be mistaken for twins. All three sisters had the amber brown eyes inherited from their British dad and the dark glossy hair from their American mother.

Dove smiled as she thought of their parents, the close-knit community and the simplicity of life back then. As children in the States, the girls had enjoyed a large extended family, meeting up for weekends full of food and music festivals. Lucky, she had been very lucky.

* * *

They drew a blank at the next two hostels and decided to head back to the station early for the next briefing. The best leads at the moment seemed to be the possible boyfriend, Marc, and anything Gaia might be able to add to the investigation as a significant witness.

Dove grabbed coffees for them both before they sat down in front of the bank of computers. Another team had been going through Agnes's social media and had pulled up a photograph captioned:

Me and Marc #truelove #romanceinparis #couplegoals

They had emailed the picture to the entire team. Dove peered at it. It was a glossy, filtered image of Agnes and a blond man sitting at a café table, a bottle of wine and two full glasses between them.

The man had piercing green eyes and a strong bone structure. He wore a white vest which left his tanned, muscular shoulders and arms bare. Agnes had a hand in his and wore a red flower-print gypsy top, her long hair touching the table. He looked to be at least thirty, making her look even younger.

How much was real and how much was just another glossy for her travel blog, Dove wondered. According to the email, this was the only image they had pulled up for anyone called Marc. Had they fallen out and she decided to escape a broken love affair? Perhaps it really was that simple.

DC Amin appeared at the door and raised a hand. Dove left her desk and met him halfway across the room. "Thanks for picking that up. How did it go?"

DC Amin was young, probably early twenties, and very good-looking. He grinned at Dove. "Got some good stuff. Your sister had everything ready for us. CCTV footage from the night we assume Agnes went missing, paperwork, everything. Shit, she's incredible."

Dove smiled. Clearly her sister had made an impression, and it seemed she had kept her aversion to the police under control. She could see her sister overwhelming this boy totally.

DI Blackman joined them and those present were called together for a quick update. "This is a significant development, but we are still trying to find out where the victim was staying while she was in the UK. We need to get in touch with the supposed boyfriend, Marc."

"I'm on that," DS Lindsey Allerton said. "I speak fluent French, which might help." There was a definite smugness to her tone and by the way several officers rolled their eyes, Dove deduced she wasn't the most popular member of the team. But who cared, if she got the job done?

DC Amin, prompted by the DI, stepped forward and cleared his throat. "We spoke to the club owner at California Dreams, Gaia Smith-Milson. She gave us plenty that should be useful. These are Agnes's sign-in sheets, her original application form and a list of anyone she did private dances for. Agnes arrived on 2 April, just wandered in and asked at the desk if they were hiring. Apparently, most of the club's employees come in like that." He glanced down at his phone. "So with the confirmation from Border Control on her passport, she's been here three weeks, and started work at California Dreams the day after she arrived. According to the owner, she filled out the application form on the spot, did a quick audition and started work the next evening."

"Did she mention anything about her travel plans that Ms Smith-Milson noted?" DI Blackman asked.

DC Marsh scrolled through his own notes. "According to her employer, Agnes took the Eurostar, because she said there was some mix-up about booking her ticket. She'd finished with Paris and wanted to come here early, apparently."

"That tallies with the dates and times from Border Control. Did she say why she wanted to come to the UK early?"

"She gave the impression her love life was pretty busy, and she mentioned a row with her boyfriend, Marc, whom she'd met in Paris. Ms Smith-Milson also said, '*I wish I'd paid more attention now, obviously, but she was full of chatter. Bubbly and happy with life is how I'd describe her, but she was a professional flirt. That could have rubbed someone up the wrong way. Not here, because that's what they're paid for, but if she did it on the outside . . .*'"

Dove could almost hear her sister speaking, her sharp tones tempered with a low, husky laugh. Gaia was a businesswoman, brisk and organized, and had clearly dredged up every last thing about the murdered girl from her mind. Dove had expected no less. She and her younger sister were alike in so many ways, despite constantly butting heads over day-to-day life. Quinn, when he met Gaia for the first time, suggested afterwards that being OCD must run in the family. Dove told him it was just a question of being organized and in control.

DC Amin consulted his notes again. "The victim was backpacking around Europe, then going to the USA in August. From there, she was going on to Asia. Ms Smith-Milson said it wasn't uncommon to have someone like her looking for a job, and she gets a lot of backpackers wanting casual work. They're usually using Lymington-on-Sea as a not-so-exotic cheap stopover."

"Within easy reach of London, Brighton, travel links, so it works well for them," DS Allerton added. "Not to mention the bus station is a national coach drop-off and pick-up point too."

"Did the club owner think she'd worked in this particular industry before?"

"Yeah, she said she had." He glanced down again. "She stated Agnes *'wasn't shy and she had all the tricks. I'd say she was well used to working in clubs.'*"

Steve tapped his pen to his lips. "When did her employer last see Agnes, then?"

"Thursday night she worked until 3 a.m. There was a private party in from midnight and she danced for them." DC Amin glanced at his phone. "She signed out at half three. Two private dances logged from earlier in the evening . . . A regular and a couple . . . Security didn't note any disturbances, but you can see the CCTV for yourselves. We've got the USB stick with everything on."

Dove nodded, blinking her sore, gritty eyes as a wave of fatigue swept over her. "Anyone she upset during her time there? Maybe a customer who wanted more . . . We spoke to a cleaner at Beach Place Hostel, who also works at California Dreams. She mentioned the boyfriend, Marc, but the last time she saw Agnes was Thursday evening about six. She said Agnes always came in early for coffee and a chat before work."

DI Blackman nodded. "DC Amin, let's have a look at that CCTV from the early hours of Friday. It might well be our last sighting of her."

The younger man bent over the computer and they crowded round. Later, at the proper briefing, it would be shown on the big screen, but now it was important to get quick updates, sifting leads as they came in.

"Normally, from the other footage we've seen, Agnes gets a taxi home or gets a lift with one of the other girls. Ms Smith-Milson said Kiki Hall was friendly with her."

All the girls and anyone else working at the club would now be interviewed as a matter of course. Dove felt a tiny flicker of encouragement. They were making some headway at last, she was sure of it.

They gathered around the screen, peering at the slightly blurred grey-and-white images. The cameras were positioned all over the club and outside from every angle.

DC Amin turned back to the desk, and pointed at the screen. "That's her dancing, and then if we switch rooms, this is her at the private party on Thursday night . . ."

Agnes was a good dancer, and she was laughing and flirting with the party. At one point she sat in a man's lap and he fed her strawberries.

"Who's that?" Dove asked.

"Uri Maquess. He's a Russian broker, and owns a few yachts down at the marina. Apparently he's a long-time client, and quite often books a private party."

"We'll need to chat to him and all the other party guests." DI Blackman nodded.

"Steve and I can do that, if you want? Can we see the camera outside when she leaves?" Dove asked.

"Sure. We were told the girls use the back entrance to keep them away from the punters." DC Amin fast forwarded to three thirty, and Agnes appeared with two other girls.

"Kiki Hall and Ellie Peroni," DC Marsh supplied, consulting his notes.

The girls seemed in good spirits and kissed each other goodbye before the pair got into a taxi, leaving Agnes alone on the street.

Agnes seemed to be waiting for someone, leaning against the door, smoking and looking down at her phone.

At quarter to four, a man in security uniform came out of the door and they had a brief conversation, before he went back inside.

"That's Dennis Maitland. He's been working at the club since they opened."

"Really?" Dove's attention was on the screen, studying the man.

Finally, at four a.m., a black BMW drew up and Agnes opened the passenger door. She didn't get in straight away, but appeared to be arguing with the driver. At one point she leaned forward and jabbed a finger at them.

Eventually she threw her arms in the air in a clear gesture of annoyance and slipped into the passenger seat. The car drew away, plate number clear in the street light.

"That'll be easy to trace." Dove peered at the grainy image, excitement fizzing in her chest. This was a good lead and a recent one. If they tracked down the car driver, they could place her somewhere twenty-four hours before her body was discovered.

DI Blackman took over. "Okay, DC Milson and DS Parker, you're on the car owner. DS Allerton and DC Shipton, I want you to have a chat with the club manager, Colin Creaver. His home address is in the notes. He's a fairly new recruit and has previous for theft and various other petty offences. Nothing violent and no sex crimes."

Dove frowned, distracted from pulling up DVLA contacts. A new hire? Gaia never said she was hiring a manager, but then why should she? Their conversations were usually initiated by peacekeeping Ren, and never progressed beyond the basic civilities.

Flicking over to the spreadsheet, she clicked on the hastily assembled list of club employees, all with photographs she guessed had been lifted from their employment records. Instead of the standard, passport-sized squares, these were full-length pictures. The girls posed like models, pouting like reality stars, but Colin Creaver was smiling, relaxed and muscular, hands in pockets for his shot.

His blond hair hung to his shoulders and he had light green eyes, a tanned face and big smile. Both arms were covered with intricate tattoos and he wore several plaited leather bracelets. For a second, she almost thought he could be Marc from Agnes's Instagram post, but his face shape was wrong, too square.

"Look at this." She tapped Steve's arm and he too frowned at the pictures.

"It isn't the same man, but they are very alike. Maybe related?" he suggested.

She wondered how well Colin knew the girls, and if Agnes had also noticed his likeness to Marc.

CHAPTER TEN

I smile again, and pick up my bag — the signal for the team to move in. Keeping just out of range in case he throws a punch, I snap back into being myself and fade carefully into the darkness as Elijah steps out from behind the bus shelter, still filming.

Our van pulls up alongside "Matthew's" car. We never block them in, and we always let them escape. Our traps are to entice, but not to hold.

Taj jumps out. The man swears and turns back towards his vehicle. Taj is also filming.

"Hey, Matthew. Would you like to explain why you arranged to meet a thirteen-year-old girl down here tonight? Can you tell us why you asked her to send naked pictures online? You do know that's illegal, right?" He's grinning, firing the questions like bullets. Like me, Taj is doing this for revenge.

Matthew shoves the others away, swearing at them, at me, looking around wildly. "What the fuck is going on? What is this? Lisa?"

But I've vanished round the side of the bus shelter, yanking on my thick black hoody, hiding my hair, pulling on jeans, until I'm just one of the gang again.

Following the usual pattern, Taj continues to ask Matthew to explain himself, and Matthew staggers back into his Micra. He tries to shield his head from the cameras pointed at him, and puts the car

59

into reverse. There is a satisfying crunch as the car hits a bollard, but he spins the wheel and drives away with a screech of tyres.

Our prey is now metaphorically bloody and wounded, terrified of what we might do with the footage. He probably has a family, a job, friends who would be horrified by his secret fantasies. We melt into the background, high-fiving at another capture. Sometimes it's enough. Enough to persuade them to keep their fantasies locked inside their sick brains. But sometimes they simply can't control the urge, and they come back, scarred and defiant, ready for another round. Funny thing is, we've never caught a repeat offender.

There is a third option available to the prey, though, and this one keeps me checking the shadows and loading up with pepper spray . . .

Sometimes they come for us.

CHAPTER ELEVEN

The paperwork that Gaia had given them was resting on Dove's desk now, with a smiling photograph of the dead girl clipped neatly to the first folder.

Agnes looked older here than she had appeared in the glass coffin, with her wavy blonde hair cascading down around her shoulders, and red lips posed in a sexy pout. But there was no doubt that this confident, happy girl was the same girl who had met her death just weeks after the shot was taken.

The interview with Agnes's parents Samuel and Elsa was just as Dove had supposed — horrific. They were both understandably so distressed they hardly seemed to know where they were.

It was tough, walking the fine line between wanting to comfort them and promise their daughter's killer would be brought to justice, and remembering to stay professional. Promises could not be made if there was a chance they would not be kept, but Dove's heart hurt for them.

After the preliminaries, DI Blackman went gently over the timeline leading to Agnes's murder, coaxing answers from them. He was respectful, calm, and they clearly appreciated that a senior officer had taken the time to speak to them. Their English was excellent, heavily accented but fluent.

"Did she mention any boyfriends at all?" Dove asked, watching the expressions. Often in murder it was a family member responsible, but she could read nothing but genuine pain and anguish in these two. It mirrored the pain of her own family.

Elsa shook her head, holding a tissue to her trembling mouth. "No, I do not think so . . . Oh wait, she went out with a boy called Marc recently. He is French and when we spoke on Facetime, she was just going out to dinner with him. She was fussing around selecting an outfit. I told her she looked beautiful." Her blue eyes, so like her daughter's, were bleak, dull and hopeless. "She always looked so beautiful."

Elsa and Samuel knew no other details of Agnes's love life and couldn't shed any further light on Marc's whereabouts.

"Finally, is there any reason you can think of that Agnes would not have told you she was coming to the UK early?" DI Blackman asked them.

"No." Samuel rubbed his hands through his blond hair, wedding ring gleaming in a stray beam of sunlight, his face haggard. "Ever since you first asked, we have been thinking of why. As for working in that club, well, it is a shock but I can see she perhaps thought it was an adventure. Everything for Agnes was an adventure, always exciting. She had no reason to hide anything from us, and she was mostly honest. And happy, Agnes has always been happy . . ." His voice broke and he hid his face in a handkerchief, blowing his nose loudly.

They wrapped up the interview and found DS Karen Smith waiting outside in the corridor, ready to escort the grieving parents back to their hotel.

DI Blackman watched them go. "I don't think they know anything, or if they do, they won't remember until after the initial shock has worn off."

"Grief does that to you," Dove agreed, remembering vividly that moment when she had been told Hayworth had admitted to murdering Eden. Hope had died in an instant. She could only compare the pain with the moment the chisel had entered her body during the attack. But for Eden, there had been no rescue. "I didn't pick up on anything but genuine horror and grief at the situation."

"No problem. As long as you're okay as well?" His face was bleak and for a second she wondered what tragedy had touched his life. They walked back upstairs to the main offices.

"Fine, thanks, boss."

Steve met them at the door. "Got it! Tom Jenson is the registered keeper of the vehicle. His address is listed as 59 Millfield Road, Abberley. It's on the road past the theatre, so not too far from the hostel. Want me and DC Milson to check him out?"

The DI nodded. "Take a couple of extra bodies just in case, though. Does he have any previous?"

Steve shook his head. "I looked and there's nothing apart from a couple of minor traffic offences."

Dove and Steve were on their way out when DS Lindsey Allerton stopped them. "The strip club Agnes worked in belongs to your sister, doesn't it?" she asked, a trace of incredulity in her voice.

"Yeah, why?" Dove flicked the other woman a glance. She was used to having to defend Gaia's business choice, even if she didn't actually like it herself. It was a constant source of tension between them.

"No reason, I'm just checking so I know all the facts. I also wanted to let you know that Agnes's address on file at the club is listed as Bengards Apartments on Eastern Road."

The DI, on his way into his glass-walled office, glanced round. "DS Parker has already checked and they claim she never stayed with them. They *do* have a booking in her name for the end of June, though. We've got uniform round there at the moment to get the records."

"Easy to scribble down a handy address if you know it's unlikely to be checked," DS Allerton commented, giving Dove another hard look before returning to her computer.

* * *

"I reckon he'll do all right, the new DI," Steve told Dove as they clattered down the main staircase.

"I'm sure he will. What's up with DS Allerton?"

"Told you before. She's spiky by nature and desperate to climb the career ladder. Come on, Lindsey's all right and a good officer, but I reckon she has a bit of a thing for our new boy."

"Really? I'm sure he'll be dead pleased to hear that." Dove grinned at him, before returning to the job in hand. "We didn't get anything useful from Agnes's parents. They're so cut up, poor things, but I suppose they might talk to the FLOs later on. I feel like from nothing to go on, we're suddenly getting lots of little threads and more questions."

"This is how it works, and believe me, it's all good. Once you start digging, all kinds of shit comes out, but we'll get some good stuff and nail this sick bastard."

"Hayworth was a serial killer," Dove said as they exited into the sunshine.

"You're waiting for another body?"

She shrugged. "If I'm honest, yes, I reckon most people are. If you copy a crime to that extent, and go to that much trouble, it just seems like they would carry on and go the whole hog."

He glanced sideways at her, concern flickering across his face. "Don't take this the wrong way, but I think we need to be careful with the Hayworth comparison. This could be all about Agnes Nilsson, and a pissed-off boyfriend or something. There is enough about Hayworth online to gather every last detail of his crimes, and to someone's twisted mind it could look like the perfect final solution for an ex-girlfriend."

"Glad we aren't dating if that's the way your mind works," Dove told him, going for upbeat, even as his words stung a little. Was she obsessing about Hayworth to the extent of missing something right under her nose? "So what about this Jenson bloke? If he is involved, it was pretty dumb to let the CCTV catch his car."

"Perhaps he just didn't think about the cameras. People forget, because they're everywhere now," Steve suggested. He chucked her the keys and slid into the passenger seat. "You drive, and I'll call Jess and see if there's anything new from her end. A fiver says Tom Jenson's our man and we have this case wrapped by lunchtime."

"Done, if you have money to lose. Jess'll get pissed off if we keep bugging her. She knows we're desperate for anything. She already told me all the samples have gone up to the central labs, and the pathologist will call if he gets anything at all." Dove adjusted the rear-view mirror. "Anyway, back to this Tom Jenson. It took a hell of a lot of planning and an equal amount of care to get Agnes into the state she ended up in, so I'd say we're looking at a very smart killer, not some hot-headed boyfriend who rowed with his girl."

"Never assume anything in this job," Steve said.

"Profound, I never heard that before," Dove smiled. "Come on, let's go and find this bloke." She passed a new bag of jelly sweets across to her partner and he pulled a face.

"They are so disgusting. You know those things will make your teeth fall out?"

"Kind of you to worry about my dentistry, but as addictions go, I think it's pretty mild."

"I'll stick with cigarettes," he told her. "Although not for too much longer. There hasn't really been a moment to mention it, but Zara's pregnant."

"Oh!" A quick rush of emotion rose in her throat. She shoved it away. "That's great. When's the baby due?"

"October. We were waiting until we had the twelve-week scan to let everyone know."

"That's so exciting." Her voice was shaky, and she had to control her hand from creeping to her stomach. He would be a great dad. She started the engine. Time to focus on finding Agnes's killer.

She pulled into Millfield Road. The extra uniformed officers introduced themselves, and all four headed across the scrubby grass square to the block of flats.

Tom Jenson lived on the second floor. The flat was one of the larger corner ones, and should have been airy, with views of the sea. But what appeared to be a communal hall-way was crowded with bikes, three surfboards and a pile of stinking trainers.

In answer to their knock, Tom answered the door in his pyjamas, blond hair tousled and a day's growth of stubble on his face. He was clutching a large carving knife. His eyes opened wide at the sight of the police officers, knuckles whitening on his weapon.

CHAPTER TWELVE

"I didn't do anything wrong!" Jenson shouted, brandishing the knife in one hand and what was revealed as a packet of ham in the other.

Once he was persuaded to relinquish the knife and had calmed down, Dove's heart rate slowed. It soon became obvious to all that Tom Jenson was about as threatening as a pet hamster and, from the smell of the flat and his behaviour, also slightly stoned.

The knife was for chopping his lunch and being a bit out of it, he clearly saw no reason not to answer the door with a blade.

PC Ellis muttered to Dove that they would stick around for a bit, but when she gave the nod and was happy, the two uniformed officers would get back out on the street.

"Thanks. Let's just have a quick initial chat with him and a look round," Dove answered.

Tom waved them through to his kitchen. "Sorry about the mess. My flatmates, you know . . ."

Dove picked her way around empty pizza boxes and ready-meal cartons. The flat also stank of sweat and mould. It was clearly an overcrowded sublet. Through the open doors she could see the two bedrooms had been roughly portioned to make four even smaller ones. Sleeping bags littered the floor and clothes were stacked in cardboard boxes.

"I thought you might come over, it was just a shock to see a load of you at the front door," he slurred. "I was going to ring you when I heard about Agnes. I really couldn't believe it when I saw her picture on Twitter." Suddenly his personality changed and he beamed at them all before sinking onto a threadbare couch, toppling a pile of sports magazines to the floor.

"Well, here we are, saving you a phone call. It's only a murder investigation, so no urgency at all." Tom just looked at her, clearly not connecting. Dove wondered if he was a regular user, or if he was just not the brightest. "How did you know Agnes?"

"Met her in a club a couple of weeks ago. Not the one where she worked, California Dreams, it was Crazy Plaza off North Street. She said she needed a place to stay, because the hostel she was going to stay in was all booked up and she was kipping on someone's sofa, so I offered her a space here. She moved in the next day. She was basically sofa-surfing. It's cheap and easy, but I offered her a room-share. One of my . . . friends is moving out at the end of the month, so she would have got the bed." He dropped his eyes, biting his lip. "I really was going to call you when I realized it was her on the news. I just don't want any trouble, you know?"

Dove mentally calculated. Two weeks ago, so where had she been staying for the first seven days of her UK visit?

"Did she tell you whose sofa she was sleeping on before she came here?"

"Don't think so. I didn't really ask."

Steve wandered over to the window. The glass was covered in a thick film of grime. "Is this your own flat?"

"Yeah. Well, I rent it from the agency. Sometimes I have my mates stay over."

Dove ignored this for the time being. "Did you pick her up from her previous address, help her with her stuff maybe?"

"Nah. She just said she'd come and she turned up. I didn't think she would, but turns out she had been promised a hostel place and it never happened. I think she answered one of those online bulletin boards for places to stay. She said that it was a great way of finding a sofa or floor to crash on. You know she was backpacking, right?"

"We do. Talk us through your time with Agnes. Which day did she move in?"

"Monday the seventh, I think. I had some . . . other mates staying and it was pretty crowded. She didn't like that, but she worked most nights anyway. I think she had a boyfriend." He gave a harsh laugh. "I thought I was well in there, but after she moved in, she told me she didn't like me like that and wanted us to be friends."

"Sounds like a lot going on in a couple of weeks. Go to Thursday night this week. Did you see her?"

Tom sighed. "Yeah. She was working late at some party in the club. I finished my shift at McDonald's at midnight so I said I'd pick her up. I'm a musician really but gigs are hard to come by and I've got to pay the rent somehow." He indicated a guitar case in the corner of the room. "She was late, though. I sat out the front for an hour, and I kept calling her. Finally she rings and tells me to meet her at the back entrance."

"Did she seem upset?"

"Just kept apologizing for being late and saying she wanted to get home."

"How did you feel when she kept you waiting?" Dove asked.

"Well I was pretty pissed off by then so we had a bit of a row." A flash of fear crossed his face, clearly penetrating the weed-induced stupor. "But I didn't *kill* her! I knew it. That's why I didn't call you as soon as I saw her on Twitter. You bloody cops are all the same. Fuck, that *is* what you think, isn't it?"

CHAPTER THIRTEEN

"We're not thinking anything at the moment," Dove said. "We just need the facts so we can rule people out of the investigation."

"Did you drive straight back here, after you picked Agnes up from the club?" Steve asked.

Tom nodded, wrapping his skinny arms around his chest in a classic defensive pose.

"How did she seem when she lived with you? Did she ever mention she was scared or worried about anything? Someone at the club? Or her boyfriend?"

"No. She was a real pretty, smart girl. I sort of got the impression she had a lot of casual sex and she was out to enjoy life, you know? But she had a more regular bloke on the go, too . . . I think he was more her boyfriend than most of them. He came by to pick her up on Tuesday last week. They were going out along the coast for the day to see some castle, but I didn't see him because I was working. She was always on about her Insta account too and how she needed to take pictures for it."

Steve made a note. "Do you have any contact details for her boyfriend?"

"No. I think she called him Marc. But it was casual. She was on loads of dating apps, and she had the pick of the blokes." Again, there was a slight edge to his voice. Did he feel rejected?

"Which room did she have? We'll need to send someone over to check through her things," Dove said. She was watching Tom's face.

"I kind of thought you would, so I put her stuff in a bag for you." Tom indicated a black bin bag next to the couch. "She was sleeping here, when she was in the flat. Like I said, she wasn't here much. She must have taken her phone with her, when she . . ."

"We'll need a list of your other flatmates, so we can talk to them," Steve told him.

"I can give you some names but I dunno when they'll be around. Most of them work shifts and that." He cringed under Dove's hard stare. "We keep our heads down and get on with our thing. This has got nothing to do with any of us. I just let her stay in the flat, that's all."

"Tom, this girl has been *murdered*, and it seems like at the moment you were the last person to see her. This isn't a case of someone illegally subletting a flat, it's a murder investigation," Steve said.

"Yeah . . . I know that. I guess I'm just shocked. I liked her, not just like that. Like I said, she was so full of life and happy. Even when she was eating takeaway on the floor the other day, she was talking about stuff she was going to do, places she wanted to go. She was just . . . so alive. And she was hot."

"Okay, thanks for your help. We'll be in touch," Dove said. She smiled at him but she was assessing him. She saw the relief in his face as they got up to leave.

Back in the car, Steve passed a fiver over to Dove. She looked at him in surprise. "What's that for?"

"You win. This isn't going to be easy. What a twat. I can't believe he didn't call us straight away. Plus I now stink of weed from that shithole of a flat."

She snagged the note and slipped it into her pocket. In the passenger seat this time, she put in a quick call to the DI to update him on their findings. "We still don't know where she was for the first week of her stay. Steve and I can come back and start checking out the backpacker websites. Jenson gave us a couple he knew most of the kids use, so we can start with those."

"Sure, if you think it might be useful. Be ready for the next briefing at shift changeover," DI Blackman told her.

Dove slumped in the passenger seat, wishing she had got more sleep the night before. "Stop at the next drive-thru, I need coffee. And maybe a burger with fries. And a gherkin."

"Nice. Any new thoughts?"

"She was on Snapchat, Instagram, all the usual places. I can't help wondering why, from a girl who seems to put her whole life online, there isn't anything more about this Marc, or about her three weeks over here. It's almost like she was hiding . . ." Dove sighed. "Pretty travel pictures and a pretty girl. Lots of followers."

"That's what Hayworth kept saying, wasn't it?"

"'Where have all the pretty girls gone?'" Dove quoted, feeling another shiver run through her body. Any thoughts of food fled, leaving that deep, gnawing pain in the pit of her stomach. "It was his catchphrase. He kept saying he spent ages searching for 'the pretty ones, the perfect ones'."

"Well she fits the profile, so someone *is* following in his footsteps fairly closely. It's just a case of working out who it was. I honestly think, gut instinct, that Tom Jenson is too thick and too weedy to have pulled it off."

"Unless he *was* more pissed off at the rejection than he let on, because she wasn't interested, and he got his flatmates to help with the plan?"

"Could be, I suppose . . ."

"We said before it would take a lot of effort to get the glass coffin up the hill to Gibbons Copse, even on something like a motorized sled. It would certainly be easier with extra manpower," Dove suggested.

Steve indicated left and pulled into the McDonald's drive-thru. "Come on, I need that caffeine hit before I do any more thinking."

* * *

The black rubbish sack from Jenson's flat yielded a backpack, toiletries and an iPad. No phone, but the telecommunications company reported that the last signal from Agnes's phone triangulated somewhere in the area of Tom's flat.

"What do you think of him?" DI Blackman asked Dove. The team were gathering for the next briefing.

"Jenson? He's either genuine or an impressive actor. I really think it's the former, he was pretty doped out. Actually, I reckon he was more worried about us being onto his sub-letting scheme than the murder of a flatmate. He seems to have lost interest in Agnes when he realized he wasn't going to get in her knickers."

"Possible motive?" Blackman asked.

"There is nothing to say he did murder Agnes, and he has a watertight alibi from two of his flatmates slash lodgers, who both say he and Agnes got back to the flat, had a drink and they all went to sleep. Another flatmate confirms she saw Agnes on the sofa asleep at 7 a.m. when she got back from a night shift. The last bit of information seems to be from Jenson who claims he went out at about ten, when the others were either asleep or also out, and Agnes was gone when he got back at eleven thirty."

DI Blackman added this to the timeline on the whiteboard, leaving a question mark between the time Agnes supposedly left the flat, and the time her body was discovered on Saturday morning. Eighteen hours when she was unaccounted for. The time when she met her killer and was encased in glass.

"Anything on the websites you and DS Parker were checking out?"

"Nothing yet, boss. There are hundreds of posts and it's going to take a while to narrow them down."

The DI nodded, and then raised his voice to be heard by the others in the room. "Right. I've tracked down Uri Maquess, the party host from Agnes's last night at work, and he will be back in Lymington-on-Sea tomorrow by ten. He will be down at the marina, and I want DC Milson and DS Parker to head over for a chat. I believe we are on the way to ruling out ninety per cent of the client list from California Dreams, but I want us to keep on it. Also tomorrow, I want to run an appeal for information." He paused and took a quick gulp of his coffee. "We need to know where Agnes was staying for the first week of her arrival. After the handover, I want you all to go home and get some sleep. We'll need clear heads to press the fast forward on this case, and not only because the media are watching every move we make."

Soon it would be nearly forty-eight hours since Agnes had died. The pressure was on. DI Lincoln and the night shift were starting to arrive and more staff had been drafted in to cover the phones as calls from helpful members of the public stacked up. In the briefing room, with numbers temporarily swelled, many had to stand. They lined the walls, cups in hands, pens and phones at the ready.

DCI Franklin looked exhausted. His pale face looked flabby and unhealthy in the glow of the lights, and his sparse grey hair was sticking up on one side. The DCI was often pegged by mountains of paperwork, and given the MO of this murder, Dove could imagine his role was exceptionally difficult right now.

He smiled at the assembled team. "Let's make this quick, then. We've got the SOCOs round at Tom Jenson's flat, and we need to follow up on the flatmates before they all do a flit. We have spoken to Agnes's parents. They had no idea she was in the UK, despite regular communication, although as we already know, she did tell them she was intending to come over here next month. She had booked and paid for a room at Bengards Apartments hostel online, despite them saying they had no knowledge of her booking."

At a nod from his boss, DI Blackman took over. "We now know that Agnes had been in the UK for three weeks, working at California Dreams. We have her arriving on the Eurostar alone and getting the train to Abberley, also alone. What we still don't know is where she was staying for her first week and why she came early, despite telling her parents she was still in France. There is also the French boyfriend, Marc, who hasn't come forward, despite the media attention." A blow-up of the Instagram shot appeared on the screen. "Agnes's employer, Gaia Smith-Milson, thinks that the girl mentioned some kind of row with Marc, and got the impression this might have been instrumental in her leaving France early. The cleaner at California Dreams, Janet Green, also mentioned a boyfriend, and we have this one shot from Agnes's social media account."

"We'll get on that," DI Lincoln said. He studied the neat list of names beside each stage of the timeline. "What about the new manager at the club, Colin Creaver?

"The initial chat points to him having an alibi, and I've left you some extra notes on that one to follow up. Other leads . . . It's possible she met someone on a dating app and he was over here in the UK so they hooked up, according to one of the other girls at the club. She didn't know what, when or who, but she thought Agnes might have mentioned it," DCI Franklin added.

"Tom Jenson mentioned two online notice boards for backpackers who wanted to sofa-surf. He was fairly convinced that was how Agnes found her first accommodation. The hostel has confirmed they were fully booked until the night of her original reservation," Blackman said. "And before anyone asks, no, the lab results aren't back yet."

The briefing broke up, and as people grabbed bags and headed home, or broke out the coffee for the night, Dove paused next to DI Blackman.

Dove caught several members of the team passing loaded looks. She was discovering that there were a few big egos in the squad, but that was nothing new, and certainly nothing she hadn't handled before. The key was not to let them get to her. She waited until the buzz of chatter had reached normal levels. "I thought Steve and I might check Hayworth's old address before we clock off. It's not far to go . . ."

DI Blackman nodded. "What's your thinking? Anything coming through from the last cases?"

"Copycat slash hero worship and so maybe the killer spent time in this area, or lives in this area and was soaking up the memories? I don't know. I haven't watched the recent documentary on Hayworth, but it seems plenty of people did. It might be worth chatting to the production company, as a long shot," Dove suggested.

"Go ahead with both those things. Oh, hang on a moment—" DI Blackman held up his hand to Dove and answered his phone.

She waited, heart pounding, hearing from his half of the conversation that the preliminary lab results were back.

"Thanks, Jess." He put the phone down, and called across the office. "Okay, people, the lab results are in. She tested positive for ketamine, but there was no semen present and no sign of sexual assault. Cause of death is confirmed as suffocation, which we already knew from the preliminaries."

There was a flurry of activity, and Dove caught DS Allerton giving her another hard look. Did she know about Dove's connection with Hayworth or was she still incredulous that Dove's sister ran a strip club?

Dizziness, which she told herself was lack of sleep, made her grip the doorframe. Hayworth had also used ketamine to control his victims. This was a perfect copycat, but she clung to the fact that the girl hadn't been sexually assaulted. Hayworth had raped all of his victims, so either this perpetrator didn't have a taste for it, or couldn't get it up.

Eden's face spun across her vision, all bright eyes and wide, trusting smile. And now there was another girl, another set of grieving parents.

CHAPTER FOURTEEN

It's Monday evening and I'm back in front of my screen, reading my messages. Each site requires careful access, and each time I leave or enter a new chat room, I check my own security. Most of the users are familiar with the Dark Web, and they have advanced cloaking software that can never be traced.

But some are dipping a toe for the first time, and they get trapped by Bollo, who's a tech genius and professional hacker. He can trace these people, get them shut down and, again, sometimes that's enough of a warning.

I wander back into the Sugar Teens site, clicking on the link that takes me into the illegal chat forums. This is not one where I post. This is a site for those seeking underage pornography, and I am here to watch. Familiar names occasionally pop up and we can link them back to other sites. I know Taj and Ellie are on here, but I'd never spot them. Deep cover is what this is all about.

Alan1 is back with more photos, and others cautiously offer to trade. I skim down the chat to where BigDaddy is posting a link to a paid live chat.

These are always horrifying, involving child abuse, and I struggle to watch. Taj and Bollo will take over and get as much information as possible, before passing it over to the police.

I spot another familiar name, Jase&Girls. "Taj, I think I've got another one," I call over to him. One of the bigger players is putting a call out for girls. They do this sometimes when they have something major planned.

"Where is he?" Taj is next to me, his dark eyes gleaming with excitement.

"UK, I think. Hard to tell." It always is, these sites attract perverts worldwide. "He's looking for anyone under fourteen — oh, boys and girls this time . . ."

"All right . . ." Taj skims through the forum posts. "Yeah. Keep on it. Maybe try a few posts on some of the chat sites he's on and post as Kerry."

Kerry is one of the names I use when I'm online. Kerry is a frequent visitor to online chat rooms but she hasn't trapped anyone yet. Her web history is untarnished. She's just a normal, lonely eleven-year-old girl looking for a bit of fun on forums like Teen Chat and MyMate.

The excitement of possibly reeling in a vast and vile predator keeps me buzzing until two in the morning. By then, Kerry is deep in conversation with "Kyle" who claims to be a fifteen-year-old boy. He's a catfish, and there are enough alerts on his profile and in his messages to make me link him to Jase&Girls. Either he/she trades with Jase, or this is just another identity of the big player.

I sign off, telling Kyle I need to go to bed. He sends me a GIF of a kitten throwing kisses. Another sign that this is not a fifteen-year-old boy.

CHAPTER FIFTEEN

"Jesus! So she was still alive when he shut the lid on the glass case. That's a fucking awful way to die." Quinn, Dove's boyfriend, still in his dark green uniform, slumped on a chair in her living room and dragged a hand through his hair. "Although I suppose if the ket was still working, and he'd given her a decent dose, she wouldn't have been fully aware what was happening . . . Babe, I'm so sorry this had to be your first case. It's a bit freaky, isn't it?"

Dove handed him a mug of coffee and perched on the chair opposite. Quinn had just finished a run of night shifts, and his shadowed eyes and drawn face matched her own. "Yeah, well, murder is never nice, is it?"

"Must be bringing up memories, though. How's Ren taking it?" His dark eyes showed concern. Her elder sister liked Quinn, but Gaia, for whatever reason, did not.

Dove pulled a face. "Not good. I spoke to her earlier and having this in the news is tough for all of them. Delta's been having nightmares, too. Ren's been off her meds for at least a year now, but Alex is talking about getting her an appointment with the counsellor for next week. She went down so fast last time. Before we realized it, she was suicidal, and it nearly tore them apart." She shuddered. "I would hate for that to happen again."

"Yeah, of course. Alex is a good bloke . . . I can't believe the dead girl was working for Gaia. That also freaks me out a little, so God knows how you must feel."

"I went over to Hayworth's old house on my way home," she said. "Me and Steve just drove over to get a feel, not really because I thought we'd find the current killer sitting on the doorstep."

"You did? Babe, he's dead," Quinn said softly. His fingers linked into hers, comforting and familiar, the other hand stroking Layla's soft fur. The cat was purring rustily, enjoying the gentle caress.

"I know, I'm not thinking his ghost is walking around committing murders . . ."

"Just one, and no, you're right. No ghosts." It was a firm statement.

"Anyway, we checked his old house, and then we parked next to the industrial estate." She met his concerned gaze. "I had Steve with me, so it felt okay. If this is about hero worship, the killer might have gone so far as to visit the places where his idol lived. The lab results came back and so far, we have nothing. The MO is classic step-by-step Hayworth apart from the fact the girl wasn't sexually assaulted. The glass casing was made in the same way, the method of subduing the victims is the same . . ."

"But you told me the place where he kept the girls was destroyed, and there must be new people living in the house?"

"Yeah, that's true, and the new housing covers the road he lived on. His place was knocked down and these little red brick bungalows stretch right up to Hallows Hill."

He nodded slowly, then changed the subject. "You around tomorrow night?"

She raised an eyebrow and he grinned. "Okay, dumb question. Let me know if you get some free time and we'll go out for dinner to that Italian place on the seafront. Or do a takeaway in front on the TV." He leaned in for another kiss.

"Don't forget, Dove, you can't lose yourself in this one, no matter how tough it gets. We're all here for you." He paused. "Don't take this the wrong way, but it couldn't be anything to do with Gaia, could it? Like, her past catching up with her and somebody killing one of her employees as a warning . . ."

Dove sighed. "The DI did ask about Gaia, and I know she has a criminal record, but she's been out of drugs for years. The club was her way of cleaning up her act. After Eden, I just don't see it. It affected all of us so much, and with Gaia, it was like she felt she needed to work harder, make more money, just not on the wrong side of the law."

"Okay, babe, just a thought. I didn't mean it like that."

"I know." For a moment, the silence was easy, the cat purred and Dove felt herself reaching out for him, slipping an arm around his shoulders, feeling the warmth of his body, his breath on her cheek.

It was like turning back the clock, and she almost opened her mouth to ask him to move back in. But he hadn't ever asked for them to live together again. Maybe he was having second thoughts.

"Steve's wife is having a baby."

His muscles tensed under her arm, and she looked up, watching his face. The dark eyes stayed steady. "How did that make you feel?"

She shrugged. "Weird still, I suppose. But I can't freak out every time I see a baby in a pushchair, or when someone else gets pregnant, can I?"

"Have you spoken to Jess recently?" His voice was soft.

"Yes. She mentioned the adoption thing again."

He turned, gently moving in her arms so that they were nose to nose. His heartbeat was strong and steady against her chest, and he reached up with a familiar little gesture, pushing her hair away from her face. "You know I'd be happy to go with whatever you feel is right."

"But I don't want you to do that, Quinn. I want you to be part of any decisions, not just going along with stuff to make me happy," she told him.

81

"You know I still love you, and when you're ready, I want us to live together again." He dropped his gaze, playing with her fingers. "I would never pressure you, though. Take all the time you need."

"I know . . ." She couldn't quite do it, couldn't quench her alarm at the thought of him being with her when she had a nightmare or a panic attack . . . There was still a strong urge to see what she experienced as weakness, to keep it a secret, and at the moment she couldn't override it.

He pulled away. "Okay, I need to head off now. See you tomorrow, babe. Oh, by the way, I got you this . . ." He pulled a jumbo bag of jelly sweets out of his bag, and winked at her. "Just to keep you going."

She nodded, keeping the tone light. "A takeaway tomorrow sounds perfect. I'll call you." She leaned in for a quick kiss before he left. But as the front door shut, she felt like bursting into tears, like flinging open the door and letting him back in.

* * *

Ren would be back from the coffee shop by now, so it was a good time to drop in and see how things were. She grabbed her car keys, leaving her empty coffee mug on the table. Thank God the evenings were getting lighter now. She hated the winter. Eden had died in the snow, Ren had tried to commit suicide at Christmas, and she herself had suffered her breakdown in November. All bad things made worse by the relentless grey and cold.

It was a ten-minute drive to Ren's place, and Dove was relieved to see Alex unloading furniture on the driveway. She could grab a quick chat with him before she saw her sister.

"Hi, love, how's it going?" Alex was blond, tanned, heavily built and wore glasses which were permanently slipping down his nose. "Cuddly" was a good description for him, but Dove also knew he was tough as hell when he had to be. The good-natured rough and tumble of the market fascinated her. The close-knit traders braved all weathers to breathe life into the old cobbled square.

"Okay, I guess. I just came by to see how you were all doing. Is Ren back?" She held her breath, almost afraid of his answer.

He hauled a polished wooden dresser down the ramp, heaving it deftly onto a trolley. Dove noted the red "sold" sticker. Clearly it had been a good day. "She is. She picked up Delta from college on her way."

"I thought Delta stayed late on a Tuesday for swim training?"

"It was cancelled, I think. Anyway, Ren didn't want her to get the bus home." He glanced up, wiping sweat from his face, taking off his glasses and squinting at her, before rubbing the lenses on his grubby white T-shirt and replacing them. "She also said she doesn't want Delta going out to the beach party on Saturday night."

Dove frowned, picking up the worry that tinged his voice. After Eden's death, and Ren's downward spiral ending in a suicide attempt, she had been admitted to a facility for eight weeks' treatment. One understandable reaction to her elder daughter's death had been to smother her remaining child with love, hardly letting her out of her sight. Which hadn't been too bad when Delta was younger. But now she was a young woman heading towards university after her college course.

Alex finished piling a stack of cardboard boxes on the next trolley, and hit a button near the tailgate of the van. The hydraulic ramp neatly folded itself away, and he slammed the doors shut. "Come in, love, and have a chat with her yourself. I really don't know if I can go through all this again. Seeing her in that state, and Delta too, kills me. You know she still blames herself?"

"*Delta* does? Ren said she was having nightmares again."

"She always felt it was her fault because she never passed the message on about pick-up. They were going through an awkward stage, her and Eden." His face contorted with pain for a moment, and he rubbed a big hand around his face.

"I remember. They'd had a row, hadn't they, and that's why she didn't tell you about picking Eden up earlier from her friend's house?" Dove remembered the exact details. She also recalled Delta's horror at her realization that her actions had helped to put her sister in the wrong place at the wrong time.

"We told her so many times that it wasn't her fault. It was Hayworth." He almost spat the name. "That man said he saw her walking past the car park. She fit his profile and that was it."

"It was fate, bad luck, whatever you want call it," Dove said. Her heart ached.

"I still want to vomit every time I think about it. You can't ever heal from that, can you? When someone has taken your child, the first thing you think is that you failed to protect her, but it's just the cruellest glitch of fate that had her in that exact time and place that day." His voice cracked and he pulled a packet of cigarettes out his pocket.

"It wasn't your fault either, Alex. Hayworth was evil, and he was the one who committed the crimes, not anyone else," Dove told him. But there was always a chain of events, always a way for the parents to blame themselves, because that's just how it was.

If your child died, a piece of you died too.

CHAPTER SIXTEEN

Dove wasn't surprised to see Ren was washing her kitchen floor. The smell of lemon disinfectant mingled with the scent of baking cookies. Under stress, her sister became fanatical about cleaning and baking, rushing around all over the place, trying to distract herself from whatever issue had occurred. She once said it was an attempt to escape the pain and sheer panic in her head.

"Hi, Dove. I'll be with you in a minute. Just want to get this done." Her black curls were tied in a knot on top of her head and she was still wearing her red Coffee Fix T-shirt from work.

Treading carefully, so as not to get dirt on the shining tiles, Dove moved onto the carpet of the living room. The house was modern, open-plan and, on a sunny day, flooded with light. It was the opposite of Dove's battered Victorian renovation project.

"Mum's been cleaning ever since we got home," Delta informed her, scowling from her position at the table. Her homework books were out, and her tablet, but she was tapping a message out on her phone. "She didn't have to come and pick me up, did she?"

Delta was tall and slim, with straight brown hair, which she'd had tinted red, and Alex's blue eyes. Her skin was tanned a golden honey colour from all her outdoor sports clubs. Today, in her ripped jeans and blue-check shirt, she looked just like her sister at that age. But then, even as babies they had been beautiful . . .

"All the pretty girls." Dove's throat clogged and she felt her hand had crept to her stomach. She snatched it away, fidgeting with her hair.

Alex came through the door, taking his boots off and carefully lining them up on the mat.

"I guess I thought it would be better to pick you up," Ren told her daughter, her cheeks flushed with effort as she wrung out the mop and straightened from her task. "Safer."

"Just because another girl's been killed it doesn't mean I'll be next. You told me that Eden was unlucky, that it wasn't anyone's fault, so it should be the same with me. If something's going to happen, it's like karma, you can't stop it!" Delta snapped. "I'm not stupid, and I'm old enough to take care of myself." Her voice softened. "And you worrying so much about me makes me stress out. I can see how shit it is for you and Dad after this new murder, and how much it hurts. I miss her too . . . So much."

Alex walked over to the table and gave his daughter a hug, chin pressed on the top of her head. "I know, love, I know, but we have to accept Eden will always be with us, even though we can't see her."

"You mean like a ghost? Leave it, for Christ's sake, Dad, I'm not ten." Delta blinked her tears away, but she was almost smiling at her dad. "She'd have thought that was so funny."

"How about like a guardian angel?" Dove suggested, and Delta bit her lip, her eyes shining again, before she nodded, playing with her necklace.

"Yeah, I guess that works better."

Ren was taking cookies out of the oven now, banging the tray against the oven door with unnecessary force, her face red as she straightened up.

"And, Delta, nobody is suggesting that you are stupid. Of course you can get the bus home from training as normal." Alex flicked the kettle on and sent his wife a warning glance as they passed each other. "It's just a question of being careful. Any updates you can share, Dove?"

"Not really, and we're still in the early stages of the investigation. Everything we know is already public. Have you had any journalists round?" Dove asked.

"A man called this morning but I put the phone down on him," Alex admitted. "I might unplug the landline for a bit if they start again. We could do without the extra hassle."

"Gaia told me the girl worked at her club," Ren said. "She said she'd left you a couple of voicemails but you hadn't got back. I know you haven't been close for a while but . . ." She fingered the scars on her wrists, unconsciously smoothing the ridged skin over and over, before wrapping her bare arms around herself.

Dove shook her head. "It isn't that, and I will get back to her. It's just that she is now a significant witness in the murder investigation, and as I'm on the team, I can't be seen to be muddling any evidence."

"But you wouldn't do that!" Delta said.

"Not intentionally, but I have to make sure everything is word perfect, going by the rules, so the prosecution couldn't find any little loophole when we finally catch this person and it goes to court," Dove explained to her niece.

"Why don't you get her to meet you for coffee at Ren's place?" Alex suggested. "It means you aren't anywhere near the club and they can't possibly expect you won't see your sister at all!"

"No, they don't think that. I'll call her and work something out," Dove agreed. As they spoke, every so often one of them would glance at the gallery of Eden's photographs. She seemed to be staring right at them. It was heartbreaking. A headache nudged behind Dove's eyes.

Desperate to help her family, but unable to do so, Dove cut her visit short and headed home.

She drove quickly, still buzzing from adrenalin. Sleep had always evaded her, even before she joined the police and forced her body into endless shift work, but tonight she really could do with six hours. The sleeping meds she had been prescribed were still in the cupboard. She popped two with a glass of water.

It was bad timing that her investigation was getting underway just as Quinn had days off, but they could have an evening together tomorrow. Too bad she couldn't turn her phone off tonight to ensure complete peace. She smoothed a finger across the screen, smiling at a GIF from Jess, and then set it gently down on the table. She couldn't miss a call, but it was different now.

She knew when she answered a call there wouldn't be the heart-pounding intensity of dropping into character, of knowing what she said and how she said it could mean life or death. Sometimes she found herself searching for her phone in her dreams, combing the house as it rang unanswered.

It had been like losing a limb when she first stopped working as a source handler. She had been so used to living under the spell of the ringtone.

Occasionally she wondered about her CHIS and how they might be getting on, what they were doing. It had been like losing family when she finally separated herself from their lives. But for her own wellbeing, she couldn't continue to live like a ghost, carving herself into several different identities. After Eden's death, things affected her more, her judgement was erratic and she had got deeper into the criminal world that CHIS inhabited. Too deep.

She dragged out her yoga mat and tried to force herself to calm down. The app that was supposed to accompany meditation went on and she sat cross-legged, earbuds in, breathing deeply.

It was a massive struggle, but she couldn't afford to get sucked down again, to lose her career when, her therapist had assured her, she could control it, could prevent her mental health from disintegrating again. It was just a question of giving herself what she needed, whether it was short-term meds, sleep or counselling. Self-care, it was called, and it was something everyone struggled to do, not just her.

As Dove locked up before her early night, she paused at the kitchen window, looking out onto the road. Although she had paid a fitter to install new windows right after she moved in, the house was still in disrepair, and the faded original flowered wallpaper framed her view. It hung in torn strips like skin from a wound, exposing a startling choice of red paintwork below.

The street was crowded with parked cars as the nine-to-fivers had returned home. One car at the edge of the road had its headlights dimmed, engine running. She noted it, her vision losing focus as the sleeping tablets began to kick in.

Surely they would get a proper break on this case tomorrow. Colin Creaver, Uri Maquess, Marc the elusive boyfriend . . . It was sickening to feel the days slipping away without an arrest. She still thought Creaver was a possible suspect, especially if you took into consideration he had started at the club practically the same time as Agnes.

After a shower she checked the road again out of habit. The car was still there, but the engine and lights had been switched off. The driver, no more than a shadowy outline in the street lights, could have been watching her.

It was no more than a prickle of unease, a breeze ruffling a cat's fur, but she turned away from the window, aware that with the light on, her own shadowy movements could be tracked from outside, the blind providing scant cover of any occupants.

It was paranoia, no more. But her hand crept to her scar, and her fingers smoothed the ridges of the now-healed injury.

Nobody is watching you, she told herself.

CHAPTER SEVENTEEN

"Got you a chicken korma and some naan bread, chick." Ellie chucks the brown paper bag down next to my computer.

"Thanks. I'll give you the cash later," I tell her, without taking my eyes off the screen. The luscious smells emanating from the bag are distracting, but I'm so close to hooking this one.

Jase&Girls has been a bit quiet the last couple of days. Kyle suddenly ghosted me, and BigDaddy had his live feed busted. Well, anyway, the event didn't happen and there were loads of pissed customers who had paid but hadn't been able to watch.

I've been chatting to a boy called Charlie, who is supposedly fifteen, a footballer and from right here in my hometown. This particular forum matches you to other users in your area.

Charlie wants to meet, and again through various alerts, I'm pretty sure this isn't a fifteen-year-old boy. It's pretty quiet tonight, and I agree to meet Charlie on Saturday night at the corner of Eve Street and Shore Road. There's a corner shop open till late and a taxi rank further down. If he's genuine, I'll leave him to be stood up, but if he's not, we'll have him. Plenty of time to set up a stake-out.

Scooping up curry with pieces of naan bread, and trying not to drip sauce on my keyboard, I dive back in as Kerry, and get a bite straight away.

'Hey, babe. Seen you around here, and think you look hot. Want to DM?'

I agree and he sends me a personal message, telling me how gorgeous my profile picture is, and admitting he gets really shy in person so doesn't have a girlfriend. He says his name is Jack, and his profile name is @J_Jackson.

Too much too soon, and Bollo's software pings me four alerts on this profile. His own profile picture is pinched from a genuine profile on Facebook, and he also frequents Sugar Teens.

He's pushy, and seems desperate, which I suppose could be quite flattering if this were real. But it isn't. This is shadowland, and I get the feeling he thinks he might be winding me in. Usually they take their time, building a relationship, but he's full of flattery, flooding me with compliments, asking loads of questions, and telling me all about his life.

I pull back, saying I've enjoyed our conversation but need to get on with my homework.

He sends me a photo, clearly catfished, of a teen model. I tell him he looks fit and he tells me it's my turn. I trawl the stock, pull up my "Kerry" pictures, and DM him two.

* * *

Next evening he's back, sending me a hopeful message via the DM box.

"Bollo, can you do a few more checks on this one, please?"

"Sure, send me the link." Bollo is ploughing his way through a family-size packet of fruit pastilles. His dark blond hair is messy and his green eyes are fixed on his screen. My stomach flips. I've never told anyone but actually Bollo is my secret crush.

I really need to grow up a bit. There is no time in my life for boyfriends. I send the link and continue my chat. By the time I've finished my fish and chips, Bollo is hovering over me with a printout.

His shoulder touches mine, and I catch a whiff of chlorine and aftershave. Bollo swims a lot and plays rugby. He's a big bloke, older than me, and he's Taj's best mate. There've been a few times recently when I've thought we might be more than just mates, but I'd hate to make things awkward between us.

"So I've got matches on five sites for this one. He's a bit careless with his privacy and he dips in and out of lots of sites. Mostly he's online UK time at night, between ten and one, so looks like he is actually in this country at least, or he's masking."

I study the sheet. "Sounds like he might be perfect for a meet-up. What do you think?"

Bollo grins, showing his white, even teeth. "Let's do it, girl."

* * *

The first meet-up on Saturday is a bust. Charlie is a real kid, not at all like his photo, but still a real, hopeful teenager. We stand him up.

My midnight meet-up with pushy Jack Jackson is a few miles out of town. I told him I'd get the bus to Climpington, where he supposedly lives, and meet him outside a B & B. He thinks I'm fifteen. I know he's not.

I'm not dressed as a schoolgirl tonight, but I've made an effort in a red crop top, tight flared jeans and high-heeled boots. My hair is down and flops heavy and comforting across my back. Lots of make-up is required for this date and the prey will expect it. Sometimes I wonder who I really am, and why I find it so easy to drop in and out of my many personas. Perhaps "I" don't really exist at all.

Bollo's off sick, Ellie hasn't showed up and Taj is busy, but Elijah takes the van down to Climpington, and I arrive, as promised, on the bus, slipping into the shadows next to the B & B. It's a pretty house, tall and white, with flowerpots outside the front door. I sit on the wall, checking my phone, my bag on the ground next to me.

Twenty minutes late, a car slides to a halt next to me. "Are you Kerry?"

A large man with hard blue eyes and a round face is smiling at me from the passenger window. The driver is in darkness. Two men.

I nod.

"Hi, Kerry, I'm Jack's dad. He sent me to pick you up, because I was having a quick drink after work. Hop in and I'll drive you to our place."

"How far is it?" I ask him, working through my questions, stalling.

"Denne Road. Ten minutes. It's right next to the football pitches, so lucky for the kids . . ." the man starts to say, when without a word, the driver revs the car and screeches off down the road.

For a split second both men are lit by the street light, the orange glow showing the passenger arguing with the driver.

As Elijah appears from behind the garden wall with his phone, I still can't breathe. My life is torn apart. Again.

"Fuck, what happened? Why did they take off?"

I cling onto Elijah for support, and throw up right there on the roadside, shaking, eyes blurred. My mind is spinning, horror is my primary emotion. Has it been him all this time? Is this a coincidence?

* * *

Grabbing my coat, I call goodnight to Taj, who never seems to sleep, and head out. Our HQ is behind a fish and chip shop, in three office rooms that back onto a bricked-up yard. It's a rundown part of town, and it makes us invisible. The only way in or out is by going through the garden flat to the left of the chippie. The flat is empty, and owned by Taj. He uses the address for legit stuff only.

I should have confronted Taj and told him what I know, what I suspect. But I can't. Not yet.

I use my key to go in the back door, pinch a can of Stella from the fridge, and go out the front door, hearing the lock click behind me.

My hands are still shaking and my mind racing with fear and confusion. I down the beer quickly, hoping to blot out the evening. How could I never have suspected, never have dreamt . . .

There's no fucking question what needs to happen now, but have I got the balls to finish it?

There's a rustle and footsteps as I pass the high fence that separates the road from another yard, and I tense, ready to scream, to fight . . . But the voice stops me from making any quick decisions. My name seems to echo through the silent street, bouncing off the buildings, when in reality it has only been whispered.

"Hey," the voice says, "I think we need to have a little talk."

CHAPTER EIGHTEEN

Uri Maquess was charming and welcomed them aboard the luxury yacht while his staff brought tea, coffee and pastries.

The large marina was busy, with a water sports centre to one side, and dozens of smaller craft moored up in neat rows.

"You are Gaia's sister?" Uri smiled at Dove. He was a tall, broad-shouldered man with a pelt of silver hair, immaculately dressed in a shirt, chinos and deck shoes. A yellow pullover was slung across his shoulders.

"I am." Dove wondered exactly how many people Gaia talked to about her sister, and her job. It was a surprise, because going on past experience she had always thought Gaia was embarrassed by Dove's choice of profession.

"I rang her as soon as I discovered one of her girls had been murdered, and she told me that you would want to talk to me." He smiled again, showing perfect white teeth, offering the plate of pastries to Steve, who declined. "I wish I had something to add to your investigation, but I have been thinking so much about that last party. Everything seemed normal."

"Can you tell us a bit about your parties at California Dreams?" Steve asked.

"Of course. I have known Gaia for many years, did she tell you?" His raised eyebrows and mischievous glint in the brown eyes meant he hoped to shock. "Yes, I put some money into the club when she first bought it. Gaia bought me out last year, but I still have a vested interest."

"And the parties?" Dove prompted, making sure her face was expressionless. Gaia had never mentioned Uri as an investor.

"Around one a month, depending on where in the world I am. I like to arrange a special night for various customers, and I think you have managed to get in touch with everyone present that night?"

"Yes, thank you. Gaia was able to give us names and email addresses. Everyone has been very cooperative," Steve said. "Had you met Agnes before?"

"No. She hadn't been working at the club long, had she? I didn't remember her especially . . ." He spread his hands again, palm upward, charming smile lighting up his handsome face. "The girls are all good at California Dreams, and the bubbles were flowing. I think Agnes seemed happy, but I didn't notice her especially. Pretty blonde girls are always at the parties, you understand . . . I like everything to be perfect when I throw a party and Gaia makes that happen."

Dove nodded, making notes, sipping strong coffee, and trying to ignore the gentle rocking of the craft as it bobbed on the mooring line. As someone who was seasick just stepping onto the ferry to France, this was not going to be the best start to the morning. Funny how she loved the sea, could spend hours on the waves on her board, but put her on a boat . . .

They persisted for a while, but either Uri was telling the truth, or he was an excellent liar. His patter was a little too perfect, his eagerness to help maybe too exaggerated, and yet, it fitted with his personality. Dove would certainly ask Gaia more about her "investor".

* * *

Back at the station, Dove filed the interview with Uri, and dropped it into the office. She quickly checked her emails.

Interestingly, Tom Jenson had pitched up at the station at 8 a.m. demanding a proper interview so they could talk about Agnes. He had brought a solicitor and said he wanted to make a proper statement and help find the killer in any way he could.

But far from having something major to reveal, as it turned out he just thought talking to them with a solicitor, and having it all on tape, meant he was now absolved from any crime.

All it really confirmed was that he wasn't the sharpest tool, and even his solicitor had looked a bit impatient when he rambled on about how hot Agnes had been. Nothing new and almost definitely a waste of time.

Ruling people out of the investigation was as important as pulling in new leads, though, so she supposed that at least she could draw a line through Tom's name on her list, for now anyway. He did have an alibi, and when she went through the timeline again and checked through the statements from the flatmates, it seemed to hang together. The flatmates didn't really socialize and were used to constant new arrivals and departures.

Tom had admitted he advertised on a couple of websites as having a space to rent, and Dove found his posts on both Sofa Surf and Kip Space. Both websites had hundreds of posts in their forums and although she tried to narrow the searches to Abberley and Lymington-on-Sea, it seemed to be hit and miss whether the search engine pulled up the correct location. She switched back to the notes on numerous witnesses.

The night shift had noted that the hostel in Paris where Agnes had been staying had been extremely helpful and had CCTV. They were liaising with French police on this one, trying to track the girl's movements. She had spent two months in Paris. Checking the email from the hostel, she could see Agnes had been staying there the whole time. It tallied with what she had told her parents and her photographs on social media. So why go rogue suddenly?

The girl's Instagram account was packed with travel photos, but since her arrival in the UK she had only posted retrospective ones of her time in Paris, not even mentioning she was on the move again. Why?

Dove bookmarked her searches and flicked through the club employees and customers from California Dreams. Colin Creaver. DI Blackman had told her he had an alibi but he was concerned about both his likeness to Marc, and also the fact he'd started work at the club just a week after Agnes.

She studied the notes from the interview, noting that he seemed to be saying all the right things. His alibi was that his car had broken down that Friday morning at ten, when he was on his way to Tesco. He had waited for a breakdown truck, been caught on CCTV at the garage, and finally went out with a couple of mates and stayed over at their house on the Friday night.

Everything tied up, just as it had with Tom Jenson, which meant she should be drawing a line through Colin's name, but she couldn't. There was something that she couldn't put her finger on.

A quick call to Border Control revealed that Colin had arrived in the UK six weeks ago from Berlin. He had been staying with family for three weeks' holiday, and his sister confirmed he had been playing tourist all that time. She scrolled down. Before that, he had been living in Plymouth, Devon.

Knowing her hunch might be a total waste of time, she started digging.

"You've got that look on," Steve told her, pushing a packet of biscuits across the desk. "What have you found?"

"Colin Creaver bothers me," she muttered, shoving a chocolate digestive into her mouth and speaking through the crumbs. "I wonder what Agnes thought of him looking just like her ex . . . Exactly what are the chances of that being the case? He was supposedly in Berlin while she was in Paris. Not a million miles away."

"I've found another three addresses in the area from Sofa Surf," Steve said. "Might be worth checking out?"

"Can you let the DI know and give me five minutes on this?"

Dove dived into HOLMES for Creaver's social media, his previous addresses: everything looked clean, and had been checked out thoroughly, but still . . . Shrugging, she gave up and checked her phone. Her gut clenched. There were four missed calls from her brother-in-law.

"DI says for us to go and check these three addresses out. You okay, Dove?"

"Fine. Sorry, Steve. Let's go. I just need to make a quick call on the way."

Waiting for her brother-in-law to answer, she bit her thumbnail anxiously, hoping Ren was all right, telling herself that whatever it was, it couldn't be worse than last time.

"Dove! At last, I've been trying you for the last hour. Delta's disappeared." Alex's voice was trembling. "Dove, she's fucking gone!"

CHAPTER NINETEEN

Dove froze, standing in the stairwell, the bright sunlight that streamed in hurting her eyes. "Tell me what happened." Her heart was beating hard, painful strokes, her hands shaking. "Disappeared *how?*"

Steve had stopped too, his expression serious as he listened to her conversation, aware of her sudden horror.

"She went out last night, after she had another row with Ren. To her mate Taj's place, I think. They've been friends for ages and she mentions him quite a lot . . ." He stopped, and Dove could hear his ragged breathing as he fought to control himself. "She didn't come home, and then this morning she didn't turn up for college. I was working on the stall, so I didn't really think until Ren called and asked if she wanted dinner or if she was going out again, because she hadn't had a reply from the text she'd sent. I realized she hadn't been around since last night!"

"Okay." Dove bit down hard on her nail, drawing blood from the skin around her thumb. "Don't jump down my throat but could she just have stayed at Taj's — is he her boyfriend, and they overslept? If she was still mad at Ren for trying to keep her inside, maybe . . ." The buzz of activity from her colleagues, the noise of traffic on the road outside the police station receded as she pictured Delta's angry face. It was just a teenage row, surely. They were all emotional at the moment, understandably so.

"She's not answering her phone! And I don't know Taj's number. He lives down near the river but I don't know exactly where. She's always been so careful and so good about keeping in touch, ever since . . ."

"I know, ever since Eden. How's Ren taking it?" She hardly dared ask the question. Part of her railed against the teenage selfishness that Delta had succumbed to, yet she hoped that was all it was. The other option was too terrible to bear.

"I haven't told her. She's gone over to that rehab place for another appointment with her counsellor, and she doesn't get back until five. She doesn't skip college, Dove, you know that! I rang Gaia when I couldn't get through to you and she hasn't heard from her. Fucking hell, I can't tell Ren Delta's gone as well. What am I going to do?"

He was crying, and her heart felt like somebody had just ripped another tear in it. Not again, surely not again. This would be a classic case of a teenager running away in response to all the emotion surrounding the recent murder. It had to be.

"First, check round any of her friends that you do know, and call me if you get any updates. How has she seemed recently? Any other major arguments, or anything that had upset her? Apart from the obvious . . ."

"That's just it, isn't it? You know how she's been lately, and I'm worried she might have done something stupid. It's a lot to cope with and sure, outwardly she's been doing okay, but I'm so scared that Ren struggling and this latest murder has screwed her up." His usually strong, confident tones had been replaced by helplessness. "Dove, I don't think I can deal with this again . . ."

"Alex, listen to me. I'll file a missing persons report and speak to my boss, and you speak to any friends you can think of, if you have their numbers. Try hard to write down anything she might have said, places or people she might have mentioned in the last couple of weeks. I'm not going to say try not to worry, because we both know that's bullshit, but she's a smart girl, so hold on to that."

Alex rang off, and Dove updated Steve.

"I can grab one of the others to visit these addresses, you sort out your niece," he said.

She nodded, running back upstairs, banging the doors behind her. It was Eden all over again. Could this killer be targeting Eden's sister? She saw Delta, sitting defiant in her shirt and jeans, replacing her with Eden, at the same age. They could have been twins, just like her and Gaia. It would be twisted as fuck for someone to come after a relative of the first murders. But did that make it more or less likely?

"What's up, DC Milson?" DI Blackman took in her blanched expression.

She told him.

"Do you think there is any possibility her disappearance could be linked to Agnes's murder?" the DI asked. "I know it's tough, but you said the family has already been distressed by the new reportage, and it must be affecting Delta too. It's likely that she has run off to a friend's house to get her head around all this."

"On the opposing side, I think we need to consider there is a link in all this between the killer and my family," Dove said.

"Explain."

"Eden was killed by Hayworth, Agnes worked at my sister's club, and now her niece has gone missing," Dove said, her voice shaking. "I feel like maybe someone could be targeting Gaia."

"All right, we'll bring her in for a chat. I assume she will know about her niece already?"

"Yes, Alex said he rang her."

"We'll make this a priority because of the history," DI Blackman said, turning to pick up the phone. "And because I don't believe in coincidences."

101

With the MCT already working at full stretch, the DI began to split the duties. DS Allerton would be the FLO for the Matthews family, with an additional officer added if needed. This was an unusual move, as normally a FLO would not be allocated for a missing person, especially an eighteen-year-old who had only been missing for a few hours, but it was proof DI Blackman was taking Dove's suggestion seriously.

DI Lincoln would be in charge of Delta's case. Meanwhile, the rest of the team would continue to work on Agnes's murder.

Dove, devastated by the events, insisted she would rather remain at work chasing down the killer than at home wondering what had happened to Delta. The theory that someone might be targeting Gaia was aired and she knew that whatever reservations she had, her sister would put everything into helping to find her niece.

She rang Alex at six, waiting as news from the search teams filtered in, hoping for good news.

Her brother-in-law answered the phone quickly, his voice eager. "Dove! Any news?"

"There is a missing persons report on Delta now, and one of our officers is going to keep you up to date."

"Yes, she came round earlier . . . Lindsey. We saw the dog team in Norris Woods, and I know they were there because I said she sometimes cuts across the footpath to her friend Andi's house. It's like Eden again . . . I really don't know if I can take this, Dove." His voice was alternately quick and eager, and weighed down with worry.

"Did you have any luck with her friends?"

"Nobody's seen her since the weekend. She hasn't logged on to any of her social media accounts and her phone is switched off. We keep ringing every hour or so, just to check."

"Oh God, I should come round, but I really can't until after work." Dove felt the familiar pull between her family and her job. "How's Ren?" She braced herself for Alex's response.

"When I told her about Delta, she almost fainted dead away. I played it down and said she's probably just run off for some time out, with everything that's been happening, but she isn't stupid. To be honest, I don't think Ren herself really knows what's happening at the moment. She's on loads of meds again. But at least that means she isn't stressing too much."

Dove remembered the last time Ren had been that dosed up. The light had gone out from behind her eyes, and her lovely warm glow had vanished. She had been a robot in a brittle shell, but as Alex had pointed out, she was calm, and unaware or unable to feel the terror that was currently scratching hooked claws into her heart.

"All the pretty girls."

CHAPTER TWENTY

The morning briefing had already started when the call came in, and the DCI raised his voice. "Right, people, we've got another Glass Doll murder. Uniform have just called it in. Same MO, and I'm sending the details to your phones."

Dove clutched the doorframe with sweaty hands. *Please God, no.* It couldn't be. The buzz of her colleagues' excited chatter rang in her ears and she found she was shaking from head to foot. Not another panic attack. Not here.

"Bloody hell. You stay here, DC Milson, and I'll get DS Conrad to go out to the scene," DI Blackman told her when he saw her.

Dove steadied herself. She had to, for her niece, for her sister. "No! Boss, I need to be there. If it's Delta, I promise I'll keep out of it, but if it isn't, I need to keep working."

He stared at her, lips pursed with worry, then nodded. "Okay, but if we get there and find out the victim is your niece, you get the hell out of there and come back to the station."

"Yes, boss."

Steve tried hard to reassure her. "The description of the victim says she's a redhead, and you just told me your niece has brown hair."

Dove pressed her lips together, closed her eyes briefly and then opened them. "She has red streaks in. Lowlights or something, she called it."

"Still not a redhead." Steve held up his hand to stem any arguments. "All right, I'll shut up."

They arrived as Jess pulled up in her van and the team headed together down to the beach. Normally the CSM would arrive later, but such was the pressure on these murders, everyone was wired, desperate to solve the case. Jess's expression was grim and as they walked, unseen by the others, she squeezed Dove's hand. Their boots crunched on the shingle while the grey sea crashed below the tide line. The early promise of spring sunshine had vanished, leaving icy rain that spattered in the gusts of a wintry wind.

The body was neatly positioned in one of the many little coves that were dotted along the coast. The glass case was pulled high enough to be out of reach of the water, even at high tide, and the slightly secluded position, coupled with the unseasonal weather, was probably the reason it hadn't been discovered sooner.

Dove yanked on her protective clothing, ignoring the gathering of curious onlookers, and followed Steve and a uniformed officer up to the body. Her heart was drumming so fast she felt light-headed, the tumbling waves echoing her tumultuous thoughts. *Please, God, don't let it be Delta.*

Blue eyes, long hair in bunches, but the skin was too pale to be Delta, the hair curly and almost ginger. Freckles on her face, naked shoulders and arms, and again, she looked to be in her teens.

Someone shouted from the clifftop and she looked up at a man balanced precariously on the grass near the edge, trying to get a better look. "Can we get a cordon up at the top of the cliff as well? Those bastard journos are going to be crawling over this," Dove said to the officer nearest to her.

The other woman nodded, and picked up her radio. "We've got a team up there, but he must have slipped through . . ."

Directed by Jess, a CSI was photographing the body, and she called to Dove. "Looks just the same as the last one. Everything is very neat and professional. No damage to the body and the case looks like it's sealed in the same way."

"The bastard!" Dove said, ashamed of her limb-weakening relief as she gazed down into the blind, terrified eyes of the victim. "There must be some way he's slipped up this time. Who found the body?"

"A surfer, apparently. He's over there." Steve pointed and they made their way back across the beach.

Dove glanced across to the lifeguard hut, where the flapping blue tape provided scant privacy from the crowd beyond. A helicopter flew overhead, and the lifeguard was standing by in response to the alert. Another body was big news. Twice now, the perpetrator had eluded police, so he must be feeling pretty confident. How closely was he following progress on the previous murders, and did he hope to commit more?

As Steve paused to speak to the DI, Dove made her way back along the shingle, trudging against the wind. It would have been near impossible to drive on this terrain, and the way down from the cliffs could only be taken by a climber. Certainly not someone with a heavy glass case to manoeuvre.

She thought how perfect the casing had looked. No chips or scratches that indicated a cliffside descent. A boat, then. The killer could have loaded his victim further along the coast and brought her here under cover of darkness. It would be easier, if still hard work, to slide the case off a boat at high tide . . . She made a mental note to check tide times for last night.

The surfer was male, and he had his back to her. Tousled blond hair and a navy wetsuit, but something about the set of the shoulders was familiar.

"Colin Creaver?" Her voice carried across the beach.

He swung around. "Yes? Can you believe this? That poor girl . . ." His green eyes were red-rimmed, either from shock or saltwater. They widened for a moment as he took in her appearance. "Sorry, you look a lot like someone I know . . ."

106

Gaia, of course. "I'm DC Dove Milson. Can we have a quick chat?"

"Of course. I've given all the details to your colleague, but anything that helps you catch this bastard . . ."

"Do you have any idea who the victim is?" Her voice came out hard and harsh and she saw him wince.

"I . . ." He paused and swallowed hard, eyes narrowing. "Yes, I'm afraid I do. She's called Evie."

"How do you know her?"

He scuffed at the pebbles with his foot, and dragged a large hand through his wet hair. "She's been working at the club I manage, California Dreams, for about six months, I think."

Dove bit her lip in shock. Another one from Gaia's club. How could that be a coincidence? "Okay. Come and sit over here," she indicated a battered wooden bench on the concrete at the top end of the beach.

"I already told your colleague everything I know," Creaver said, with a trace of defiance. "Evie was a lovely girl."

"I'm sure she was, and it must be a huge shock for you to find her body. I just need to ask you a few more questions. You might remember more than you think as we go over it again. It would be very helpful to us," she added with a smile. "And anything you know about Evie's character, what she was like at work, just to build up a picture."

Creaver's face softened. "I haven't been working at the club long, but Evie was good with the men. She was . . . um . . . a bit of bitch with the other girls as far as I could see. She had endless rows with whoever she was working with and nobody wanted to work with her. I believe my boss, Gaia, was thinking of letting her go, but she did so well with the customers." He sighed. "It doesn't seem possible she's dead. And so soon after Agnes. It really is horrific, isn't it? These are nice girls."

Another girl from the club, and Delta missing. Dove was trying to balance the two in her head, make some kind of tentative connection. *Was* this personal? If so, it was entirely possible that someone was targeting her sister. Gaia moved in very different circles from her two sisters, and if there was a grudge match going on, this could be an elaborate way to get at Gaia. And that would mean they had a motive for taking her niece, too.

Uri Maquess had put money into the club. Perhaps other characters from her sister's past had also helped her launch her new business. She was sure Gaia wouldn't have taken on a new manager if she was struggling financially, so it couldn't be debts. An ex-lover?

Creaver was still watching her anxiously. "I might have touched the glass when I found her . . . Sorry, but I just couldn't believe it was happening, you know? It didn't seem real to have a dead girl in front of me."

CHAPTER TWENTY-ONE

"The victim's name is Evie Pollard. She's originally from Cardiff, but went to university in Nottingham. Dropped out of her degree course in English Literature last year and has been a bit of a drifter ever since. Her mum is on her way down here, and at the moment we can't locate the father. He's apparently on a fishing holiday in Norfolk with his mates." DI Blackman glanced up briefly at Dove, and then continued. "Evie has been working at California Dreams for the past six months. She rented a flat on the Greenview Estate on the west side of town, so geographically nowhere near the previous victim. Her flatmate reported her missing yesterday morning, when her boss said she didn't show up for work. It seems she also had a day job as a cleaner at the Abberley Road Theatre."

Dove narrowed her eyes. "The dog walker who found our first victim works at the theatre, too. Victoria." She glanced at the map pinned up on the whiteboard. "It isn't far from the club if you cut across Moore Road."

The DI nodded. "Okay, so we'll need to talk to her again and find out if there's any link there. She has a minor drugs conviction from 2018, so that might be another lead."

"Do we think the killer is targeting the club owner, Gaia Smith-Milson?" DS Allerton shot a glance at Dove, who kept her face neutral. After all, it was exactly what everyone was thinking.

"It's a definite possibility, especially if we add Colin Creaver to the mix. At this stage, we desperately need something on this killer. But I don't have to tell you that. I want us to go over the evidence again. The lab is making Evie's results a priority."

"Colin Creaver works at the club, but he moved down here just a few weeks ago," Dove said, recalling his green eyes and nervous chatter after he'd discovered the body. "He had an alibi that checked out for Agnes, but finding this latest victim puts up a red marker on his name."

"Go over his statement again. See if there's anything we've missed. Whoever is doing this is laughing at us, enjoying his power trip," Blackman said. "The press are attacking us from all sides, and the DCI wants this finished before anyone else dies. Let's nail this bastard. Two murders and a missing teenager with no decent leads is a fucking joke."

DCI Franklin cleared his throat and took over. "We also have, as mentioned already, a possible linked case with missing local teenager, eighteen-year-old Delta Matthews." He glanced at Dove and his expression was compassionate. "Delta hasn't been seen since Wednesday night, when she apparently rowed with her parents. Her sister, Eden Matthews, was one of Peter Hayworth's victims, so it is likely that this case has stirred up emotions."

DI Blackman added Delta's timeline underneath those of Agnes and Evie's. "The reason this is possibly connected, and we are making it a priority, is that the club owner at California Dreams is also Delta and Eden's aunt."

"Jesus, that's twisted," someone said in an undertone.

"Yes. So because of the unusual number of connections to our homicide cases we will keep the missing person case in house. DI Lincoln and DS Conrad are now leading on Delta Matthews."

Relieved her own connections hadn't been emphasized, Dove walked back to her computer. Where would Delta go if she needed to be by herself? The girls all surfed, and the coast was perfect for water sports. It was rocky with pebble beaches, and tiny hidden coves. Although Dove had lived in the city for years, Ren, soon followed by Gaia, had made her home in this southern corner of the UK so Ren's daughters had been brought up on the coast.

There was muttering as the team broke up and the frantic tap of fingers on keyboards filled the room. Outside, the rain had now set in and was drumming rhythmically on the windows.

Dove phoned Alex, who answered on the first ring, his voice urgent. "Yes?"

"I haven't heard anything. Sorry, Alex, but we've been tied up with this new murder."

"I know. When I saw it on the news, I thought for sure it was Delta . . . But then I thought if it was her, you would have come to see us, wouldn't you? Not just left it to Lindsey." His voice was almost childlike in its plea.

"Of course, and it wasn't her." Dove paused. "Did you manage to give Delta's tablet and laptop to the search team?"

"I found it on a shelf at the back of her wardrobe. God knows why she has to be so secretive about her technical bits and bobs," Alex said, a note of anger creeping into his voice. "Why did she do this, Dove? If she has just run away, didn't she think what it would do to us?"

"I don't know, I really don't know, but like you two, I'd give anything for this to be a teenage tantrum," said Dove soberly.

* * *

Blackman beckoned Dove in for a chat at half five. "Did you get anything else this afternoon?"

Dove frowned. "Colin Creaver. His alibi for the first murder looks good on paper, but as manager for the club, he would stay in the back room most of the time. Especially with a private party going on. So for this murder, he's at the

111

club while the victim's working, and then he also finds her body the next morning. What are the chances of that? He's very chatty and keen to help, but there's just something a bit off kilter about him."

"And he makes another connection to Gaia. She was really open about her past when she came in, by the way, and I don't doubt anything she told us. If someone is targeting her, I do believe her when she says she has no idea who it could be."

"Thanks. We don't talk that often, and with this going on, I haven't spoken to her since Evie was found."

"Okay. I think we need to bring Creaver in for another chat, but I won't bring you in because of the club connection. We need to be very careful with this. Any sign of personal involvement, and I will have no hesitation in taking you off the case, for your own sake as well as everyone else's. And DS Milson?"

She turned on her way out.

"I'll keep checking for news of your niece."

Dove nodded, managing to curve her lips into a semblance of a smile. Where the hell was Delta?

She called Quinn on her way home. "Hey, it's your girlfriend, remember me?"

"Shit week you're having, babe. I've missed you. Any news on Delta?"

"None. And now another murder. I almost run down journalists every time I drive in and out of work, and Ren and Alex are tearing their hair out."

"What about Gaia?"

"I haven't spoken to her. According to my boss, she's been super helpful, though."

"That's unusual. Gaia helping the police, I mean. I suppose if she's doing it for Delta . . ."

"She is. Whatever her faults and her past, Gaia loves Delta and Eden like her own kids."

"Like you do." His voice was gentle. "Don't let it drown you, Dove. You're really good at your job, but don't disappear again, all right?"

She knew exactly what he meant. "I won't. Are you going down the pub with the boys tonight?"

"You know me so well. The football's on and I haven't had any better offers from any gorgeous women so . . . When you're ready, just call me," Quinn said.

She was nearly home when another call came in, and she glanced at the number, shocked. Her old boss didn't make social calls.

"Chris?"

"Evening, Dove, how's it going?"

"Good." Chris had never been one for small talk, but as unit boss, he had always insisted they were all one big happy family.

"I've got a little problem. Well, more *you've* got a little problem."

"Stop talking in riddles. Are you pissed or something?"

He laughed. "No. We've had contact from one of your old CHIS. He claims to have some information for us, but will only speak to you. Obviously he knows you aren't with us anymore, and I'm not one to let the bastards dictate terms, but he says the information he has is linked to the murder of Agnes Nilsson."

"Shit." She mentally paged through her old contacts, her mind whirling. Just as she thought she'd got a grip on things and was moving on, the past dragged her back.

Chris's voice cut through her panic. "That's what I said too. I chit-chatted with him for a while, but he's adamant he only trusts you, and will only give the information to you." He paused and she detected a hint of strain, a tiny blip in his usual confidence. "I would never normally do this, but I hear you've got two bodies and no arrests, so I'm actually doing you a favour."

"You are?" Dove's heart was pounding, her thoughts still all over the place. Thank God he couldn't see her. "So who's the CHIS?"

"Adrik Hammond."

She leaned back in her seat, eyes closing, visualizing his face, hearing his voice. Of course it would be Adrik. "I don't get it, though. If he's got information, just offer him more money. He always needs the cash."

"Didn't work. I've got another proposal. I'm just throwing this out there, mind you . . . First, do you reckon you could co-handle? Just until we get the information off him."

"I don't know. God, what a punch in the guts." She was feeling her way. "I suppose so, to get the info, but I'm not a handler anymore, and his checks will be out of date for a start . . ."

"We could sort it, if need be. Think about it, and let me know in the morning."

It was completely dark by the time she pulled into her road. Her house had no driveway and she was forced to park half a mile away. Swearing under her breath, she grabbed her bag and marched along the pavement, buffeted by the salty wind, her hair blowing into her eyes.

Nearly home. A footpath branched off the road, losing itself in a twist of deeper darkness. Somewhere away to her left, a dog barked. She almost missed the voice. The name from her past, coming softly from the blackness.

"Kelly."

She hadn't heard him approach, hadn't seen him step out from the shadows, but he was there, outlined against the night sky.

CHAPTER TWENTY-TWO

But Dove was still a professional, no matter what state she was in mentally, and she snapped back into character. "Adrik. Long time no see."

That was Kelly, nonchalant and unconcerned, as though she'd half-expected his menacing presence in her own street. Which, fresh from her conversation with Chris, she kind of had.

"I need a chat." His hood was up, face almost hidden by the folds of fabric, but his eyes gleamed in the street light. As ever, he was glancing up and down the road, shifting on the balls of his feet, always ready for an attack.

"Adrik, mate, I don't work for the unit anymore. If you want to chat, you need to speak to another handler. I gotta tell you, creeping up on me in the road doesn't get you brownie points." Her heart was pounding so hard, she felt sick. How had he found her? If he knew where she lived, surely he must know she wasn't really called Kelly.

"Whatever. I needed to find you. I haven't talked to anyone else. Nobody except you. It's been over six months, and I've got stuff to tell, but I'll only speak to you. I miss our connection. I already rang in and told them I got something for you." His voice was hopeful.

"You know it doesn't work like that." Her shock was cooling to anger. He should have stayed on his own patch and out of her new life. The ghosts were out of the box and dancing on the street. She had broken the rules, but survived. The last thing she needed was Adrik back, whatever Chris was saying about breaking the case.

"Make it work, then." He came closer, and she stood her ground, meeting his eyes. "I know stuff about Agnes Nilsson, and it's good enough that you might catch the fucker who killed her. It's a big piece of junk, Kelly."

"You've got junk? That I wasn't expecting." Dove let out a long breath, shoving her hands in her pockets, maintaining eye contact. Adrik Hammond was a low-rent criminal, constantly lurking on the fringes of the bigger stuff, but never progressing into anything that could cause him major trouble. His family were into drugs, and his brothers were dealers, carjackers and everything in between.

Adrik's speciality was as a tech dealer. He had a knack for anything electrical, from mobile phones to laptops and other gadgets. In another lifetime, with the right opportunities, he could have probably forged a career in that industry. As it was, he kept his head down, his true intelligence hidden. His long-term girlfriend, Aleesha, had tried to push them out of the area, even suggesting they go abroad. But Adrik would never leave his brothers.

Kelly's cover was that she had been the girlfriend of a mate of his, and when the mate was killed in a pub stabbing, he had promised to look out for her. It made sense and she had been widely accepted.

It a world where death and promises were cheap, Adrik was surprisingly loyal. Most of her other CHISs had been backstabbing, double-dealing snakes, twisting and squirming and requiring constant checking to make sure they weren't feeding false information, and taking double payment from the very criminal gangs they were supposedly informing on.

Adrik was a CHIS because it was a good way to make money, and he got a buzz from occasionally informing on rival family members. Out of all her contacts, he was the closest to a friend, although she wasn't supposed to be friends with any of them.

He had also been there for her when Eden was murdered, when she had slipped up and blurred the lines between professional and personal. She hastily shoved the memory away.

Dove worked hard to keep her face blank. She was desperate to ask what he had on Agnes Nilsson. He spoke again, low and urgent.

"I know your real name. I know who your sister is, so I know what's going on in your life right now, like I know what happened before, as well."

She realized she had wrapped her hands across her stomach, was standing awkwardly in front of him.

His expression was gentle, his voice soft. "But I'd never use it against you, because, you know, me and Kelly are mates. You've always got my back, so I reckon I owe you. Don't freak because I found you, all right, I'm not some weirdo stalker, you know that."

"Yeah, I know, Adrik. But I've got to follow the rules. *You* know that. I'm not an informant handler anymore and I don't work for the IU or even for Nantich Valley. You can't just hunt me down, come up to me on the street and tell me you've got something. That puts both of us in danger."

"How else was I meant to contact you? You've got no phone anymore, not for me anyway." His eyes glinted in the street light, lips curving into a smile. His hood slipped back a little, revealing spikes of ice-blond hair. "Don't stress, I checked it out and we're good."

"I can't just take information from you on the street." Her mind was working to reach a way out of this. "Okay, tomorrow I'll ring my old boss at the unit, and . . ."

"I ain't telling nobody else." He was stubborn. "It's good, sound junk. You need this, Kelly."

"Junk" was his word for tech, and she suspected it was a mobile phone, which was his usual way of providing information. So many criminals only cared about the latest flash kit, tossing the old stuff aside when a new model came out, so they could show off how well they were doing. The old stuff often went to Adrik, and the owners were frequently careless enough to leave all sorts of juicy details on back-up disks and memory cards. What was thought to be deleted, if you were Adrik, was never truly gone.

Running her conversation with Chris over in her mind, she half-wondered if her maverick ex-boss had set this up to get a result. Surely even he wasn't that crazy, though?

"I was actually going to say I'll ring my boss tomorrow and see if we can set up a co-handler. That way it's still me, but there has to be someone else as well. You know exactly how it works. If you just mouth off at me in the street, you won't get paid and we can't use any information. It's got to be done properly." The wind was icy, cutting into her face. She pushed her hair out of her eyes.

"Yeah, I remember. Like, we've got that protocol to think about, haven't we? I've still got my old number, Kelly."

"I'll call you tomorrow, and we'll sort it out, Adrik." He came closer and peered into her face, touching her arm. She shook him off, feebly.

"Yeah, I don't want that bastard killer to get any more girls. I know you lost family and that's partly why I came. You know I don't like that shit. Sicker than I've seen in a while." Adrik raised a hand in farewell and walked quickly down the road, leaving her speechless, heart pounding.

In her head, she could hear her Chris's voice as she stood in his office for the last time. "*You might be moving out of the city, Dove, but you'll never really leave the Source Unit.*"

Fucking bastard, she'd thought at the time, but now what could she do? If Adrik had information, and she had no doubt he did, despite the whole load of paperwork and pro-tocol involved, she wanted whatever he had to offer.

A CHIS could be as stubborn as a handler and with Delta now missing, she would take anything, whatever the cost to herself.

CHAPTER TWENTY-THREE

"As you said yourself, you don't work as a handler anymore. This could potentially be a really awkward situation," DI Blackman said, in response to her urgent late-night call. "Can't you get him to liaise with someone at Nantich Valley?"

Calming down after Adrik's street ambush, she had realized she needed to talk to her current boss before she spoke to her old one.

"I could. I know the rules, but Adrik has been, sorry, *was* one of mine for four years. He gave some good stuff and it was proper heavy information that checked out. As far as I trust any of the CHIS, I would trust him. Okay, tracking me down is not ideal and believe me, I'm a bit freaked out, but he really believes he's got something."

"I know how hard this must be, trying to work the murder case with the history and with your niece still missing. If the personal angle is getting too much, just say the word, and I'll take you off the case."

Dove gripped her phone in frustration. "I'm fine, and I'm just going on gut instinct. Boss, my family is falling apart and I can't help them unless I do my job and Delta is found."

"What do you suggest? Nantich Valley aren't going to be thrilled to share a CHIS, are they? Especially one who's been off the books for six months. All the checks will need to be done again, and if they agree it means you taking on co-handling duties as well as the current workload." His voice was heavy with concern. "Not to mention the mountain of paperwork we'll need to process."

"I get what you're saying, and I really will tell you the moment it gets too much, but I'm hoping it doesn't." Should she tell him Chris had already called her last night? No, let them work it out. All she needed was that information, and it wasn't like she'd even have to co-handle for long.

"What do you propose, then?"

She had thought most of it out before she rang him, and tried to sound calm and in control, when actually her hands were still trembling at the late-night encounter. "I'll tell Chris Sanderson, my old boss, to set it up so I can co-handle Adrik. Adrik will agree to a co-handler but he won't give up his info to anyone except me. I can make him see that this is the only way. It isn't a forever situation, it's just to get this current information, which you must agree would give us a boost. We're still hanging our hopes on Creaver or this phantom boyfriend, Marc."

"I still don't like that he's been following you, knows who you are. Does he fancy you?"

"*Adrik?*" she laughed, hoping it sounded convincing. It had just been the one time, but once had been enough to burn the connection soul-deep. She had met Quinn shortly afterwards and grabbed at the lifeline of a potentially normal relationship. "No. He's always seen me as a sister slash mother figure. When his first kid was born, I was there at the hospital with a bottle of fizz and flowers for his baby mama. Each time one of his family gets in shit and loses their lives, I'm there as a shoulder to cry on. It's intense, and I'd like to reiterate *I'm* freaked out that he tracked me down, but it's not impossible and he's clever with his tech. I haven't moved far, just one borough over. These people have ways of finding anyone they want, you know that."

"All right. Talk to Chris tomorrow. Christ knows we could do with some good news."

"Thanks, boss." Dove finished her call, and once again looked out over the dark road. No silent watcher tonight. She figured it must have been Adrik checking the place out, but she was telling the truth when she said it didn't worry her as much as it should. He was a good bloke on the whole, and if he could help break the case it would be worth setting the ghosts free. It was something she had missed on the MCT, her link with the criminal world, her information squeezed through the cracks — or, more likely, vomited on a side street.

The random warnings, the solid gold nuggets that led to preventing stabbings or to arrests of those who consistently danced outside the law — whatever she had told herself, a part of her soul was still in the shadows, deep in the heart of the criminal underworld. Not even Quinn, *especially* not Quinn, knew how close she had become to being one of them. Instead, she had nearly become a casualty, another life lost in the darkness.

There was much more at stake now. If they could find Delta, Ren and Alex wouldn't be torn apart again. And if she could find the perpetrator of the current Glass Doll murders, she might be able to lay her ghosts to rest, bolster her career. Despite the reassurances she had given to Alex, in her heart, she was screwed up with terror that the killer had taken Delta.

She spent the night waking from recurring nightmares of babies crying, and of the chip, chip of chisels on stone. She woke at 4 a.m., clutching her stomach with shaking hands, her face wet with sweat.

Layla surveyed her with interest from the chair by the window, her purr reassuring and steady, breaking the silence. Dove got up, and with a soft word for the cat, headed for the shower.

* * *

121

"Chris? It's Dove."

There was silence and then he laughed. "I knew you'd do it. Even being a murder squad girl, you're still one of us, really."

"Fine. I thought it over and I think you're right, I could co-handle. Oh, and Adrik turned up at my place last night right after your call, just to reiterate that he had some good stuff for me."

"He turned up at your house? Fuck me, that's weird. Are you all right?"

Was he shocked enough? She wasn't sure. This man would do anything to get a result for his unit, and in his mind, his unit probably still included Dove.

She gritted her teeth and forced herself to play nice. Chris was another man locked firmly in her past. She had made sure she didn't give him any encouragement, but there had been a couple of times — when they were deep in conversation, when he was being serious — when she had considered it, even allowed him to get closer. The physical attraction had been instant and electric, but even in her twenties she had known a relationship needed to be more than that, and it had never progressed further than a bit of flirting.

Her refusal to play along with his sexist games had made her the target of his endless tasteless jokes. It was a shame, because Chris was a bloody good copper, he just didn't know how to work with women. In his mind, they couldn't be friends or colleagues without getting the sexual attraction over first.

"For you, anything. It might come with a price, though."

Fuck you. But she told him how she thought it might work, adding, "I spoke to my boss last night and he is aware of what's going on, so the two of you just need to sort some paperwork first."

"Yeah, I reckon Jon'll go for it. He's a top bloke and he needs this case. As long as he understands where the credit lies for this one."

"I doubt he's going to care who gets the medal as long as the job gets done. Like I said, you two talk it out and let me know," she told him, jaw clenched.

"You know, if you get a taste for it again, you might just want your old job back."

She said nothing to that, and he laughed again. "No? It'll be tough to set up, and we'll be bending the rules slightly, won't we? Different borough, splitting a CHIS in half, so to speak. Much as I'd like to do that physically to most of the fuckers we deal with, it's going to take a lot of paperwork. I reckon it'll be worth it, though."

Dove took a deep breath, and spoke calmly. "I'm sure Adrik can deliver. He's done it before and like you said, it could break this case. My niece is missing too, and although it would be mind-bending to imagine that her disappearance is related to this recent spate of killings, I can't rule it out until we get a solid suspect and ideally an arrest."

"Okay. Last thing . . . Are you going to find time to handle — okay, co-handle — a CHIS when you're up to your neck in a murder case? I'm not being pissy, I'm genuinely worried it might be too much." His tone was serious now. "And before you answer that, don't forget we've got checks to do on Adrik Hammond again, as he's been quiet for a bit, so you dipping your toe back in won't be all over in twenty-four hours."

"I *can* do it. We've got two teenage girls dead and one is still missing. Believe me, Chris, I can fucking do this," Dove told him, her voice still even, despite the fact that her whole body was now shaking with the intensity of the conversation. Unspoken emotions seemed to be travelling between them.

"I was also thinking of your injury, the attack. You don't just get over something like that."

"I'm not over it, but I'm doing fine. That had nothing to do with Adrik; in fact, as I remember, he was the one who told you where to find me." She repeated her reassurances and eventually he agreed to have "some conversations" and let her know.

How had she ended up trying to persuade him to let her co-handle, when the whole thing had been his idea? God, he was a tricky bugger.

She checked her voicemail and winced as she heard Ren's wail. "Dove, I can't find Delta . . . I can't find my baby girl . . ." She stopped, tears choking her voice, and the call was cut off.

Her second voicemail was from Alex, who reassured her Ren was okay and he was with her, apologizing for letting her leave a message. Dove swallowed hard, her emotions welling up, but she had no time for that, she needed to nail this bastard by doing her job.

At least she wasn't stuck behind the scenes this time. She was out on the street, hunting him down.

CHAPTER TWENTY-FOUR

Steve Parker was waiting by the car as she scooped up her coat and ran out into the morning rain. She gave him a quick update on Adrik and the proposal that she should run him as co-handler to get the information.

"Bloody hell, Dove, he actually knows where you *live*? That says stalker, not someone who wants to help out." Steve's eyes flicked over her face, concerned. "And yet you don't seem that bothered."

Dove frowned. She had been terrified, but it wasn't like she had been hiding away since she left the unit. "I can't explain it, but I'm going on gut instinct. If we get an arrest for the murders, and Delta is still missing, my family can at least stop wondering if she'll turn up in a glass coffin. Adrik's got a good record."

"Rather you than me. Just be careful." He pulled out a packet of jelly sweets and chucked them over. "Have some sugar. Creaver's coming in today and the DI is going to grill him on both murders. I got a hit from night shift on the sofa-surfing websites. We're going to have a chat with Ben Corners, who has confirmed he let Agnes sleep on his sofa when she first came to the UK. He claims he didn't think it was the same girl when he saw the murder, but they tracked him down from his posts on the website." Steve pulled up outside a block of flats. "He doesn't live here. He's a property developer who rents out the places he's doing up to unsuspecting backpackers and students. It looks from the notice boards like you either get lucky and end up in a posh pad for a few pounds, or in a demolition job with no heating."

"Wow. What is it with these people that they don't come forward?" Dove said with frustration.

"I suppose they just don't want anything to do with us, or any scandal," Steve suggested.

Ben's flat was a complete contrast to Tom Jenson's. It was more of a riverside apartment, overlooking both the grey waters and the theatre. It was technically part of Abberley, but the town had pretty much lost its own identity with all the new development that had merged it with Lymington-on-Sea.

"Are you arresting me?" Ben asked, as he showed them inside, before plonking himself nervously on a white leather sofa. He was tall and slim, with short dark hair coiffed with gel. He wore expensive designer jeans and a smart, tailored shirt and he'd overdone the aftershave.

"No. If we were, we wouldn't be having a chat in your flat, we'd be down at the station," Steve told him pleasantly.

"Nice to meet you, DC Milson," Ben said, turning to Dove. "I'm really sorry I didn't come forward, but I rent places all the time, and my portfolio changes on a daily basis. I just didn't recognize her, because I only spoke to her a couple of times. It was only when you called, DS Parker, that I checked the booking and realized it was Agnes Nilsson."

"We understand, but you must see that for us, this could be vital information. It puts Agnes in Abberley, specifically in your flat on the day she came to the UK," Dove told him.

"So what do you want to know?" He looked slightly worried, but no more.

"Can you talk us through what happened when Agnes arrived to rent your sofa?" Dove asked.

"I left the key in the usual place. This place is nearly finished, but the other bedroom needs work and there's no hot water. I always tell them when I take a booking. I'm not the landlord, so there's no forms to fill in and I'm just offering what it says on the website, a sofa to sleep on." He indicated a battered red tweed model. It was large enough, and had a zip-up bag with a duvet and pillows next to it.

"How did you get into this business? Of letting sofas?" Steve asked, a note of slight disbelief in his voice.

Ben looked sharply at him, eyes narrowed, but answered steadily enough. "I went travelling a few years ago and used a few of these sites myself. When I got into this business, I let my mates kip on the properties for a couple of nights. It's not illegal."

"Did she talk to you about herself? Why she was in the UK, maybe?" Dove asked.

"I just got her text to say she was here, so I popped in the next day to check she was okay. We had a quick chat." Ben's expression altered, and a flash of amusement crossed his face. "She was very flirty, but she was wasting it on me. My boyfriend always says I have more luck with girls than guys."

"And she booked your sofa for a week?" Steve asked, glancing at his notes.

"No. It's a one-night thing. If you want to stay longer you re-book by three that day. But she did re-book to stay all week."

"Did she have any visitors that you noticed? I saw you'd got CCTV," Dove said.

"All my properties have CCTV and I use a private company. Yeah, I checked when you lot said you were coming round, and there weren't any visitors. She worked nights so it was just her. The rest of the apartments are still at first fix stage, so not safe for anyone to rent yet."

"The whole building is empty?"

Ben nodded.

"Did you know Evie Pollard?"

"The second girl that got murdered? No, and Agnes never gave me any names of friends or boyfriends. It was strictly business. I was with my boyfriend both nights the murders happened, too, because I know you're going to ask me. The first night we were at an all-night party, the second at my sister's." His mobile phone rang and he looked at them apologetically.

"It's fine if you want to take that, we're just leaving. We might need to chat to you again. Obviously ring us if you remember anything that might be useful." Dove handed him a card. "Can you also send us the CCTV from the week that Agnes was here?"

"Sure. I'm sorry about the girl and really sorry I can't be more helpful," Ben said, answering his call and launching straight into a negotiation about the price of some houses.

They sat in the car for a moment. Dove pulled out her phone. Nothing from Chris, and nothing from her boss confirming the CHIS status of Adrik Hammond. *Damn!* There was a voicemail from Janet Green, the cleaner from California Dreams. She quickly switched her mind back to the investigation.

"She says she wants to tell us more about Agnes." Dove looked at Steve.

"It's on the way back, so we might as well stop off. You want to call the DI and tell him about Ben?"

"No. I'll tell him when we get back. There's nothing major there, just join-the-dots information, isn't it? We've confirmed Agnes stayed there, so now we know where she was from her very first day in the UK, but I don't think Mr Ben Corner has anything else to add."

Janet's house was on Thyme Farm Estate, an ugly block with peeling window frames. But the inside was spotless, and Janet seemed pleased to see them, apparently welcoming the chance to gossip.

"Was it something in particular you wanted to talk to us about?" Dove asked her, as she and Steve accepted mugs of tea and helped themselves to the inevitable plate of biscuits.

"I only work at the club so I've got a bit of extra money to go on my holidays," Janet said. "It's pocket money for a trip to Benidorm, if I can get there. I like to travel. That's what I talked to Agnes about, mainly. She was a nice girl, but she took risks with men, from what I gathered. Now Evie's dead too, I've been racking my brains to think of any connection between them and this is the only one I've come up with. Evie and Agnes used to talk about drugs a lot."

"What kind of drugs? Were they dealing?"

"They mentioned some kind of dating app, and Evie said she hooked up with a man who sorted her out some gear. They shut up when they saw I was listening, but Agnes was talking about getting extra money and 'doing it again' two days before she got killed." Janet rolled her eyes and tutted.

"I don't suppose you know what she said she'd 'do' again?" Dove asked.

"No. Lots of different names they mentioned, but not one stands out. I thought at first she'd had sex for money with one of the high rollers. Uri Maquess has a girl he takes off with him sometimes . . . He's a nice man, that one. Agnes was on a high, travelling around, getting her first real taste of freedom, moving from country to country . . . Not like Evie, who was just a bit thick. Evie was the kind of girl who took every compliment from a man and thought he was in love with her. No offence, as she's dead." Janet didn't look guilty.

"None taken. Did Evie mention any special men?"

"Not really. She would talk to me, but she was a bit of a madam. There were a few of them who could turn it on for the punters but had nothing outside of work. To Evie and plenty of the others I was just the cleaning lady." There was a touch of bitterness in her voice.

"What about Colin Creaver? How did you get on with him?" Steve asked.

Janet laughed. "Lots of muscles and not much brain. I must say, I was surprised Gaia hired him. At first I thought she might be sleeping with him, but I don't think so." She shot a loaded glance at Dove. "But he's a good manager, the bits I saw. He's called in sick since Evie was killed, but you can't blame him for that. Shock, I expect. I heard he found the body?"

"Yes. Did Colin get on well with the girls?"

Janet sucked a loose tooth, making Dove's stomach turn. "Seemed to. He hasn't had much of chance to settle in, but he is very efficient. Those big parties Gaia keeps hosting for corporate clients are worth a lot of money, and he took over one of them straight off in his first week. Can't say as I noticed he spoke to Agnes or Evie especially. They were all pretty nice to him, because they know who will be organizing their shifts." She cackled cynically.

"Thanks, Janet, that's really helpful," Dove told her.

The car had steamed up, and the rain continued as they started back to the station.

"What do you think of the drugs angle?" Steve asked.

Dove looked out of the window, watching the water droplets dance sideways across the glass. "Gaia used to be a dealer," she said.

CHAPTER TWENTY-FIVE

Back at the station, they found Colin Creaver yelling at the desk sergeant, and two PCs trying to calm him down. The press, who were still camped out by the gates, were busy trying to get long-range shots as Dove and Steve snuck inside.

"I told you everything I knew. Don't try and pull the wool over my eyes, because I know you're trying to frame me! My name was in the paper this morning, and my neighbours think I'm a suspect. They chucked paint over my car. How did those journalists find out who I was?"

"Mr Creaver, we aren't trying to do anything except find the person who killed these two girls. If you had called us, we could have sent someone round to deal with any vandalism. We certainly didn't tell the press who you were, but consider how many people were at the scene when you found Evie's body. Even if you mentioned it to close friends or family, it is entirely possible someone leaked your name," PC Ellis told him firmly. "Why don't you come with me and we can have a chat."

Colin's eyes were wide, his mouth set in a thin line, but he deflated a little at her soothing words. "Do you think someone could be trying to frame me for the murders? I suppose there might be someone . . . I never thought of that.

If I find out who told the bloody papers . . ." A flicker of fire appeared again behind the green eyes. "Do I need a solicitor?"

The other PC smiled at him, towering over the short, muscular man. "You are not under arrest, and you are free to walk out of here at any time. Call your solicitor if you want to, but I suggest we have a chat, and you report any damage made to your property. I also suggest if you have somewhere else you can stay temporarily, it would help you keep a lower profile with the press. I believe that DI Blackman informed you that we would need to speak to you again, but we aren't trying to pin anything on you, just rule you out of the investigation."

"Fine, I guess." Colin saw Dove and Steve making their way past.

"Hey, you were on the beach! DC Milson! Can't you do anything about my car being vandalized?"

"I'm sorry, I need to check it with my boss. PC Ellis will take care of anything you need."

"I need you to bloody do something!"

"I can understand how upsetting it was to find the body, but you need to calm down, and if you came in to file a report, then do just that," Dove told him firmly.

"I suppose." He was clearly a very worried man. He had said in his witness statement he had a regular date with his surfboard several days a week, and even if he worked the night before, he liked to surf the next morning to clear his head. The mood swings between cooperation and anger were sudden. Could he be violent, or was it just fear?

There was no news of Delta, despite the search teams widening their area. Gaia had remained silent, not communicating since the phone call when she had alerted Dove to the fact Agnes worked in her club.

It had been the same when Eden went missing. Gaia ignored Dove completely unless she was putting pressure on her to find their niece. Their relationship hadn't survived the almighty row after Hayworth confessed to Eden's murder. Gaia had accused her sister of failing the family, putting her work and loyalty ahead of saving Eden.

It had hurt so much Dove couldn't even speak to her younger sister for months. They had only reconciled recently, when Dove moved away from Nantich Valley. Ren, the peacekeeper, had finally pointed out that she and Alex had lost a child and her sisters were making their lives worse with their feud.

Alex in particular had said privately to Dove he would never forgive himself for not being able to pick Eden up earlier. Half an hour was all it had taken for her path to cross Hayworth's. Outwardly, the family had recovered as much as they would ever be able to, but inwardly, it wasn't possible to get over the loss of a child. And one loss had been more than enough for the family. The thought of losing Delta as well chilled Dove to the bone.

Finally, just after six thirty, Dove got the call she had been waiting for.

"You'll be co-handling with DS Zak Yasid. You haven't met him, but he's good. Don't screw this up, Milson, because I've put my neck on the line for this. The DCI isn't happy, the MCT aren't happy and your current boss is pissed with me too," Chris told her.

"Nobody is ever happy with you anyway, and you want a result as much as anyone else," Dove told him, a burst of relief making her smile at Steve.

"I'm taking credit for the unit if this works out, and you owe me big time if it breaks the case."

"I don't owe you anything, and you can fight that out in the playground with the other children. Does it really matter who gets to say it was down to them, if we get a result?" she said, her mind already back on Delta.

"You've gone soft, Dove. It's all about the funding now. I win, I get more money for my team. No contest."

* * *

The first call with her new phone. It was like travelling back in time to see the two phones lined up on the kitchen table.

Different setting, same job. Fear jolted her and for a brief second she contemplated not doing it, changing her mind. But she couldn't, not now.

"It's Kelly."

"All right, mate. How's it going?"

"Fine, you? How's Aleesha? Did you say she had another baby on the way?" It came fine, not too sharp, and she had no trouble breathing. Everyone had babies every day. It was no big deal.

"Yeah, in another couple of weeks. Tommy's in trouble again. I'm worried for him."

Tommy was Adrik's youngest brother. "Anything I can do?"

"Don't think so. He just keeps pushing until people snap, if you know what I mean . . . I keep telling him to stay cool but he wants to make a lot of money, fast." Adrik sighed. "It's good to be able to talk to you again. I can't say this shit to anyone else, and I don't want Aleesha worried with the baby coming. So, do you wanna meet up?"

She told him where and explained she would have a friend with her.

"Whatever it takes. I'll bring your present with me, girl, okay?"

"Yeah."

She put the phone down. Her whole body was shaking. This was the reverse of a snake shedding its skin. She had wilfully added a layer, one that had come close to suffocating her previously. But it would be worth it if she could catch the killer. A gift from the past, maybe.

"All the pretty girls."

CHAPTER TWENTY-SIX

Two bodies in such a short space of time and Delta still missing made the public nervous, and the press were frenzied in their reports of police incompetence. The truth was, they were all working as hard as possible. Their usual numbers had been swelled by some twenty more officers. Not one tiny piece of potential evidence was discarded, and the phone lines were constantly ringing.

Standing in front of the team, DI Blackman looked exhausted. He indicated his board, the timelines merging in various places as he went through the new evidence.

"The search team handling the Delta Matthews case has been responding to potential leads from the nationwide alert. DI Lincoln is still handling that investigation. DS Allerton will remain as FLO to the family."

"Delta hasn't been active on any social media, her phone is switched off, and we have interviewed all her friends and family except one," DI Lincoln said. He stepped to the head of the table and indicated the timeline. "The family are convinced she had a boyfriend called Taj, and other friends have confirmed she often went off during the evening to meet him. There are no photographs of either her or him on her social media. She is very careful, and doesn't share much of herself online. Unusual for someone her age."

"Her family have told us that she blames herself for her sister's death, and feel that these latest murders have triggered rows within the family, which probably led to Delta removing herself from the family home," DS Allerton continued. "She took her wallet and a bag containing clothes and food, and seems to have been intending to stay away for a while. Her bank card hasn't been used. Her tablet and laptop are with the forensics team, and they have confirmed no red flags are raised by the preliminaries. Her mobile remains switched off, and the telecommunications company have confirmed it was last active in the area between her home, Goddards Wood, and Short Street. Our ongoing investigation will focus on finding Taj, pending any other leads. There is every chance that the two murders are not linked to Delta's disappearance, and we have reiterated this to the media."

DCI Franklin nodded. "Good. So far, all our efforts concerning Agnes Nilsson and Evie Pollard have established they both used the Sofa Surf website, which gives us another link. Colin Creaver is now our main suspect for the murders pending further enquiry. We are also still looking for Marc. It might be worth cross-checking to see whether Delta Matthews used any of the same sites as the other two girls."

DI Blackman wrapped up with a quick rundown on Colin Creaver. "Creaver is manager at the club where both victims work, and he called in the body of Evie Pollard. His appearance is strikingly similar to Agnes's boyfriend, Marc." He flashed up the headshots of both men. "Most of the Creaver evidence is circumstantial." He paused for dramatic effect and smiled. "Apart from his semen sample, which has just come back from the lab with a positive match to that found on our second victim's body."

There was a buzz of appreciation at this news, and the DI's smile deepened. "We'll see what Creaver has to say about the match. I know this is a tough case, so good work, everyone. Let's finish this."

* * *

Dove checked her phone, as she collected her iPad for the interview, leaving Steve pondering the choice of Fanta or Coke from the rickety vending machine. No time to call Ren as she had hoped, but what could she say? *Sorry, we still haven't found your daughter.* Lindsey Allerton was a good copper and would do her job.

Colin sat nervously with his solicitor beside him. His huge, muscular shoulders were hunched, and he was picking his fingers, pulling at the dead skin in a way that repulsed Dove.

DI Blackman made the introductions for the tape.

"Look, I did know Evie, I told you, but I'd never kill her," Colin said. His eyes darted from one officer to the other.

"Tell us what happened the last time you saw her," Dove said.

Colin glanced at his solicitor, who nodded quickly. "Okay, I met her for a drink after work. She worked at that party, as you know, and after I'd locked up, we went to a club on Broad Street. She knew it really well, but I can't remember what it was called . . ."

"Paranoia?" DI Blackman asked.

"Yeah! Yeah, that was it. We had a drink and then started walking home, and . . . well . . . . We had sex in a side street near my house. There was nobody around and I'd had a few drinks. She was really full-on, and I wasn't going to say no."

"And afterwards?"

"She said she didn't want to make a night of it, and got a taxi to her place. I did ask if she wanted to come back to mine," Colin added.

He didn't want to be seen as a loser who had a quick shag in an alley, and then blew the girl off, Dove thought. "Did she call or text you later?"

"No. Well, you've got my phone so you will have seen. I went home to bed, and got up early to go surfing."

"And then you found her body," DI Blackman said.

"I didn't kill her!" His solicitor put a reassuring hand on his arm.

After the interview, DI Blackman grabbed them both coffee and indicated the door to his office.

"Do you think he did it, boss?" Dove asked.

"Possibly. I think we still need to find Marc," he said.

Dove was pleased he too seemed to be on the fence about Creaver. "For someone to carry out the whole murder, to snatch them, make the mould and the glass case, takes at least twenty-four hours. I checked with the professional who was present at the autopsy, and it's not a quick process. If he just wanted to kill them, it would be fairly easy, but this elaborate charade is bizarre." She frowned. "I still feel like the killer might be a Hayworth worshipper, to go through all of this, and to be smart enough not to get caught so far."

"Unless it is Creaver, and we have caught him . . . Nothing new on your niece. How are you holding up?"

Thanking her lucky stars DI Blackman was turning out to be a good boss, she shrugged. "Okay. I keep telling myself that she must have just run off. When Evie was found, I was convinced it would be her, but afterwards I realized even if she was taken the night she went missing, it wouldn't have been enough time for the killer to . . . to do his thing."

"No." He was watching her face. "DC Milson, don't take this the wrong way. Your sister has been extremely help-ful, but could someone be trying to send her a message, or harm her business in an extreme way? Creaver could even be part of it . . ."

She felt her hand twitch, and kept it firmly clasped to prevent any nail-biting. "It has crossed my mind, but there honestly isn't anything I can add from a personal point of view, and I would, for sure. Gaia hasn't always been on the right side of the law, far from it, but she's been straight ever since she opened the club." Dove sighed. "Just because she

138

owns a strip club, people tend to think she's some kind of pimp, but for her, it's just a business."

"All right, thank you."

Dismissed, Dove slumped back in front of her computer. She had an email from Gaia. Texting Ren to say she'd come over tonight, she pondered Gaia's email. It was short and blunt, urging her to get her backside into gear and find Delta. Like she was actually lying on the sofa at home eating chocolates, instead of slogging her guts out, Dove thought, a flicker of anger curling through her chest.

As the day shift went home and the night shift queued at the coffee machine, Dove moved on to her next assignment. She threw her neat suit on the bed and dragged out jeans and a pink crop top, adding a long white cardigan. Her hair went down, thick curls cascading across her face.

After she had blended her make-up, it would have taken most of her colleagues at the station a double take before they realized she was the same woman who shared their office. It was one of her talents as a former informant handler. She could blend in anywhere, change effortlessly between one character and another, and tonight she was Kelly again.

Adrik knew her real identity, but for their story to continue he needed to pick up with Kelly once more.

* * *

"This is Zak. He's going to be co-handling Adrik with you." Chris slid a hand up her arm and patted her on the back, like she was some kind of favourite pet.

"Nice to meet you," Dove told Zak, who looked pissed off, but was trying to hide it. He was good-looking, with gelled messy hair and deep blue eyes. There was a dimple right in the middle of his square chin. His bone structure was square too, and with his broken nose in no way marring his attractiveness, he looked like a prize fighter who had turned to modelling to pay the bills.

"You sorted for this meet, then? The idea will be that although you're there, it really is just for show, and if he has good information, we'll get him back on side and working with Zak," Chris said. "Checks have all come back good, but I've fast-tracked them through so watch yourselves. This had better be good."

Zak was nodding. "It's a difficult one, but I can see why Adrik would prefer to have a pretty girl handling him." Both men laughed and Dove scowled at them. "But we're bending the rule to get this show on the road. Whatever he has on this case, we want to get it quickly."

They were treating her like she was a novice at this game. All those years of being a handler was hardly going to be forgotten in six months, was it? And she was thirty-six, not fourteen, a fact which she felt needed to be made clear to Zak. She straightened up and met his eyes. On the level he was a couple of inches shorter than she was.

"Fine, whatever. But I think it's best if you let me take the lead on this one, Zak. I know Adrik, and I'm really just introducing you at this stage. He knows what's going to happen, but he doesn't like it. I made it clear this is the only way he can give me, us, the information, and he's going along with it, but the last thing I want to do is upset him."

"Dove, I've got no intention of interfering, but you and I probably have different ideas on how to treat a CHIS. Let's go straight down the middle on this one and see what happens," Zak said. He smiled at her. "All you need to know is that my way gets results fast, even if I don't have time to build any bridges, and Chris is totally up for that."

"So tell me your story," Dove demanded. Every handler had numerous stories, false names, and every CHIS had a "legend" created around them, to protect both them and their handler.

"I'm Jack." Zak slipped neatly into a Scottish accent and Dove was pleased to see his whole demeanour change. It was imperative that each character assumed by the handler seemed totally real. The CHIS weren't stupid, and they knew what was going on, but hell, half the time they operated under numerous different names too.

She filled him in on "Kelly" and the story behind her relationship with Adrik, and he nodded. They got in the car. Dove stared out of the window. She should have been running over her backstory, slipping into Kelly's persona, but as they drew closer, memories rolled back.

It was during one of Dove's last meetings with a CHIS that she had been attacked and taken hostage for a terrifying twelve hours. A gang member related to her CHIS had taken her to a warehouse and interrogated her while he carried on with his work as a stonemason for the family business. It was his voice that spoke to her at night, and his scars she carried.

The chip, chip, chip as he moulded the gravestone . . . A stone angel opposite where she was tied had its blind eyes fixed on hers throughout. The monotonous voice kept asking her questions, demanding answers. Then more pain and dust from the stone making her eyes water, she denying all knowledge of his family, of the investigation.

She saw now, looking back, that she had got too close to the darkness, and been punished for it. But it had been a wake-up call that stopped her from pushing herself, from letting fate decide. Back from the brink, after therapy, she had decided to make a move to the MCT. It was a good choice, and she needed to hold on to that.

In the interview with DCI Franklin, she had been honest about her breakdown, about the way she saw her future career path, and he had taken it as given, not pressuring her with questions about the past. It was something she was immensely grateful for. Second chances didn't come along too often.

Eden hadn't had one.

CHAPTER TWENTY-SEVEN

The meet was at a small hotel in Cattling, right on the border of the two boroughs of Lymington-on-sea and Abberley. Their team had been in position for the last hour. As always, nobody knew who could be following a CHIS, and surveillance was essential both before and after meetings to prevent things getting nasty.

The hotel room was drab and smelled damp. The carpet curled at the edges, and the bed covers were discoloured and tatty. Adrik arrived a few minutes after the agreed time, head down, hood up, his quick, bright gaze taking in Zak, who sat legs crossed, sleeves rolled up, in an armchair.

Dove elected to stand rather than sit on the bed. "Hey, Adrik. Nice threads, mate."

Adrik gave her a grin, flashing perfect white teeth. "You wanna jacket like this, you gonna have to pay for it, girl."

She dismissed money with a quick, rude gesture and Adrik laughed, falling easily into their usual banter. She kept him talking, while moving on the conversation with skill to get to the real reason they were all crowded into the hotel room. It was another rule for source handlers to keep things moving so smoothly that the CHIS felt they were the centre of attention, the star of the show.

"So this is Jack, and like I said on the phone, he's my mate, a friend of Nathan's. Same rules, you just get two for the price of one." Nathan was the name of Kelly's supposed boyfriend who had been stabbed to death four years ago.

Zak smiled. "Kelly isn't mates with everyone, so you must be something special. Nathan always told me to keep an eye on her, so here I am."

Adrik nodded at the other man, his expression cool and watchful. "Nathan's been dead four years, man, where've you been?"

Zak shrugged. "Around, mostly in Glasgow where I do a lot of business, but she's a pretty girl so I thought I should check she wasn't in any trouble now I'm back down this way." He winked at the other man.

Dove flashed him a furious glance, not just because that's what "Kelly" would have done. Wanker, with his "all boys together" chat. Zak widened his eyes and leaned over to give her a one-armed hug, smiling at the other man.

None of the unfriendly exchange, or her stiff response to his physical contact, was missed by Adrik, who stood nearest the door, one hand on his pocket, eyes flicking from one officer to the other, shoulders set and tense.

Dove moved things on. "You told me you had something for me?"

"I got a phone in. Not sure who brought it because it came in a bag with a job lot, so don't ask. Likely from the bins in this area, but can't say for sure."

Dove, used to Adrik's jerky speech patterns and his sudden, brief silences, kept quiet, allowing him to talk, but Zak jumped in. "Come on, mate, move it along. You want to get paid, so you need to give us the good stuff and we can all get out of here. I've heard you're solid, so let's see it in action."

Dove scowled at him again, but he ignored her.

"Kelly says she's gotta work with you, so I'll go along with it, but you're already fucking me off. Yeah? I always give good stuff, Kelly knows that." Adrik straightened slightly, chest broadening as he flexed his muscles.

"It's okay, Adrik, he was just being a dick," Dove told him.

"This is the phone." He tugged a blue plastic bag containing the device out of his pocket and handed it to Dove, bypassing Zak's outstretched arm. "It must've belonged to Agnes Nilsson. I recognized her from the news photo. Loads of photos, emails and texts on there, and I knew right away you'd want it." He shrugged. "It came in Friday."

"Are you sure you don't know who brought the job lot in?" Zak asked.

"No. I paid cash and got the bag in a drop chute. Like I said, it came in on the Friday morning . . ."

"But . . ."

Dove nodded at Zak to shut up. "Thanks, Adrik."

"Yeah, ta for that. Here's to working together." Zak smiled at him.

"It's just what we need," Dove added. "Let me know when that baby makes it into the world, and I'll be round."

"Yeah, mate, thanks, I'll let you know when she goes into labour, and if I get any more juicy stuff, I'll let you know . . . let you *both* know." Adrik's face lit with a flash of mischief. His words were laced with sarcasm.

For an hour afterwards, Dove and Zak, as Kelly and Jack, stayed in a rundown coffee bar in the centre of Nantich Valley. The conversation was exactly as it would have been if they were really meeting up for the first time in years, talking about Nathan, Jack's business deals, and Kelly's cousin in Spain.

After an hour had passed, Dove went off to wait for the number sixty-two bus which would take her out to Merringdean. From there, she would be picked up and taken back for the debrief. It was the usual protection, just in case anyone was watching.

When she and Zak finally met up again, it was past midnight. Chris was waiting for them in the car and as the driver took them up the motorway, she felt herself relax.

"The phone has gone straight over to the lab and they'll call Blackman after a preliminary look. How did you feel it went?"

Dove shrugged. "All right. Adrik seemed his usual self, and there was no sign of any adverse activity. He seems pretty happy to be back working with us."

Zak nodded. "Yeah, unless you noticed anything from the outside, boss, I think we had it sealed off. The chat in the café was a nice touch, too."

"How do you feel about continuing for a while, as co-handlers?" Chris said.

"I'm not sure," Dove jumped in. "All this was just to get one piece of evidence, wasn't it? And it looks like we hit the jackpot with her phone. I think we planned that now I've introduced Zak, I'll just fade gradually into the background. I'll have to stick around until the baby is born, because Kelly wouldn't miss that, but we can use that to make sure Jack is really part of the story." Dove paused. "This isn't a long-term thing, is it? It can't be."

Chris smiled at her, and winked. "Nah, I'm just kidding."

Zak raised his eyebrows, clearly picking up on the tension between his colleagues.

"It wouldn't work long-term," Dove told her old boss, whose eyes flickered with something that might have been annoyance. Those had been his exact words to her when she had told him honestly that she couldn't continue with the IU. He had said he thought she might enjoy the MCT for a bit but it wouldn't be a long-term career move. He had then offered her a small pay rise and as much time off as she needed, but she had still said no. Chris had wanted to hold on to her not because he felt any compassion, but because she got results.

Thank God neither Chris nor anyone else had ever known about the true depth of her relationship with Adrik. His silence had been a measure of their bond, and his way of comforting her over Eden. That memory would stay in the shadows.

CHAPTER TWENTY-EIGHT

My footsteps echo on the wet pavement, and the street lights cast dancing lights across my path. The bus stop is only a fifteen-minute walk, and although rundown, this area is well lit and has a busy road.

I hold my rucksack tightly, phone in my other hand, walking briskly, head high. A car goes past with a swish of tyres, splashing water onto the pavement, soaking my trainers. Another, driving slower, approaches. I glance to my right, checking the vehicle's reflection in the puddles at my feet.

A taxi depositing a customer. I can hear laughing from one of the houses on my left. A door pops open, and loud music bounces out onto the street.

I'm passing waste ground now, fringed by the river, eyes focused on my phone. The text I thought I'd sent about grabbing a lift hasn't gone, and perhaps my voicemail sent an hour ago hasn't been picked up. Frustrated, and shivering in my thin top and leather jacket, I try again, but the signal is weak.

As the rain continues, the sensible part of me suggests I go back and wait at the party, phoning from there and getting a pick-up outside the door. The idiot in me continues walking towards Tesco. I need to clear my head, which is full of the party and my boyfriend. My boyfriend, who now thinks we need to "take some time out", the total bastard. I walk faster, stamping my boots. That's another reason I can't go back and wait at my friend's house. He will probably still be there, drinking.

And that's how it happened. One little mistake, one wrong choice defined the rest of my short life. I was a normal teenager, and then, in a split second, it all changed.

Past the derelict sheds on the edge of the waste ground, I see a familiar car. What's he doing here? But relief at the prospect of getting out of the cold means I don't think as I walk into the car park, rounding the corner of the building to see three figures.

I'm about to call out when I realize something is very wrong. For a moment, my mind can't process what I'm seeing, before the horror and disbelief wells up like a fountain in my chest. It must be a mistake . . .

They spot me as I start to run, my polished brown boots slipping on the snow and slush, my heart pounding with such intensity I think I might die here and now.

I hear footsteps behind me, gaining on me . . . The man who grabs me from behind wrenches my arm with such force he almost breaks my wrist. His breath is rank in my face and he is unfamiliar, which means that someone else is standing, watching . . .

I yell his name, my voice hoarse with terror, twisting round to see where he's gone. But the van is already moving, bumping away from me across the dimly lit tarmac.

Then I know I'm on my own, and I fight back with everything I have. But my captor is a tall man, and he throws me bodily into another van. He grips my wrists cruelly, wrapping them with tape. I lean my whole body weight back, kicking out at my attacker, still screaming for help. He wraps another length of tape across my mouth with a practised slap, and I am silenced.

I realize the inevitable is coming, but I continue fighting. My bound hand catches against a clip on my rucksack, and in a moment of clarity I fumble at it, managing to release the catch.

A pink pompom drops into the dirty water at the side of the road as the van door is slammed shut.

He will know what happened to me, but I know now he won't save me, because he was part of it. His eyes were gleaming, his face contorted with excitement, and something else. I almost didn't recognize him, but no matter how hard I try to convince myself, I know the truth.

Dazed and terrified, my heart beats so hard it seems to shake my entire body. I lie in the filth in the back of the transit van, sliding around as we drive away. I realize I'm not alone.

There is another girl in the back, the one who was sitting up on the tailgate of the van as I entered the car park.

Her dirty blonde hair is fanned out across the floor, her eyes are dull and she makes no effort to speak. Instead she lies huddled in the gloom, her face turned towards me, but there's no flicker of humanity in those sad green eyes.

What happens when you see something you shouldn't have?

CHAPTER TWENTY-NINE

Ren greeted Dove with a smooth, blank expression, her movements slow, as if she had suddenly aged forty years.

Alex was fussing over her, arranging her cushions so she could sit propped up on the sofa, bringing tea and generally treating her like an invalid, despite the fact he had been told not to last time it happened.

"Have you solved the murders?" Ren asked dreamily, as a news item popped up on the TV.

Alex hastily changed over to the *Antiques Roadshow.* Dove bit her nail, ignoring the question. It could be the slightest thing that set Ren off, despite the medication, and she didn't know if she could cope with her sister having another breakdown in front of her.

Alex and Dove moved to the kitchen table to talk as Ren watched TV. Alex looked awful. His big square face was pale and drawn, his blue eyes bloodshot and his hair greasy. He kept running his hand through it and fidgeting with his phone.

"I keep thinking she'll call. All the time, this is just how it was with Eden." His eyes filled with tears and he scrubbed them away. "It's been four days now, Dove. What the fuck are the police doing?"

Dove felt a catch in her heart and wiped her own eyes. "We're doing everything we can and so are you. Gut instinct says she's just had enough and taken off for a few days. Focus on that and it'll keep you sane."

"But what if he *did* take her? This killer? Is he targeting our family?" His face darkened. "I saw in the local paper that Gaia's club manager has been questioned . . ."

"His name has never been officially released. We would never do that. He has been helping with enquiries, that's all." That was the very question she had hoped he wouldn't ask, and the reason they tried not to name names until they had to. "A lot of people have been questioned, and we're still ruling people out, Alex. I don't have the answers right now, but please believe me when I say we are working so hard on this, to find both Delta and the killer. I heard Gaia's had to get extra security in on her club, did she tell you?"

"She called yesterday. I thought she'd be freaked out that another girl had been killed but she seems to be handling it okay. She's coming over to be with Ren tomorrow morning so I can go to work. That colleague of yours is good. Lindsey. She's been coming over and keeping us up to date. Sorry I asked, because I know you can't tell me anything, anyway." He was weary, his voice flat and dull.

"At least you won't have missed much trade today, it's been pissing down," Dove said. She switched the subject back to work, aware that neither of them was really listening to the other. The conversation was paper thin. Just words spilling out without any depth. And all the while her sister sat on the sofa, curled in her blankets, staring in silence at the TV screen, her hair falling in tangled curls down her back.

Dove ached to comfort her, but was terrified of show-ing emotion in case she set Ren off again on that terrible trail of destruction. Instead, she reassured Alex as much as she could, wondering how long it would be before he, too, started showing cracks. The signs were all there. He had been the one shoring up the family last time, refusing help or counselling, but this second blow must be bringing him close to the edge.

She gave him one of her awkward hugs. "We've still got hope, Alex. Hang on to that if you can."

He nodded, unable to raise a smile.

CHAPTER THIRTY

DI Blackman, despite the bags under his eyes, was immacu-late as ever in his white shirt and striped navy tie. He looked round at the team. "Creaver has been arrested, so we need to nail this case now."

The team were red-eyed and exhausted. Fuelled by junk food and caffeine, their discarded cups and wrappers cov-ered the desks and the briefing room table was scattered with paperwork.

There was murmured approval and excitement at the news that the end was perhaps in sight, but the DI held up a hand. "Okay, we're not through yet. The blue van that was our possible transport vehicle in the first murder hasn't been traced yet, and in the second murder, there is no evidence that the same vehicle was used. In fact, we're considering the killer might have used a boat. Our CSI team found no evi-dence of the case being dragged or transported from the car park to the cove. It wasn't lowered from the clifftop, either."

He clicked on a slide and a smiling photo of Agnes Nilsson came up on the screen. "Following information from a shared op with Nantich Valley, we have Agnes Nilsson's phone. It is currently with Forensics, but they have given a quick prelim report. She was on a Sofa Surf app and seems to have communicated with various known drug dealers. The website seems to have not only been used as a place to find a bed for the night, but also a way to mule drugs. Interpol has been very useful on this and I know there is more to come, but we can do this." He took a deep breath and smiled round at the room.

Sharing his relief at the case finally moving forward, Dove smiled back. She couldn't help but feel that after days of struggling, of tangled strands leading to dead ends, there was now a glimmer of hope. It was just frustrating that there were still ends to tie up.

She glanced down automatically as her phone buzzed with a text.

How u doing 2day? Hope all ok didn't hear from u last night?

Adrik had always been needy, requiring constant reassurance. She supposed it was because in his world, people often didn't come home, weren't where they said they would be . . . It was intense and cloying.

He had come through with Agnes's phone, though, and she was getting used to responding to his little texts throughout the day or night. Even a line would do, just so that he knew she was safe. Dove had once asked Aleesha, partly joking, if Adrik was one of those men who liked to keep tabs on his women. She remembered Aleesha's flicker of annoyance, as she'd admitted her texting him all the time seemed to keep him happy.

She tapped out a quick, discreet reply, then turned her attention back to the briefing. Exhaustion was giving her that sick, floating feeling.

The DI was still talking. "We have texts between Agnes and various friends, all of whom check out. Alex Corner, who rented her a sofa for the first week of her stay, has an alibi for both murders." He nodded at Dove for her input, and she pulled herself together.

"Texts between Marc and Agnes go back as far as February this year and indicate they met via the forum on Sofa Surf, and casually dated. His phone number no longer exists. The last text conversation between them is here, and it

153

does point us further in the direction of a drugs mule," Dove said, indicating the screen as a slide flashed up.

U need to collect from me at 5 x

My train is at 6? Can u do earlier? When do I get paid?

When u get to Euston go 2 the Costa shop and u will be found. Give them the package and they give u the money x

Still not sure . . . Told you I wasn't going till next week.

Done it loads of times. He needs this NOW. U wanted extra money didn't u? Triple pay if you do it tomorrow xxx

Ok xxx

Dove continued. "The messages give the impression that Agnes was bringing something into the UK illegally. Probably drugs, stolen goods, or something small enough to hide in a rucksack, because CCTV shows she only had the one bag when she arrived. Unfortunately, when she went into Costa at Euston, she just bought a takeaway coffee and came straight out again. From the coverage, she never actually met anyone for the drop-off at the station. If she was using drugs as a way to supplement her income while she was travelling, it could explain why she didn't tell her parents she was in the UK, or why she came early."

"Interestingly, after that, all conversations between Marc and Agnes cease. Did something spook her? Nothing turned up among her possessions at Tom Jenson's place and her locker at the club was clean," Steve added.

"So we have nothing concrete to suggest Marc came into the UK as well. Tom Jenson seemed pretty certain Agnes was going on dates with Marc, but as he never saw him, we don't have any ID potential. Was the second victim into the same thing?" DC Conrad asked, frowning.

DI Blackman shook his head. "The cleaner, Janet Green, claims both girls talked about drugs a lot, and as Evie was also using Sofa Surf, it is possible that the whole case is drugs-related, and the Hayworth template was chosen because of the shock value. Both girls were injected with ketamine to sedate them prior to their murders, but there was no evidence of any recreational drugs in their systems. Of course, that doesn't rule it out, just means it wasn't recent."

He changed the slide and continued. "Back to Creaver. He has no convictions, but according to his deleted browser history, he has been looking on Sofa Surf during the last three months. There are millions of users on the forums, so for us this is just another thread. He claims he was thinking of planning a trip across the USA on a budget and came across the site that way."

"No news on our missing teenager, but we're working with the family," DI Lincoln said. "Her last phone signal and CCTV from the top of Short Street places her there the night she went missing. We will be organizing a reconstruction and appeal for information, again with the family's cooperation. This is likely to be set for tomorrow morning."

Dove said nothing in response, careful to ignore the few curious glances that were thrown her way, grateful for Steve's solid presence on her right. The fewer people who knew she was bending the rules and co-handling the better, but she'd bet the word was out already on how Agnes's phone had been acquired by the police.

"One final note," said DI Blackman, "it seems that Tom Jenson, landlord of our first murder victim, managed to get himself into trouble last night. He's looking at a GBH charge and currently cooling off in a cell downstairs. DC Milson and DS Parker, you can lead on that one, as you spoke to him initially."

* * *

Dove wandered out to the vending machine in search of a sugar boost. She was just kicking the trapdoor to make her selection fall down when Jess appeared from the stairwell.

"Are you trashing that thing again?" her friend asked.

"It's given me Nik-Naks instead of Jelly Babies. I bloody hate those things."

155

"Stroppy cow." With a deft tap on the glass, Jess managed to make the correct packet fall into the chute. "How's things, anyway?"

Jess, whom she trusted with her secret, had been uncertain about her friend's venture back into handling.

"Okay." Dove glanced up and down the empty corridor. "I was actually thinking of asking Quinn to move in with me . . ."

"That's great! Really great." Jess peered at her, shoving her glasses higher up her nose, swiping a lock of blonde hair away. "What about the co-handling thing?"

Dove tore open the sweets and offered the packet to Jess. "Fine, I guess. Intense. My co-handler is an arse."

"Chris just wants you back — you know he does. I bet he wet himself with excitement when Adrik approached him and said he'd only work with you. I only like the red ones." She selected her sweets, frowning. "You need to make sure you don't get locked into something, Dove."

"He wants results and funding," Dove said. "But you're right, I do wonder if he could've set the whole thing up when Adrik first contacted him. He's already asked if I'd go back, but he made a joke out of it, like it didn't matter one way or another."

"Don't we all want funding, but I can't stand Chris. He's such a twisty bastard. Clever, but twisty."

Dove laughed. "How's Dion and the kids?"

"Kids are gorgeous but hard work, and husbands are such a pain sometimes. He's building a new man cave in the garden, complete with bar."

"Sounds all right to me."

"Not when he has his mates round and shuts me out."

"So have the girls round and stage a takeover!" Dove told her.

"Maybe a celebration for when you and Quinn move back in together?" Jess asked, amusement in her voice.

"As soon as this case is done," Dove promised, and instantly her heart felt lighter. The decision had been made, now she just had to hope Quinn still felt the same way. "And Delta is found."

"She will be." Jess looked at her straight. "Keep hanging in there, Dove. I'll be stuck here until four, so text me if you get a break." She pinched another couple of sweets and headed off back down the corridor.

* * *

The interview room was hot and stuffy. It smelled faintly of vomit and disinfectant. Dove vowed to get this interview over with as quickly as possible. Steve, sitting next to her, was scanning through his notes.

Tom Jenson sat with his shoulders hunched, cradling his left arm. His expression was sheepish and his cheeks had the slightly grey-green tinge of someone who had caned it the night before. He had refused to have a solicitor present.

Dove read the usual blurb for the tape recorder, and began with an easy question. "Tell us what happened last night, Tom."

"I just lost it. Some of the blokes in the pub, they were going on about Agnes being a slag, and saying that because she was a stripper she got what was coming to her. There was a journalist there, too, and these boys were giving him all this stuff that wasn't true."

"So beating one of them up was a belated white knight gesture?" Steve asked dryly.

"You what?" Tom's lip was swollen and he had cuts along one side of his neck. The black eye was an impressive mix of bruising and blood, and he sported three stitches in his chin. "I dunno, I just lost it. She was a lovely girl, like I told you, really happy and bubbly. I felt like it was wrong to diss her now she's dead. Nobody deserves that. And I drank way too much . . ."

"Tom, did Agnes ever take drugs?" Dove asked.

His eyes widened. "Nah. She was clean. I mean, I smoke a bit myself. I only knew her for a while, but I never saw anything." He paused. "I thought she had a lot of money for a backpacker, though. When I got her stuff together after she died, I found a lot of cash."

"Is there anything else you want to tell us?" Steve asked. "Anything you've remembered at all that might be useful?"

"Nah. I've been over and over it in my head . . . It's giving me nightmares, you know." His eyes dropped to his hands, where he was picking at his thumb. "I keep thinking that if I'd been around, I might have seen who picked her up. At least I could've seen him, the bloke who killed her . . ." His voice trailed off.

CHAPTER THIRTY-ONE

There are eight girls in the darkness. Already we know each other's voices, can tell when someone is struggling and needs someone else to crawl towards them for a hug.

Crawling is all we can do because the ceiling is so low. There is a long skinny window that stretches across the entire room. It is no more than a couple of inches deep but is reinforced by dusty chicken wire and a scaffold bar. In daylight, the sliver of brightness shows us that we are up in someone's attic.

There is the noise of a main road, always busy, even at night. Somewhere close is some kind of industrial site. Or maybe a building site. The workers arrive before it gets light and leave after it gets dark.

This much we have learned in the nine days we have been held captive here. It's dark now. The workers left about half an hour ago and without distractions, the world is reduced to our agonizing prison.

"Do you think they'll give us more water tomorrow?" Helen is the youngest. She's only ten and she cries almost the whole time she's awake. It breaks my heart.

"Yes. They want us alive. They're just trying to break us," I say.

"Fuck off already. You know what's going to happen." Tessa is fourteen, with a thin, pinched face. "We aren't stupid."

"I didn't say you were, I'm just saying we don't go down without a fight," I tell her. Her eyes gleam in the darkness. I feel her quick, dismissive movement.

"We would've had water today if you hadn't kicked that bloke in the head. He only came up to talk." Jessie's voice is strong and angry in the darkness.

"Whatever," Tessa says.

There is a tiny streak of light from the moon now, as the clouds roll back. The room stinks of sweat and piss. We have a bucket in the corner and food and water are thrown in via a trapdoor. Twice, a man has tried to stick his head up and talk to us. The first time, we all converged on the trapdoor, screaming, and the second time, Tessa kicked him in the head.

Opinion is divided over whether this was a good thing. None of us recognizes our captors. We have no idea where we are, and from talking to the girls, at least half of them won't be missed. My hopes rest on my pink pompom and on little Helen.

If what she says is true, there will be a massive police hunt taking place in her area, and media interest will surely drive out any information. Somebody has always seen something, but they don't always speak out.

Our phones and watches were taken, but we are still fully clothed, which gives me a tiny bit of hope. I'm not sure why, but I'll grab at anything now. I'm the eldest girl here by four years. I can't say why, but I keep my name a secret. I am Sarah, my middle name now, and just like the others, I am terrified.

I arrived the same night as the others, shaking and screaming for help. There is a vague memory of four men in the ground floor of an industrial unit. I didn't recognize any of them. We all have bruises from the beatings, but our faces are unmarked. All the time, once I realized what had happened, I wondered what he was thinking, now he knew that I knew. Part of me had hoped it had been a mistake, that there had to be some other explanation for what's happened.

Now I know there isn't one. I stumbled across his secret, and now I'm going to pay the price.

CHAPTER THIRTY-TWO

Dove's phone rang as she was wading through the paperwork from Colin's witness statement after finding Evie's body.

"Hi Ren, how are you doing?" She braced herself for bad news, but Ren seemed resolute and calm.

"I'm hanging in there. I know she's going to be fine. Alex is at work this morning, but he'll be home just after lunch," Ren said, her tone robotic. But robotic and stuffed with medication was preferable to freaking out and trying to take her own life. "One of Delta's friends called me earlier. A boy. He wouldn't leave a name and he said he couldn't tell the police, but . . . wait a minute, I wrote it all down . . ."

Dove was breathless. She crossed her fingers and clutched the phone so hard, her hand hurt. *Please let this be the break we've been looking for.*

"Tough Justice. She was a volunteer at Tough Justice. It's a vigilante group that catches online paedophiles and puts them on YouTube. It's run by a bloke called Taj. You know, we said that Taj is one of Delta's friends, but I had no idea . . . I thought he was someone from college, her boyfriend or something. He just told me she was safe . . . Nothing else except that she was part of this Tough Justice group. Why would he do that?"

"I don't know. Maybe her disappearance has something to do with this group, and he wanted to tell you but felt threatened by revealing that? At least he said she was safe, Ren." She took a deep breath. "Look, DI Lincoln is in charge of Delta's case, but you can tell Lindsey about anything like this too. That's what she's there for." Dove knew she had to suggest Ren told Lindsey, to avoid any appearance of breaking protocol. In reality, if something came in about her niece, she wanted to be all over it.

"Lindsey? Oh yes, she's been really good, but I wasn't sure . . . I knew if I told you, that something would get done. I didn't think of calling her, only you."

There was a trace of emotion flickering through her words, and Dove hastened to reassure her. "It's fine. You did absolutely the right thing. Have you told Alex yet?"

"No, I tried to ring him after this boy called but it went to voicemail. It's too loud down the market to have a conversation anyway."

"Okay, I'll let DI Lincoln know, and Lindsey, okay? We'll find this Taj bloke. Did the boy say anything else at all?"

"No. Just that Delta was safe, and that stuff about the group. I tried a couple of times to get his name, but he wouldn't tell me. He . . . He said he knew I would be worried, but Delta wasn't in any kind of trouble."

"Did he say *he* was part of this Tough Justice group?" Dove wondered. Maybe it was Taj himself, worried about his friend/girlfriend?

"No, but I assumed maybe he was. He was young, a teenager or early twenties, I should imagine. Well spoken."

"Any accent? Did you get his number?"

"No and no. It was a withheld number. I almost didn't answer it because I thought it might be the journalists again," Ren said. Her voice shook, and a sharper tone took over. "They keep bothering us . . . I hate them bringing the past back again, and it's not like that, is it? It's not about Eden . . ."

Dove felt a rush of panic. Had she been taking her meds? Going from dull monotone to sharper sentences, she seemed to be coming back into focus. "Ren, I thought Gaia was going to come over this morning? Is she there?"

"No. She did pop in for a chat but . . . You know what she's like and I'm so tired, I can't cope with her anger at the moment. She suggested that Delta . . ." Ren swallowed. "Well anyway, she said some crazy things but I *know* Delta has run off to get some space. She'll be back as soon as she calms down, won't she? The boy practically confirmed it?"

Dove fought hard to keep her emotions under control. "Yes, I'm sure that's it, and this information is really helpful, Ren."

Cursing Gaia, she rang Alex and left a voicemail telling him he needed to get someone to check on Ren.

Locating her colleagues was easy, as both were standing swearing at the coffee machine in the corner of the office space.

"Ren says she doesn't know the voice, and the number just came up as withheld, but Tough Justice should be easy to track down," Dove concluded, when she filled them in.

"Thanks for that." Lindsey made a face as she drank her coffee in one hit. "Disgusting, but I need the caffeine. Does your sister want me to go over, to sit with her?"

Dove felt a rush of relief. "Yes, she would, especially if the boy calls again for any reason, and if you could be there when Alex gets back . . ."

"Done." The other woman smiled and squeezed Dove's shoulder as she passed. She seemed to be thawing towards her now that she had her own important case to be working on.

DI Lincoln put a pound coin into the vending machine next door and grinned at her as he extracted a packet of wine gums. "I'll get onto Tough Justice. We'll find her. You know what teenagers are like. I've got four, and when they go to ground for whatever reason, they go to ground."

"You don't think she's in trouble?" Dove said, then cursed herself for putting him on the spot.

"I didn't say that, but all this points towards the fact she is probably alive at this moment. As you know, that's what we like to hear."

Dove also updated DI Blackman, and forced herself not to ask any more questions. It was not her case. Her case was the murder enquiry.

Back at her desk, she checked her phones. Adrik had sent a message with a photo. She opened it and saw a baby asleep in the crook of someone's arm. The baby had that sweet, crumpled look of any newborn, his tiny fingers hooked over the edge of his blanket.

Josiah Cole. Born 1 hour ago. At the Alexander till 2mro.

Even though she had been expecting the text, the shock almost winded her. She wrapped both hands across her stomach, and tasted blood where she had bitten the inside of her lip.

But there was something else. A spark of hope, soothing her pain, relaxing her body as the thought occurred to her. Jess's voice saying she could adopt, Quinn's voice telling her he loved her no matter what. Even her parents, Starr and Isabelle, joined the conversations in her head, talking about surrogacy. There were other paths, other choices if she did want a child . . . If *they* wanted a child.

Her instinctive reaction was to delete the photo. It was like switching channels every time babies were mentioned, snapping off the radio, moving away from pushchairs on the pavement. Things she had been doing ever since the attack, a futile attempt to quell the pain. But, reassured by that first flicker of hope and courage, this time she kept the picture. It felt like a massive step forward, so massive that her body slumped, relaxing for a long moment.

She needed to go and visit Aleesha and the new baby, to keep Adrik sweet, but would that be too much? Adrik, of course, knew all about the attack, but he didn't know the doctor's prognosis. Could she send Zak?

Even before she dismissed the idea, she was texting an answer. This was an important part of her life, had been for so long. The least she could do was to see it out with one last celebratory bottle for the new family. Her reaction to the photo gave her hope she would be able to cope with meeting the baby. It was a test she needed to pass.

If I can do this, I can do anything. I can find Delta, and I can rebuild my life with Quinn . . .

She made the formal arrangements to swing by the hospital, then pulled up a search engine. They were still waiting for the extra information from the lab from Agnes's phone, and Evie's phone hadn't turned up at all. Curiosity made her fingers fly over the keyboard.

Tough Justice was easy to find online, with a thriving YouTube channel. There were a lot of people who enjoyed seeing these men — and sometimes women — lured out from behind their screens.

The footage was all shot on a smartphone, and information underneath gave the name and county of the person caught by the sting. It was unlikely that all the names were real, but some people were so convinced by the comfort blanket of their online presence, they could be fooled into revealing their identities. And of course, the footage outed those who didn't.

Dove had done a short stint in the Digital Forensics Lab at Nantich Valley, and it confirmed that nothing was ever really deleted, no matter how many times you emptied that little trash icon. You also had to be far smarter than the average Joe Bloggs getting his rocks off on underage porn to become a player in the paedophile world. As the criminals got smarter and more tech happy, so did the law enforcement agencies. People like Adrik sat somewhere in between, using their intelligence for the good by dabbling in the bad.

"What do you think?" Dove asked Steve, who was now sitting next to her, munching on a bacon roll.

"Yeah, I've seen this kind of thing before. Trouble is, mistakes can be made, and by naming and shaming you're leaving them open to abuse. There was a guy last year that hanged himself because one of these groups 'exposed' him." He finished the roll and tossed the greasy wrapper towards the bin, missing by a foot. It joined the packets and wrappers on the faded green carpet.

"I'm sure Ren and Alex had no idea Delta was into this, but obviously I'll check it out. Shit, I mean, who knows what she was exposing herself to for this Tough Justice lot."

"It's easy to get totally caught up in a cause as a teenager," Steve said. He attacked his keyboard, not looking at her.

"Is that the voice of experience speaking?" she teased.

"Maybe. Let's just say I'm going to be keeping a close eye on my kids, just to make sure they don't follow in my youthful footsteps. Now shut up, leave this alone and let's get our murders solved. Did you say you needed to make a hospital visit?"

"Yeah. Give me an hour or so, and I'll be straight back." Dove straightened her back, feeling her insides spasm at the thought of the baby. A whole ward of babies. *I can do this.*

"No protection?" Steve queried.

"It's a hospital. I'll go from one of the cafés in town, and come back the same route. My IU boss knows what I'm doing."

"What about your co-handler?"

"He's meeting me there." She grinned. "I'm being very careful to keep him involved. He's pissed off we're going to see a baby."

"Do I detect a little friction?" Steve teased.

"Let's just say our professional attitudes to handling differ slightly," Dove told him. "But if you get a result at the end of the day, who cares?"

CHAPTER THIRTY-THREE

The hospital smell made her nauseous.

"I still don't feel this is necessary. I don't even go and visit my own family when they have kids," Zak grumbled.

"That possibly says more about you than anyone else," Dove told him, channelling her nerves into sparring with her partner.

"Oh fuck off, Milson."

Aleesha was sitting up in bed, with baby Josiah in a plastic bassinette next to her. He was asleep, Dove was relieved to see. Actually holding a child might send her into a blind panic. But just now, fuelled by her annoyance at Zak, she was managing.

"Kelly, Jack. Nice of you to come." Adrik got up from a chair, taking the bunch of flowers and bottle of fizz Dove had insisted on buying. There was a bunch of blue helium balloons attached to the bed head, and other gifts littering the cupboard on the opposite side to the baby's crib.

"No problem, mate," Zak said. "Nice kid. Congratulations."

"Thanks," Aleesha said. She looked exhausted, but her eyes were bright, and her cheeks flushed with happiness. "It wasn't easy, but I can't wait to get him home now."

"Yeah, congratulations. He looks just like you," Dove said.

"At least he doesn't look like his dad, poor thing." The other woman winked. Her hair was lank and cascaded down over her shoulders. One hand still had a cannula inserted.

A baby in the crib across the room started crying, triggering a whole load of screaming babies. Parents fussed and soothed, medical staff hurried around with blood pressure machines and medication, and Dove stood firm in the middle of the chaos.

I can do this.

They stayed for another ten minutes or so of small talk, Dove's nerves jangling, while Zak could barely conceal his boredom.

"We just nipped in to say congrats, so we should head off now," Zak said, taking the opportunity of a break in the chit-chat.

Dove was so grateful to him for creating a quick exit, she could hardly respond to Adrik's words.

"Don't forget to give me a shout later, Kelly."

She gave him the thumbs up, blew a kiss for Aleesha, who blew one back, and walked strong and steady through the maternity ward, out to the lifts. The heavy fire doors clanked shut, blocking out the noises of thirty fussing newborns. She had done it.

"Well, that's ticked off the list. I hope this means Adrik will be reporting to me without any fuss from now on," Zak said. He smoothed his hair in the mirrored sides of the lift.

"Yeah, I'm sure." Dove could hardly speak for the relief that flooded her body. Her strength was back. Her own reflection stared back as they rode down to the reception area. Something in the set of her mouth made her think of Delta. Now she knew she would find her niece.

I did it.

"What did you say?" Zak was watching her with a puzzled expression as the doors hissed open and they stepped out.

"Nothing." She grinned at him, enjoying his surprise. "I didn't say anything."

It was what I did that mattered.

* * *

Dove drove back to McDonald's and she and Zak chatted about the new baby, their mutual friends, anything that wouldn't matter if they were overheard. It was excruciating and Zak clearly didn't see the point of any of it, but rules were rules.

Half an hour later, she changed quickly and stashed her clothes in a sports bag, ready to head back to the station. Avoiding the journalists, she parked up, and checked her phones for messages. Steve was smoking in a patch of sunshine, and he waved her over.

Listening to her voicemails, Dove wandered across the tarmac towards her partner. Alex had called, saying Ren was getting in a bit of a state again, and asking if they'd had any luck tracing the mystery caller from this morning. He added that he had no idea Delta was into that kind of stuff, and wondered if it was even true.

Back in the office, having caught up with Steve, Dove delved back into Evie's friends and family statements, hunting for any mention of Marc or Colin Creaver.

Absorbed in her work, she was almost ready to call it a day when she found a one-liner from Kiki Bell, another of the club girls.

Evie did lots of different things, as well as working here. She did some cleaning, waitressing, and packing at the mushroom farm in Kilread. And she did a couple of odd jobs for this bloke called Mark.

Where was Kiki's number? Dove pulled it up and called. It rang for ages before the girl answered, yawning.

Dove introduced herself and explained why she was calling.

"Mark? Oh yeah, she mentioned him. I got the impression they'd had a fling. He sent her tickets for the Eurostar last month, for like a date in Paris."

"Really? How romantic," Dove said. "Do you know Mark's last name? Or where he lives?"

"No . . ." Kiki yawned again. "Sorry, I had a late one last night. She stopped talking about him after the Paris date. I'm not sure if it went badly. Don't know where they met but I remember she was extra keen he didn't know she was working at the club."

"Thanks, Kiki, that's really helpful. In case you think of anything else, can I just give you my number?"

Kiki yawned her assent and then her voice sharpened. "Do you think Mark might be the one who killed her? Fuck. It's none of my business, but we know Colin's been arrested, and you're making a mistake, there. He's such a teddy bear, and he's definitely not the bastard who did this."

"How do you know?"

"I know men, and he didn't do it, okay?"

Dove called Steve over and told him about Kiki. "I think it got missed because of the spelling of Marc, but she's sure he sent Evie tickets, so perhaps she was trafficking drugs the other way. Whatever was going on, he will have gone to ground, and if he's not in this country, our chances of grabbing him for a chat are zero."

"So we need whoever Agnes handed the drugs to over here. Presumably, it's the same person who gave Evie a package to take out to France. Or did she go out empty-handed and carry something back in?" mused Steve.

"I'll let the DI know," Dove said, pleased to have made progress, but aware that it wouldn't help their chances of getting the CPS to accept Creaver. But what if it was all about the drugs? Again, her sister flitted through her mind. She needed to have a chat with Gaia, even if her sister blew up in her face again. She had to know the truth.

By eight, Steve was ready to call it a day, and Dove couldn't stop yawning.

"Do you think Creaver did it?" she asked.

Steve shrugged. "Christ knows, and time is running out on this one. If it had just been the second victim, I'd have said yes, especially as there was semen present, but he just doesn't seem intelligent enough, and we still don't have enough to tie him to Agnes. Whoever did this is smart and has a hidey-hole somewhere that can churn out bloody bodies in glass cases.

Problem is, until we find out where that is, we aren't going to get any closer to solving this."

"What about the drugs angle, though?" Dove suggested.

"It would fit. Punishment for screwing over a dealer, maybe? A warning to rivals. Mysterious Marc with a 'c' or a 'k', who seems to have dropped off the planet . . ."

Dove sighed. "Ren and Alex went through so much with Eden, and logically I don't want to believe that these crimes are anything to do with Delta's disappearance, but what if she's got herself into drugs as well? I'm not saying she was a user, because I don't think she was, but she may well have decided to make herself some extra cash. I know she talked a bit about taking a year out to go travelling. She's not mentioned it recently, but I wonder if Sofa Surf will turn up on her browser, too?"

"What about Tough Justice?" Steve said.

"If she's got herself involved with the wrong people, anything could have happened."

"Perhaps she did it for her sister. You know, like an avenging angel, or a vigilante, taking down these lowlife sexual predators," Steve suggested.

"Avenging angel? You watch the wrong type of movies." Dove smiled. "I think it would be more that she wanted to put herself in the danger zone and see what happened, to push it as far as she could." Her heart twisted a little as she remembered suggesting to Delta that Eden might be her guardian angel.

"Now who's speaking from experience?"

"Let's call it a night."

He grinned and gave her a friendly shove. "I'm with you there."

CHAPTER THIRTY-FOUR

After two weeks in our prison, the trapdoor opens in the darkness to reveal five men. A light is switched on before they lift the door and enter. We were dozing, trying to stretch out aching backs and cramped limbs, unprepared for the attack.

All the men wear hoods over their faces. They speak a mixture of English and what is possibly Polish. I've always picked up languages easily. I wanted to travel on my gap year, to Asia, to Africa, to America. Now I hope to live just a few days longer.

The removal is swift and brutal. There is no chance to defend the youngest girls, the weakest in our group, and our strength is sapped from the lack of food and water.

Strong arms encircle us one by one. I go limp as I am pushed down the stairs, still held firmly by my captor. When we get to the bottom step, I can see we are in some kind of industrial warehouse. The metal doors are shut but a window provides possible escape. The smell of plaster and paint invades my nostrils, and I stumble over a roll of carpet.

In another futile bid for freedom, summoning reserves of strength I never knew I had, I lash out. My blows make contact, and the grip loosens for a second. There is screaming and crying from the others, the scuffle of another fight. The men don't seem bothered by our noise, so we must be far from any neighbours. Nobody heard our yells for help in the attic prison, nobody will rescue us now.

My heart is pounding, sweat dripping, mingling with my captor's blood. His hood is pushed away, and our eyes meet as we struggle. His are black, thickly lashed and almost too large for his thin, pale face.

My nails tear at his flesh, and I bite the hand that flies up to trap my wrist. There is a ripping sound as the fabric of my top comes apart at the seams, and my shoulder is laid bare. Still we grapple.

But my efforts are futile, as another man steps in to hold my other arm. We are trapped together, quiet except for the sound of rough commands. One man, the smallest, snaps a picture of each of us on his mobile phone. He shouts at Helen to smile, and Tessa tells him to fuck off. I don't smile, or speak, but I scan each man's face when the opportunity presents itself. Could he be hiding behind that hood? Is he here?

Please God, let them locate me. Amelie will have told them when I left, and my phone would have been traced to the wasteland, surely, my pink pompom extracted from the puddle at the side of the road. The police aren't stupid, they will have joined the dots.

Is this my punishment?

My racing thoughts are interrupted as I am shoved forward out of the line.

"Your turn," my captor whispers in my ear. His hand is heavy on my bare skin.

The ground floor of the building is scattered with building supplies, and there are two partitioned rooms made of plasterboard and wood. Plastic sheeting and bags of cement are lined up along the walls.

One by one, we are herded into the rooms. Tessa and I catch each other's eyes as we are pushed away. Her door locks behind her. Her eyes are blank, her face expressionless, like she's already gone. I could tell somehow she had suffered abuse before. She knew what was going to happen.

The room is in semi-darkness, and I sit where I am told, while the man points a phone at me. He exclaims in annoyance, pointing at my ripped top, and the other man rummages in a corner, before chucking a white blouse at me.

There is no doubt they want me to change in front of them. The new garment is grubby and too tight. My fingers shake as I try to get my ripped top off and button the new one without exposing any more flesh than I can help.

The man with the phone nods in approval, and begins filming. He asks me questions in slow, heavily accented English. I answer them. I do this because my original captor is now pointing a gun at my head. He stays out of shot. My thoughts of dying now and getting it over with are foremost in my mind, but some tiny spark of survival won't let me go for the gun.

Instead, I concentrate hard on the questions, on giving information to my saviours, just in case. Maybe the video will be sent to my parents, demanding a ransom . . . That would be weird. How much is my life worth?

"Say, I'm fourteen years old."

I'm eighteen, but with a gun still pointing at my forehead, I manage to stutter out the lie.

"Now say, 'I would like to find a boyfriend'," the man demands, and I say it mechanically, sitting still like a stuffed doll, fingers twitching occasionally and blood dripping down my wrist, where his nails had gouged my skin.

The man with the gun asks his colleague something in his own language, and he nods, looking hard at me.

"I am from the UK and I am a schoolgirl," I repeat my lines, thinking how alien and stilted my own voice sounds, echoing around the room.

The filming stops as screams echo around the building from the other room. I catch my breath, hearing the thud of flesh on flesh. Catching my expression, the man with the gun presses it hard against my forehead, execution-style.

They talk among themselves while I wait, staring at the wall, trying to block out the sounds of the other doors banging, of more screaming, abruptly silenced.

My own door opens, and two men slip inside, shutting it behind them. Their appearance seems to be unexpected, and in the split-second attention is transferred to the newcomers, I move as fast as I can towards the door.

But the man nearest to me catches me around my waist. I smell him, can feel his arms encircling my body, and terror whirls again. It is my captor from the car park.

"Shut up a minute, I need to talk to these men. If you stay very quiet, we might find you somewhere safe to go, but if you make a fuss,

174

we'll auction you off with the others." His eyes gleam in the spotlight. He's English, with no particular accent, pale skin and smooth brown hair.

Before I can move, he pulls a gun from his own pocket and shoots the three other men. The stench of blood and cordite hits me like a tidal wave. My mouth hangs open, eyes wide with shock.

The men lie still, their blood pooling from their wounds. He was so quick that they had no time to reach for their own weapons, if they had them. The remaining man high-fives the murderer, and there is an exchange of banknotes.

I can't breathe. I can't breathe. His hands are around my neck. I'm going to die in this slaughterhouse. The darkness drags its blanket of shadows across my vision and I know this is it.

My last thought is of my sister. I hope she knows it isn't her fault.

CHAPTER THIRTY-FIVE

As Dove made her way home, her other phone rang, and she answered quickly. "Adrik? You all right?"

"Yeah, thanks for the bottle, Aleesha was so happy you made it. Your mate Jack's a wanker, though."

She ignored this. "How's Aleesha doing?"

"She's so happy, and Josiah is fucking awesome. We should be home in a couple of days. He's got jaundice, but the doctor says it should be fine. Anytime you wanna come and see us, just let me know."

She laughed, slipping quickly back into character as sharp-tongued Kelly. "Just me and another bottle, I know. What about Jack? Unless you want him to come too?"

He laughed, as she had known he would, and told her to fuck off. "Nah, just you."

"That's good. I've got to go now . . ."

"I did have one other thing," he said. "There's gonna be a bit of a thing going off on Northwood Estate tonight. They say they're bringing knives to finish a job." He named a couple of rival gangs, and Dove noted them, the familiar names jogging her memory.

This was classic Adrik, ringing for a chat, leaving his information right to the end of the call. "Thanks, mate, and you know Aleesha is epic, right?"

"She's my girl."

Dove turned off the hands-free and pulled over, grabbing her iPad. She hastily typed up the phone call. Not just money this time for Adrik, but the secret thrills of taking down a rival.

She put a few calls through and informed her co-handler — who, as expected, was snippy about the fact Adrik had rung Dove and not him.

"This is Nantich Valley area so I'm just passing info," Dove told him briskly. She had no time for bruised egos.

"How's the murder case going?"

"How do you think?" she retorted.

"Slippery bastard, this one," Zak agreed, before he rang off.

Dove was exhausted, but she knew she had to see Gaia. She needed to satisfy herself about the drugs, to lay her doubts to rest.

"Hey, Alex, is Gaia with you tonight?"

"She's talking to Ren. Why? Is there any news?"

"No, I just thought I might drop in and see you all," Dove said.

By the time she got over to Ren and Alex's, it was gone eleven, and yet again she had that sick feeling that goes with too little sleep. Her brain was sluggish and even as she entered the house and saw Gaia, curled like a panther on the sofa, her amber eyes glittering with emotion, she had second thoughts.

"Dove!" Ren was red-eyed and pale, but maintained her chemically induced calm as Alex brought her a glass of wine.

"Have you heard anything?" Gaia asked. Her tight black sweater and leather trousers clung like a second skin.

"No. Lindsey will have told you everything we have on Delta," Dove said.

"This Tough Justice thing?" Alex looked sceptical. "Don't get me wrong, I'm pleased at anything that helps get her back, but I can't see her being involved in that kind of thing . . ."

"Don't be an idiot, Alex, she's a smart teenager, with no illusions about life. Why shouldn't she turn vigilante for a bit?" Gaia told him.

177

He sat next to his wife, one arm around her shoulders, his forehead furrowed. "Lindsey said that they've managed to track down a possible candidate for the mystery caller. David Bollington, also known as Bollo, swims with the performance team at Delta's club."

"But he's gone walkabout too," Ren said softly. "His parents can't find him, and his flatmate doesn't know where he is."

"But that might be good," Dove suggested. "If he's with Delta, then she's probably safe, isn't she?" She was trying to find a good moment to bring up the drugs question, but God help her, she couldn't. Gaia was actually speaking to her, and her other sister and her brother-in-law looked like they hadn't slept since Delta's disappearance. She couldn't do it, couldn't break that fragile bond between them.

When she said she had to go, an hour later, Gaia walked out with her, saying she also needed to make a move.

They got down the garden path past Alex's workshop, as far as the road, before Dove decided she had to ask. "Gaia, do you know anything about any of the club girls doing drugs?"

Her sister, tall and elegant in the shadows, paused, one hand brushing the hedgerow. "No. I mean they don't." She peered at Dove. "What do you want to know?"

"I want to know if there is any way your past could be coming back into this?"

"Your colleagues already asked that," Gaia said icily.

"I know, but let's say I'm worried about the drugs angle and I don't want any of this to fall back on you, especially when we're all taking a hit with Delta's disappearance and the murders."

"Fuck you, Dove. I don't deal anymore. That's what you're delicately trying to hint at, isn't it?"

She shrugged. "I don't want my family in trouble, that's all. We've been through enough. It isn't that I don't trust you . . ."

Gaia turned and stalked away without another word, slamming the car door and pulling away with a screech of tyres.

Dove stood in the dappled moonlight, shoulders droop-
ing, still feeling the icy blast of her sister's anger.

As she got into her own car, she could see a figure at
Delta's bedroom window. Ren. She was looking out while
she pulled the curtains closed. Silhouetted through the thin
fabric against the lighted room, Alex joined her and put his
arms around his wife, her head on his shoulder.

CHAPTER THIRTY-SIX

I watch my reflection in the dusty mirror, noting my dull complexion, my greasy hair and my deadened eyes. I am old and faded, trapped like a songbird in a cage.

The baby plays in the filth beside me. Somewhere outside, I can hear the seabirds scream, celebrating my special day.

It happens quickly, my birthday miracle. He stumbles in, clutching his chest, burbling helplessly. I've never seen him like this — he's always so strong and sure of himself.

Now, terror lights his grey eyes. His face is grey too, and wet with moisture. Through my drug-addled haze I realize what's happening, and although my actions are slow, I manage to pick up the child.

I judge the situation. He's still on his feet, but swaying, gasping for breath. I need to get him out the way, but I need to take care he doesn't injure the baby.

It doesn't take long before he slumps to the floor, his breathing now just a rattle, long and drawn-out, pausing far too long before the next desperate gasp of air.

I pause at the top of the stairs, giddy from the aftermath of my injection, elated by the feel of warmth on my skin, the sight of fields of heather, the wide open blue sky. But urgency drives me to turn and shut the cellar door. Putting the child down briefly, I drive the bolts home. Panting with fear and exertion, I secure the rusty padlock.

I hope he's conscious on some level and I hope he dies in the darkness in terror and agony, before descending into hell, or wherever the truly evil end up.

After so long in captivity, I am bewildered by the outside world, blinking mole-like at the sunlit heaven we have ascended to.

Elan crows with delight, running his tiny fingers through the grass and heather, his round, chubby face lifted up to the sun. My baby has my dark hair and blue eyes. He is my child and he has no father. He is the only reason I am still alive.

I don't know how long we sit there, just absorbing the light, adjusting to our new environment, breathing the sweetness of the fresh air. I can see the shack that I suppose he lived in, long lines of drystone walls, and a pen of goats. A flash of fear worms its way up as I consider that there may be others. But I've only ever seen or heard him, and he has complained forever about how bored he has been, stuck out here with just me for company.

Sometimes he left us for days on end, so he must have gone to a town or something to find entertainment and company. This gives me hope that we might be able to find someone to help us. My brain fog blurs over pictures of my family. They must think I'm dead. Everyone I ever knew must think I am dead. Except one.

He's never been to see me since I was passed to my captor, this fat, red-headed man with the bored smile and huge belly. This man who must now be dead, or still writhing in agony. I hope it's the latter.

The heather and grass stretch as far as the horizon on all sides, but I can smell the sea, taste the salt and hear the gulls riding the spring breezes. I see no people, no cars, roads or signposts. I have no idea where we are in the world. My hands are spread wide across the ground, fingers stroking the earth, the leaves, the rough stalks of plants and the delicate little white rosette flowers that have sprung up in some moss.

The days were marked by the calendars he gave me. This wasn't because he was being kind, it was so that I could see my life wasting away underground. But now we are free, my boy and me. Tears are running down my cheeks, coursing down my jutting chest bones and soaking my thin dress. I am free.

Eventually, cursing the drugs still running through my veins, making me clumsy and blurring my vision, I gather my child up into my arms and we start to explore.

For days, as the drugs slowly leave my system, I can barely function. The vividness of the colours, the strangeness of it all, leaves me breathless and emotional.

Elan is pure joy to watch, as he scampers around, half-crawling, half-walking, strengthening both our muscles in his explorations. There is canned food and water in the shack, the sofa is heaped with rugs for a bed, and we use the bathroom, revelling in the shower water splashing against our skin. I won't sleep in his bed, but I will take anything else he has to offer.

I find his mobile phone, and a stash of money in a drawer in the wooden desk. There is no signal out here in the wilderness, and I can't get into his phone through the lock code. The money is welcome, and by the fifth day, I am starting to make a plan. Although there is nothing to tell us where we are in the world, I assume some islands in the north. It's cool and often breezy. I've become convinced I can hear the sea in the far distance.

The scenery and wildlife aren't too unfamiliar, so I assume we are still in the UK. I was drugged senseless on the drive here, all those years ago, but we started off in a van, and when I was dragged out of it, we seemed to have arrived at our final destination.

It was dark, I remember that . . . I shake the memories away. If I am to survive, I need to move forward as fast as I can and never look back.

There is a rusty old Land Rover in the shed to the side of the shack, but I haven't managed to find a key for it yet. I don't even know if it works.

After a furious search, I ascertain that my captor must have the keys in his pocket. There is no other place he would have put them, and it makes sense that he would keep them close. He must have unlocked the padlock with a key on the ring.

I curse myself for not searching his body before I left him, but I must get those keys or we'll be stuck here forever. This means going down into the cellar to a dead body. I hope. He has to be dead by now, doesn't he?

The wave of sick terror that hits me triggers a full-blown panic attack, and I have to sit in the sun for a while until I've calmed down. Elan, playing in a patch of dirt, is ignorant of my loss of control and pushes his grubby fingers after a snail trail.

I wait until midday before I creep over to the cellar. The padlock is locked and he has the keys. My brain is slow to respond and I panic that I'm going mad. Common sense tells me it's just as a result of being held captive underground for so long, and fed a diet of mind-bending chemicals.

He told me what he gave me, and explained why. It made me wonder if he had a medical background, but I suppose you can look these things up on the internet, just as you can buy pretty much anything on the Dark Web.

I doubt Amazon would deliver out here, though . . . I force myself to stop dithering and fetch a saw and hammer from the big rack of tools in the kitchen.

With Elan watching, I get the door open, take a deep breath and let light flood the cellar. Part of me is convinced he will rush up and grab us both, forcing us into darkness once more.

But I'm nothing if not a survivor, so I finally walk slowly down the steps, finding the body at the bottom. The stench makes me vomit, and as I reach down to his coat pocket, I think he moves, and pull back so fast I tear my arm on a rusty nail in the wall.

The keys are in my hand, and I rush back out to the sunlight and my baby, banging the door shut behind me.

On the seventh day they come for us.

CHAPTER THIRTY-SEVEN

Quinn's flat wasn't too far away. Without giving herself time to think, Dove drove straight over, knowing he was home. She would do it now.

"Dove!" He looked surprised, but pleased to see her.

"I just thought I'd stop by and we could have a chat," she said, nerves starting to jangle.

They went inside, and he poured a glass of wine for them both. His flat was sparsely furnished, but clean and tidy.

Dove took a tiny sip of her drink, and leaned over, slipping her fingers into his. "There's something I need to tell you." Before he could speak, she told him, all of it. The nightmares, the fear of him seeing her panicking, losing control, and finally, the baby she had visited today.

"That's a lot to take in." His eyes were soft, his touch on her hand gentle and warm. "I haven't liked to push you. You went through so much after the attack. I always saw a future for us. I must be one of the only blokes I know who starts thinking about weddings on the first date." He laughed. "I did think we would have kids, but, Dove, I love you, and if being with you means we don't have children that would be all right, it really would."

Tears slid off her lashes, splashing down her cheeks. "I know. I'm sorry I kept pushing you away. I kept thinking you might find someone less difficult, someone who could have babies . . . Quinn, I want us to be together again. Will you move in with me?" She snorted with laughter through her tears. "God, I feel like I should go down on one knee."

He was laughing too. Moving his hand from hers, he reached inside the coffee table drawer and produced a small box. "Funny you should say that."

"Oh my God . . ." Her heart was pounding so loudly, she held a hand to her chest, as he slid down on one knee.

"Dove, I bought this ring a week before you were hurt." He popped open the box to reveal an antique emerald and diamond in a simple gold setting. It was delicate, tiny and beautiful. "Will you marry me?"

"Shit!" She was laughing again, crying too as she forced the words out. "I would love to marry you, Quinn."

A few hours later, they lay in his bed, moonlight brightening the small room, shining on the ring now on Dove's finger.

"I need to go home. I haven't got any clothes here."

"You look better without them," he murmured.

"Cheesy." She dropped a kiss on his forehead. "And you have to be up for work in three hours."

Quinn sat up, his hair ruffled, yawning. "Okay, but drive carefully."

She slid out of bed, still admiring the ring, tugging on her clothes. "Love you." It sounded tentative but right.

"Love you too."

Despite her late night, Dove slept surprisingly well, and arrived at work with a feeling of optimism. After much deliberation, she had tucked her ring back in its box and hidden it at the back of her sock drawer. It was so new and so private she only wanted to share the news with Quinn at the moment, to be in their own private bubble.

When Delta was home safe, when the case was over, she would tell her family and friends. But for now, she would hug her secret close to her heart.

In the office, she was greeted by Lindsey waving at her across the crowded room.

"I've found Taj. I've got an address in Leaf Road, and we're heading out now." Her expression was triumphant, but the fact that she had shared the information before chasing him down suggested another softening of attitude towards Dove.

Blackman, passing with a sheaf of paperwork, addressed Lindsey. "Bring him in. I want to know everything he knows about Delta Matthews and David Bollington."

"Right, boss."

Dove found herself biting a thumbnail and whipped her hand away from her mouth like a guilty child. The peace and happiness she had rediscovered last night was washed away in the frustration of not being part of Delta's investigation. But she forced herself to calm down. Her own murder investigation was enough, not to mention her co-handling.

Adrik had called on her way into work, talking about the load of tech he had shifted yesterday, and about how he had lost two friends in the last six months and didn't want Tommy to go the same way, but was worried about him.

He didn't offer any information this time, but it was all relationship-building. He clearly felt at ease with her again, but he did tell her straight that he wouldn't call Jack while she was around. His argument was that if there was a meet, he was happy for Jack to be there, but he felt no need to build a relationship with his co-handler when he could rely on her.

This was not how she had hoped things would progress. When she called Zak to report this, he was pretty pissed about the situation, accusing her of trying to keep a foot in each camp, which she hotly denied.

"Come off it, Dove, you can't do your job with Blackman, and keep Adrik tied to your apron strings as well. You need to get him prepared for the final cut and lay it on the line."

Furious, Dove snapped back. "I need to get him happy with working for us again before I start pushing him away.

It's pretty obvious you have a different relationship with your CHIS than I do with mine."

"Yeah, I don't have sex with mine for a start," he told her scornfully. "With my bosses or my CHIS."

In the silence that followed, Dove was glad they were only on the phone or she might have been tempted to rip his eyeballs out. Zak was showing his true colours. "I think I'm going to end this conversation. And just for the record, I've got my successes by working hard, not by shagging my way around the borough."

He ended the call without speaking again and she scowled at the phone. Smug, patronizing bastard.

Lindsey was coming through the door as Dove exited. "We brought Taj in. He's a player, and already got his solicitor in. Seems genuinely concerned for Delta, though. Just not concerned enough to come and speak to us when he found out she was missing. I don't think he trusts us at all."

"Thanks for letting me know." Dove carried on towards DI Blackman's office, glancing back with a quick smile.

Lindsey gave her a loaded look. "You aren't the only one who's lost a family member."

Dove watched her stride across the room, and felt vaguely comforted, as though an unexpected ally had appeared from nowhere.

"DC Milson. I've got the files you sent over. We'll have a quick brief in half an hour to update the whole team. Meanwhile, I want you to make sure everything is up to date on the two murders. The clock is ticking on Creaver, remember. We're going to take this whole thing apart and put it back together piece by piece," the DI said. "I don't need to remind you that we're down to final hours on this one. Every piece of evidence that you think might count, add it to the file. Any join-the-dots from the witness statements, sling them in. Okay?"

"Yes, boss."

A text from Jess made her smile, and she almost told her that she had got engaged, just for the reaction. But this was work, and she needed to get on, not go all goofy over her engagement. The secret warmed her heart.

Her phone rang again, and she reached into her pocket, assuming it would be Zak calling back with an apology. But the number was unfamiliar.

"DC Milson."

"Dove? It's Freddie. Long time no speak."

"Jesus, Freddie, how the hell are you?" Dove said, as she placed his heavy Liverpool accent, smiling as she pictured his wild red hair and abundant tattoos. "Are you still with the labs?"

"Nah, I'm at Central Database now, and much as I'd love to say this was a social call, I've got something interesting for you."

Dove's heart started pounding, palm sweaty on her phone. "Go on."

"It's from a case up in Shetland, on one of the islands located on the west side of Shetland, in the Vaila Sound. Access to the mainland is via boat." He paused.

"Sounds lovely. Go on then, I imagine there must be more to this than the travel brochure for Scottish islands."

"You haven't changed at all, Milson. Right, here it is, the juicy bit . . . A fifty-eight-year-old deceased male was discovered on one of the remote crofts out there. Looks like he had a cardiac arrest and died of natural causes under no suspicious circumstances, but there were blood smears they couldn't account for at the scene."

"Go on."

"We got a DNA match to a female on the database. Eden Matthews."

CHAPTER THIRTY-EIGHT

She couldn't speak. The room was spinning. She grabbed the edge of a table so hard it seemed to be the only thing that anchored her to reality.

"Dove? You still there?"

"You what? Fuck, Freddie, are you sure?" Dove swallowed, her throat dry, emotions rushing to the surface as a wild hope surged through her brain.

"Positive. I checked Eden's details because I was a tad surprised, then I tried DI Blackman, as it's his borough, but his line is busy. I saw your name on the list and went for you next. You never told me you'd moved boroughs. Eden Matthews was supposedly one of Peter Hayworth's victims, wasn't she? And she supposedly died in 2016."

"Yes, she did."

"Well, I can see I've done well with my news. You're speechless, and that never happens."

"Sorry, Freddie, I'm just shocked, that's all. I've been with the MCT for a couple of months now. I think the DI is at a press conference. Ironically, we're running an appeal for information on Eden's sister, Delta Matthews. Bloody hell, if Eden was still alive . . . my brain is fried. Did you get any more info?" Dove was shaking so much she could hardly hold her phone. It felt like all the blood was rushing to her head, and the noise and chatter of the large room had receded into the distance.

"No. It was a standard check, but of course when I got the match, I red-flagged it because of the Hayworth connection. You know what I'm like, I enjoy a bit of digging, and this is a right banger, isn't it? By the way, there was no match for the deceased male, and they haven't got a name for him yet."

Dove hung up, shaking. Could Eden really be alive? She went straight over to DI Lincoln, words bubbling out as she related the content of the call. "The DI's phone is just going to voicemail, so I can't let him know, but I've got the name of the investigating officer and Freddie's sending over the details he had."

"Jesus, just when I think I've got this case pegged, something else gets thrown into the mix," DI Lincoln said. He glanced at his watch. "Jon'll be back soon."

"I don't have all the details for you yet, but I just need to talk to whoever's in charge, get everything sent over." She kept talking so he wouldn't have a chance to tell her to keep away from this. His expression was one of concern, with a touch of excitement. She felt it too, a rush of hope and the electric buzz of a professional hit. This meant something, all of this happening at once. "The deceased male died of natural causes, and the bloods were sent over for a routine match because they don't have a name and there were unexplained smears at the scene. It isn't being treated as a suspicious death." She was pleading with her eyes, sensing him wavering.

"Okay, get me all the information and I'll add it to the mix. I don't know if this has any bearing on our current cases, but it's a pretty big coincidence, isn't it? And, sorry to say this, Milson, but it does seem to all relate to your family members."

"I'm on it, boss."

The investigating officer was a DI Karen Hartfield. Dove rang her mobile, praying she'd answer.

"DI Hartfield." The voice was sharp and strongly accented.

"This is DC Milson from MCT down in Abberley. I've just had Central Database on the phone and they've got a blood match from one of your current cases."

"I just got the email from Central." There was a pause, before she continued. "The match is to Eden Matthews, who was supposedly a murder victim in 2016."

"Yes. Can you give me a quick rundown of what happened and where you're at with this, because we've recently had two copycat murders in the style of Peter Hayworth," Dove told her. She wouldn't mention any personal involvement, although she was desperate to jump on a plane up to Scotland and search the island for her niece.

Eden could be alive, so where is Delta?

"Right, I saw it in the news. It is kind of strange to have a link to a previous victim and some new killings within the space of a week. We still don't have an ID for our deceased, but one of the other inhabitants on the island thinks he was called Philip. A rough estimate says he has been dead about a week, maybe longer. A guy who owns a small shop says he saw Philip maybe once a month. The story is that he was some kind of high-flyer in the city and he burned out and wanted to live a simpler life. He could do that on the island. It's a small one, maybe sixty-three acres in all, with a pier, a few watermills and a fishing village at the south end. Just a few farms at the north end, far more remote."

"Did anyone see him with a woman? I don't quite see how Eden is going to fit into this," Dove said.

"This guy lived off the grid. Just drove into town every month for supplies and mail. The locals said he was always polite but never friendly, but they never really took a lot of notice of him, and nobody knew he had a woman living with him."

"Who reported the man deceased? Could it have been Eden?"

"No. There was an anonymous 'Concern for Welfare' call to us, which is how we discovered the body. The female caller just said she hadn't heard from her friend in a while and he always kept in touch because of his location. We sent a couple of officers from the mainland round to check it out." She paused, and Dove could hear again the tap of fingers on a keyboard. "I'm sending you the report now, but to cut it short, the scene looks like Eden was being kept captive underground. Outside the main farmhouse was an old entrance to a bomb shelter. It had been updated and secured to become separate accommodation, next to several outbuildings."

"Fuck. Underground?"

"Right. Looks like she might have been kept captive for a number of years."

"If that is true, and she's alive, then where the sweet hell is she now?"

"Since the blood match came back this morning, we've had a search conducted of the island, and we got the coast-guard out, but nothing yet. It's a problem getting extra bodies out from the mainland because we've had a couple of storms recently. There is also, as you can imagine, just a few of us covering a whole lot of islands."

"Yeah, I can imagine. Please do keep me updated. We're extra interested in this because Eden's sister, Delta, has also gone missing."

DI Hartfield gave a low whistle. "Something or someone has got all stirred up, then? Are you linking this to the murders?"

"It's possible. There are too many coincidences not to consider it. Here we have one of the victims of the previous case back from the dead," Dove said.

"Right. Keep in touch and I'll do likewise. Eden can't have gone far. If she made it across the island, somebody would have seen her."

Dove sat for a moment, staring at the wall. Eden was still alive. Or she had been still alive last week. The report stated that the blood on the wall looked like someone had caught their arm or hand on a rusty nail as they hurried past. She pictured her niece released from years of captivity, running up the stairs to freedom, only to find she was on an island in the middle of fucking nowhere.

She would run. Of course she would run, and carry on running until she was sure that nobody was chasing her. Just because her captor was dead, that didn't mean there weren't others involved. Did this Philip, her captor, have a boat? Where would Eden go?

Dove went back to her computer, and smoothed a finger across her phone screen saver, desperate to ring Ren and Alex, but knowing she must wait. It would not be her breaking the news, but she would go over later. She blinked back tears. Eden was alive. Now all they had to do was find the two sisters.

A thought struck her. Had Delta somehow tracked down her sister? Did the answer lie with Tough Justice?

CHAPTER THIRTY-NINE

"This is a quick update, and you will have all had the email. The big news is that Central Database contacted us, and we have a blood match to our missing teenager's sister, Eden Matthews. It's from what was supposed to be a domestic case up in Shetland. Looks like the girl had been held captive for years. I've got some pictures from the scene . . ." DI Blackman's eyes were alight with interest as he gave them the rundown.

There was a ripple of excitement as Eden's smiling face appeared from an old shot, followed by pictures of a small stone house, steps down into an underground room, and finally snaps of the room itself. It wasn't often that murder victims returned from the dead, but it did seem that this might be the case.

The cellar was small, with a bed, filthy toilet and sink, piles of clothes, and, most horrifying, signs that there had been a child in the room, too. Crayon drawings adorned the dirty walls, and the few toiletries seemed to confirm a baby or very young child.

The final picture showed a body.

"The deceased is now confirmed as Philip Ashley. He seems to have been living off the grid for years, but is originally from Devon. No previous convictions and the autopsy confirms he suffered a cardiac arrest." DI Blackman let the information sink in, before continuing. "We presume that was when Eden escaped. Peter Hayworth confirmed Eden was one of his victims, but we never had a body, so this one throws up more questions than answers at the moment."

"Jesus, so if she's still alive, where the hell is she?" Steve asked.

Someone whistled low and long. "Maybe we were right and the Matthews family is being targeted? Agnes and Evie both worked at the club owned by Delta and Eden's aunt, and now Eden turns up alive after Delta goes missing. Fuck, what are the chances?"

Dove couldn't see who had spoken, but that same cold fear wrapped around her heart. Her emotions were already rubbed raw, and seeing Eden's photo, a copy of one in Ren's precious gallery, was making it hard to breathe. She tried to keep her struggle silent, desperately hoping her own family ties wouldn't be laid bare. She frowned, her brain making connections, like joining pins on a map.

"Colin Creaver was from Plymouth, in Devon, wasn't he? I think that Peter Hayworth was from the South-West too."

The DI nodded. "Check it out a bit more. A long shot, but geography might have brought them together. There is a link somewhere, we just need to find it."

For a team used to picking up information like hawks hunting vermin, Dove was surprised only a few had picked up on her connection to Delta. There were a few looks of pity and shock as Eden's story was relayed, but mostly her colleagues were tapping furiously on iPads or scribbling in notebooks. Energy and purpose had returned to the room.

"There are too many lost jigsaw pieces here, and they are not falling into place. We will be sending our FLO already assigned to the Matthews family to break the news about Eden, and of course, there is a search underway to find her, and probably a child. Don't forget, we don't know yet if she

195

is still alive, although it looks like she escaped and fled the scene. At this stage, we simply don't know what happened afterwards," DI Blackman said.

It made her wince every time she thought of Eden alone in that shithole, abused, giving birth, but Dove thought that if she could survive all of that, surely she must have survived her escape.

"DC Milson, any news on the possible drugs link between our murder victims?"

She shook her head. "No. The results back from the tox screenings just confirmed that both girls were healthy, and unlikely to be regular drug users from the physical evidence displayed. Some more information from Interpol is that we have a possible match for Marc, and several aliases. According to the most recent information, he is wanted on drugs offences, and his current whereabouts is unknown. I'm working my way down his list of known associates in the UK."

DI Blackman nodded. "Keep on it, please. Even if we keep ruling out, I want every little avenue investigated."

DI Lincoln leaned forward. "Regarding Delta Matthews, Tough Justice have moved all their gear, if the address was correct, and Taj's personal electronic devices are clean. He was very open and up front about his op, and he told us Delta was one of his volunteers. She's been with him for five months now. His story is that she was fine when she walked out of his place on Monday night. He does seem pretty concerned, but I get the impression he doesn't think much of the police, likes to think he's smarter than we are. We're still trying to locate his business address. He's a clever guy and also uses the name Christian Mathers."

"Haven't we shut him down a few times? I seem to recognize the name from somewhere . . ." Steve queried. "Is he just house-hopping with a few laptops, or is it a bigger operation?"

Lindsey got up from her seat, and pulled up the Tough Justice YouTube page onto the screen at the back of the briefing room. "Could be either. It's very easy to run anything out

of your back room with a bit of tech. His channel has a big following, and if we centre on the last month, we have three men
who have been targeted by the group. Jonah Bennet, Captain
Jack, and Edgar Price. Clearly, although they managed to pull
the real names of two of them, Captain Jack isn't identified."

The three men appeared as blurry blow-ups on screen
and Dove peered closer. There was something familiar about
the unknown man. "Can we clean it up at all? I think I almost
recognize Captain Jack, but I'm not sure where from . . ."

"Sure." DS Marcus Fulling was a tech genius and occasionally came into a major crimes investigation. Usually he
was part of the floating Cybercrimes unit, shared by four
boroughs. He brought the man into sharper focus.

"Shit, I'm nearly positive that's Delta's swimming coach,
Mansell Hargreaves." Dove was biting her nails again. She
had picked up and dropped off her niece at training a few
times, and Delta had pointed her head coach out. Had Delta
realized who she had trapped, or had she seen him when Taj
put him up on YouTube? Perhaps she had decided to con-
front him . . . Taj was going to need to be a lot more helpful.

"If you're sure, we'll get him in for a chat. For his own
safety, if nothing else, we need to eliminate him from the
enquiry because if the press make the connection, he'll be
lynched," DI Blackman said. He dispatched the officers.

Lindsey stopped at Dove's desk for a quick chat. "Just
so you know, I think Taj is giving us the truth. He's a cocky
little sod, and we did have to remind him a few times that
withholding evidence is a crime. I'm sure his solicitor could
do with a word about wasting police time."

"You'd think if Delta was part of their team, working
for him, he would have been more concerned when he saw
she was missing," Dove said. "I mean, what they do ruins
lives, and if they sent Delta out with a camera to catch the
wrong man . . ."

"I think underneath he is worried about her, but like
the DI said, he's probably working furiously to try and find
out what happened. He doesn't like us, and doesn't trust us."

"How unusual," Dove said, and the other woman's lips twitched into a slight smile. "When are you breaking the news about Eden to Ren and Alex?"

"The DI reckons we wait a while and see if she's found, and I'm inclined to agree. Imagine raising that kind of hope, only to find there's more to this, sorry, and she's not actually alive. It would be cruel."

"But you think she's alive?"

"Yes. You don't survive that kind of shit and then get screwed by a few Highland storms or whatever they have in Shetland. I think she's hiding out somewhere, and the quicker we find her the better."

It was tough watching other members of the team assigned to interview the swim coach, to talk to Gaia again, and to dig into Delta's last known movements. She desperately wanted to be on the case herself, hunting down the bastard who might have taken her niece. Because Delta had been playing with fire at Tough Justice, whatever safeguards Taj had in place, she had still been in contact with the kind of people who wouldn't think twice about disposing of a teenager. These were people whose secrets were about to be exposed on a YouTube channel with over five hundred thousand followers, and who had everything to lose.

Her phone pinged with another message from Alex. He assured her Ren was as well as they could hope and asked yet again if she had any news. Dove's heart ached for them. She knew how hard it was to just wait, but she could only wait for her colleagues to break the news of Eden. It was tearing her apart to be so close, yet have to keep a professional distance.

She could only imagine their joy should Eden be discovered safe and well. Their baby girl back from the dead. And if Delta could be carried home safe by her own guardian angel, it would be a good day's work.

She shoved her family worries aside. "I've got some calls to make from the information on Marc," she told Steve.

"Go for it. I'm going to be sending all the info on Sofa Surf to the drugs team. Turns out the forum is swarming with dealers and it's become a major hub for picking up mules. Not quite what the founder intended, I'm sure, unless they're making some cash from the dealers," Steve said.

"Shit."

"Yep. I think we can safely assume that this is where Evie and Agnes met Marc, and if we could get our hands on Evie's phone then I bet there'd be a whole load of information on there to link them."

Dove turned back to her own screen, but found herself scrolling back and forth between photos of the three girls, Agnes, Evie and Delta. She bit her lip as she gazed at their smiling faces. She added Eden's picture.

Two dead and two — her own nieces — maybe alive, but in danger. Even odds. There was hope, and she needed to hold on to that.

CHAPTER FORTY

It was past ten when she dropped in at Quinn's flat, carrying bags of takeaway fish and chips, and a bottle of wine. Neither of them really cooked, although Quinn could make a mean Thai curry.

"You're pushing it too hard, you know you are," he told her after a kiss.

Relaxing against him, her arms around his neck, she allowed herself to acknowledge his words. She couldn't deny it. Burnout in every sense of the word. Quinn knew about being on the front line, and he knew the mental health issues that could come with it. But much as she appreciated his concern, her overriding feeling was that she just needed to get this over with, however it was going to happen and whatever it was going to take.

"You're wearing your ring! I thought we were keeping this a secret until Delta's back home safe," he said. He moved over to the counter, and unwrapped the fish and chips.

"I only put it on tonight so I could wear it with you," Dove told him, and he smiled as he passed her plate.

"Crazy, isn't it? I'm kind of enjoying it being our secret."

"Actually, I have some more news . . ." She told him about Eden's return from the dead.

"What?" Rather than being overjoyed, he was serious, shocked by her statement. "For real? That is just too weird. Don't get me wrong, it's fantastic news if she is alive after all. But you know what I mean . . . all this going on and Delta missing. Do you still think someone is trying to recreate the Hayworth scenarios?"

"We're struggling. Our best lead was Colin Creaver, but that fell apart. There is evidence, but not enough. Everything we have, there could be a plausible excuse for, so far, and his legal team would have a ball with it. CPS won't take it forward unless it's watertight, and we've run out of time, so he's out pending further investigation."

Dove leaned back in her chair, tilting her hand so her ring caught the light, pushing work away. Her heart was breaking and bursting with joy at the same time. It was an odd, not entirely comfortable situation.

Quinn fetched two glasses and poured the wine. "What about your source unit investigation? How's that going?"

She was glad she had told him, glad that she hadn't hidden her fear of taking it on behind a show of professionalism. "The CHIS is back where we were six months ago, a bit of chat and a few tip-offs, but nothing as major as his first one."

"Which you still can't tell me about?"

"No, but it was worth it to move things along with the murder case. Trouble is, it hasn't moved them in the right direction. Sometimes I think I should get another job and get out of here. You know, like run a garden centre, or do something restful like being a paramedic."

"Cute. I was thinking of getting away for a few days," he said, eyes on hers. "Work's been crazy and I need a weekend break, maybe longer if I can blag some additional leave. I was going to suggest you come along and we make it like an engagement celebration, but this new stuff with Eden, and Creaver not being the man . . ."

When they'd first patched things up after her breakdown, she had sworn to put family and relationships before the job. As part of the vow to make time for themselves, they had taken a few trips down to the West Coast to surf and chill out, and it had been amazing.

It was their time, and they had agreed when things got stressful for either of them, before it got to the stage when they were arguing, struggling, they would just go and escape for a couple of days. But just now . . .

"Quinn, I would love to go. Honestly, with all my heart, but I just don't think I can. At least until we know what's happened with Delta and Eden. I can't rest until they're found."

He nodded, shaking vinegar onto his fish. "I know, babe. It's bad timing, but I just need a break. My nice restful job has been a total bitch these last few weeks. We just don't have enough ambulances out on the road . . . Anyway, I'll probably head down there Friday evening after rush hour. Open invitation if you change your mind."

The temptation was huge, especially in light of their new relationship status. "If I can come for two days, I will." She leaned over for a kiss. "Maybe we could talk about moving back in together."

He grinned. "Sure you want me driving you mad, leaving clothes all over the bedroom floor again? It's not too late to back out."

"I do . . . I actually do."

"So, because I'm renting and you've just bought, it would make sense to move into your place." He was watching her carefully.

"I was thinking that too." She didn't tell him that when she bought the house, she had always visualized them living there together. She hadn't given too much thought at the time as to how this might happen, but she had trusted that they would when it felt right.

She woke in his bed at four as her phone buzzed next to her pillow. Alex's number came up on the display and Dove reached for Quinn's hand. He awoke instantly, watching her as she answered the call.

"Alex?"

"Dove! It's Ren — I think she's taken an overdose!"

CHAPTER FORTY-ONE

I've done a couple of practice drives in the Land Rover, and now we're all packed up and ready to leave. I watched them drive down and find his body yesterday. It was a shock to see the vehicle, and I don't know who it was. There were two men and the sign on the side of the 4x4 looked like a coastguard one, but captors come in all shapes and sizes, and I'm not going to trust anyone now I'm free. How did they know where to come, for a start?

As my strength returns, I've ventured further from the shack, reaching the rocky shoreline in one direction, and following a cart track as far as some hills in the other.

I still can't see any signs of civilization, and I see no point in driving into the wilderness with my precious tank of diesel so diminished. No, my survival instincts have got me this far already, and I rely on what my instinct tells me now.

There are some old stone outbuildings at the base of the hills, half-hidden in the curve of the land. Tall waving grasses and stunted trees soften the skyline. One of the cowsheds still has a roof and I've moved most of our provisions out of the shack to there, our new base.

It feels good to be away from my prison, not to be watching over my shoulder all the time. But there is activity in the hills around us. Men search with a dog, and a helicopter keeps flying over. But I don't leave my shelter. I can't, even though I reason that these people must be safe, may even be looking for me.

The day they come back, we're off on another practice run. The bags are in the back and Elan is bumping along on my lap. I've just come up the steep track from the cowshed, and come to a junction in the hills. After a lot of pondering, I make a right turn. Several vehicles flash past, heading down the way we have come. I grip the steering wheel.

I did wonder if my captor kept in touch with his half-brother. He probably wasn't supposed to tell me a lot of things, but he was bored, and he had no idea I absorbed everything he said in the hope that one day I would escape. They were all related, he told me. A band of brothers. All three of them, caught up in that sick trade. I was shocked by the way my captor seemed to hero-worship Peter, the murderer, and my shock must have shown in my face. That was before I got good at hiding the real me. After that, it didn't matter what he did or said — he could never harm my soul, my core, the essence of me.

Now I know the way to go, and we accelerate onto the track, heading at speed through the hills. The scenery begins to change after an hour, and just as I'm worrying about diesel supplies, I spot civilization in the distance.

Small white houses look out over a small marina, and tiny fishing boats are strung along the shore in a colourful line.

I can't help but cry out in hope. We're nearly there, so nearly there.

A vehicle roars behind us and I look back in horror. It's one of the vehicles we passed on the hills, and it's starting the descent to this side of the island. I put my foot down, hearing the engine whine in protest.

It's a desperate race to the houses. I'm not sure if they recognize the Land Rover, or whose side they're on, but I'm taking no chances. They must have discovered what happened back at the shack. They could think I killed Philip.

Sweat is pouring from my body, and Elan is screaming. I get to a crossroads, and have no idea which way to turn. To my right, lots of people are walking along the road towards a busy pub. There's some sort of procession going on. I head towards them. I'll be safer in a crowd.

I yank the vehicle to a halt. Costumed dancers scatter, parents pull children out of the way. I ignore their horrified exclamations and twist in my seat. My pursuers have followed me.

I can see their uniforms now, and I know it's finally happening.

I cling to my baby, and slide from my sticky seat. My bare feet touch stones and I curl my toes, overwhelmed with fear and relief. A woman holds her arms out for Elan, concern in her face, but I hold him close. Others are bringing me a glass of water, a cardigan. The music burbles along, a soundtrack to my relief.

We've done it. We've escaped and now we're safe. A policewoman asks me if I'm okay, who I am. I open my mouth to speak, but the words won't come.

My mouth is dry, my lips cracked and sore, and I'm shaking like I have a fever, but I allow myself to be led inside the pub, collapsing on a chair with Elan. He nestles in the crook of one arm, sniffling.

The woman who offered to hold my baby, youngish in jeans and boots, crouches down next to me and smiles.

"You look like you've had trouble. What's your name?"

I wet my lips from the glass of icy water, swallowing hard, but my voice comes out in a croak.

"Eden. My name is Eden Matthews and I need help."

CHAPTER FORTY-TWO

Dove sipped coffee in the hospital corridor. Ren was alive. She had only been drowsy, having just taken the pills when her husband found her. Alex had been working late, restoring some furniture in his workshop next to the house.

"I came in and there she was, lying flat out on the floor." Alex was still agitated. He stood next to Dove, waiting for the doctor to come over, his face pale with exhaustion and worry. "It feels like my life's falling apart."

"Don't torture yourself," Quinn told him. "You found her, that's all that matters. She's okay." He had insisted on coming to the hospital, and she was grateful for his calm, professional presence.

The doctor, red-haired and serious, beckoned them. "Her observations are looking good. It was lucky that you found her when you did."

"That's what we were just telling him." Quinn shot a supportive look at Alex.

The doctor nodded. "The only thing is, she insists she didn't take an overdose. Previously, I can see from her notes, she admitted trying to end her life, but this time, she says it must have been an accident."

Dove tried to process this, but couldn't. The only thing that mattered was that Ren was okay. How would Ren react when she heard Eden was alive? And Alex? God, she wanted to tell them, to be the one to share the good news.

"She's in safe hands here, and we'll decide together what safeguarding needs to be put in place." The doctor smiled and moved quickly away on her rounds.

"Dove, you get to work, love," said Quinn. "Gaia's on her way over, and I'll let you know what's going on. I'll stay here, if Alex wants me to?"

"If you don't mind, mate, just till Gaia gets here. I know it's mad, but I bloody hate hospitals," Alex confessed.

Dove was torn, but nodded. "Okay, after I've seen Ren."

When she went in, Ren was sitting up, her hair curled loosely around her tired face.

"Hallo, you."

"Hallo yourself," Dove said, hardly able to prevent herself from talking about Eden. She couldn't, not this time. It wasn't her place, and if Eden wasn't alive, she would do more harm than good.

"Oh my God, Dove, is that what I think it is?" Ren squeaked, the shadow of fatigue and drugs lifting for a moment as she slipped a hand around Dove's fingers.

From outside the door, Dove could see both men glancing up in response to Ren's exclamation. She raised her left hand in a "busted" gesture, and Quinn grinned.

"Yes, it is. Quinn asked me to marry him and we are officially engaged." Dove kissed her sister as Ren pulled her into a hug.

"Are you moving back in together?"

"Yes again. We only kept it a secret because of everything that's going on, or you know I would have been straight on the phone."

The moment of joy passed all too quickly. Ren slumped against her pillows, the light draining from her expression. She picked at the sheet with nervous fingers.

207

"I'm scared, Dove. I didn't take an overdose on purpose. I don't remember doing it."

* * *

The drive to work in rush hour took ages, and Dove drummed her fingers on the steering wheel in frustration at more roadworks in the town centre. Her phone rang as she turned right by the theatre, trying a shortcut, and she bit her lip as the familiar number came up on her hands-free screen.

"Hi, boss."

"DC Milson." He was being all formal again. "I hope your sister is okay?"

"She's going to be fine. Sorry, I'm only about ten minutes away . . ."

"I wanted to call you with some news."

"What's happened?"

"Eden is safe. She and her son were picked up two hours ago. It seems they were sheltering in some derelict farm buildings. When she saw the search vehicles coming, she made a break for it, and got over to the village on the far end of the island. She's very agitated and confused, but she and the child are going through the usual medical checks."

"Shit," Dove whispered, and then jerked back to reality as a car hooted and she realized she'd drifted into the bus lane.

"One thing she has insisted on is that she wants to talk to you, and she doesn't want her parents contacted until you have spoken to her. This goes against protocol, but DCI Franklin and I have liaised with DI Hartfield and we feel that she wants to speak to you as a trusted family member, not as a police officer, so we can accommodate her request without compromising either you or the investigation."

In the first rush of emotion, Dove fought back tears, her mind racing. It was a few seconds before she could control her voice. "Okay . . . But maybe she feels because of my job she can talk about what happened? We were always close.

Did she give any reason why we shouldn't let the rest of her family know?"

"No. But it was one of the first things she said to the officers who picked her up. We'll do it via video link, obviously, due to logistics. Eden will be made aware that we need to have other officers present, but we will handle the whole thing as gently as we can. She's been held captive for four years. When she was abducted, she was a teenager. Now she's a mother."

Slightly surprised by this show of empathy, which only raised her level of respect for him, she agreed to do the interview. Her mind tracked through possibilities as to why Eden would only speak to her. The only real contender was that Eden was afraid for her family, that she had been threatened with violence towards them as part of her captor's controlling behaviour.

Dove's joy at finding out her niece was alive was now diluted by reality. What horrors had she suffered? Would she be able to recover enough to get back to normality?

"How old is the child? Is it a boy or girl?"

"Boy, and she says he's just turned eighteen months. Sorry, I realize this must be a shock to you. As you know, I'm trying everything possible to keep you personally out of this case, but I think you need to talk to her. We need to know why she doesn't want her parents contacted."

"Yes, boss. I'll be right in." She hoped her voice sounded strong and calm.

"I'll set up a suite in the main briefing room and you can speak to her via the video link. That extra reassurance of seeing a trusted family member might help her to confide in you."

Did she imagine it, or did he emphasize the word "*trusted*"? Was this about Gaia again? The thought of Gaia's past still ran like a dark thread at the back of her mind. She had been formally questioned as part of Eden's investigation, and she'd had no alibi for the night Eden went missing. Surely her sister couldn't be involved . . .

DI Blackman ended the call and Dove finally navigated onto the main road. By the time she pulled into the car park at the station, she was pumped, fizzing with adrenalin, desperate to see Eden. But she took a minute to compose herself, to wipe away a couple of tears that had escaped without her noticing.

"Eden is alive. She's coming home," she whispered to her reflection in the driver mirror.

* * *

The team were busy with new leads on the two Glass Doll murders. Steve told her that after the recent media appeal, a paddleboarder had now come forward stating he had seen what could have been the boat coming into the cove where the body was found.

"Shit, did he see who dumped it?"

"Not sure yet. He rang in on the Crimeline number an hour ago, and I'm going out to see him now with the DI. But I hear you have something else to do first?" His query was gentle.

"Yes, I'm going to speak to Eden." Even saying the name was hard. But she needed to be strong for her niece. Whatever the girl wanted to tell her, she must be supportive and not break down.

"Good luck."

Dove entered the briefing room, nodding as introductions were made, and waited for her niece to appear on the screen. Her heart was pounding. Eden was back from the dead.

And there she was, with intense blue eyes, wild black hair and her mother's dimples. Having noted how much like Eden Delta had looked the other night, Dove was shocked at how the abuse had aged her elder niece. She knew she should have been prepared for this, but it hit her like a kick in the gut. Her eyes were wet as she greeted the girl. *Stay professional.*

There was a faded bruise on one cheekbone, and just out of shot, Dove glimpsed a child's chubby cheek and fuzz of dark hair. Her heart filled and as she smiled at Eden, she could think of nothing but what would be Ren's passionate reaction to having her daughter return from the dead.

"Eden, I'm so glad you're here." She forced her voice to come out strong but calm. The effort made her body tremble, and she wondered if Eden had noticed her blinking back the tears. She swallowed. "You have a baby! What's his name?"

The girl smiled. "Dove." There was such a world of love and hope in that one word that Dove nearly lost it completely. "His name is Elan." Her voice was soft, hesitant and she kept nervously licking her lips, eyes darting from the camera to her son. She held him up, so that her aunt could see his face. "The doctors say he's going to be okay. He just needs some more food. I breastfed him for as long as I could, but the last few months, my milk dried up and I could see he wasn't doing as well as he should have been . . ."

Dove nodded, knowing that this small talk would re-establish the trust, the bond between them. "You are wonderful and brave, and I am so proud of you for surviving what has happened. Elan is beautiful and I can't wait to see you both in person."

Eden smiled again, but then her expression changed, the blue of her eyes darkening as she stroked the baby's head. "I can't talk about what happened at the moment, but I know that we'll both get all the help we need."

"Of course. Eden, don't put pressure on yourself to try and snap back to normality. You have obviously suffered the most horrific abuse and you've been away a long time. Now you need to give yourself time to heal, to adjust back to normal life," Dove told her. Was she talking to herself or her niece, she wondered? Nothing could compare Eden's traumas with her own. The girl had survived, but God knew what scars she had hidden beneath the surface. Dove felt she was treading water, waiting for the girl to tell her what she had to say. It was important not to rush her.

"Dove, there is something I need to tell you." Eden stopped and glanced around. Dove heard some soft words of reassurance.

"You can tell me anything," Dove told her. "Anything at all."

"It's the reason why I said I wanted to speak to you first. I said I can't talk about it, but you need to know how it started. You need to know how I ended up with Philip, but not what he did to me." Her expression was resolute now, and the chilling tone almost eerie.

Dove got the impression that her niece had practised this little speech in her head so often it had become second nature. She must have told herself, when she got out, she would do this.

"You can tell me anything, Eden, anything at all. Please remember, none of this is your fault."

"Okay . . ." She took a breath, and her eyes filled with tears again. She brushed them away. "I just . . . The only way I can do this is just to tell you straight what happened from the time I left Amelie's house to the time I was taken, just like a story I might tell Elan."

"That's fine, my love, just go ahead whenever you're ready." Dove hardly noticed the endearment that slipped out so naturally, and glanced at her colleagues, who both nodded. "I'm listening."

CHAPTER FORTY-THREE

Listening to her story, Dove found it hard not to let the tears go. That soft, cracked little voice, reciting the evil that had led to her captivity. The wrong place at the wrong time.

"Eden, who were the two men with the van? Did you recognize them?" Dove asked.

The eyes, filled with pain, fear, and regret, met hers.

"Yes, I recognized one of them. It was Da . . . It was Alex." She burst into noisy sobs, rocking backwards and forwards, cuddling her child.

There was an audible intake of breath from the woman on Dove's left, and, as the full force of the statement hit her, she couldn't breathe.

"It's okay, Eden." But she knew it wasn't, and wouldn't ever be again.

Following her niece's lead, she avoided using the word "dad". He didn't deserve to be called that, if this was true. "One of the men was Alex, and did you recognize the other?"

She was silent for a minute, twisting a strand of lank hair in her fingers before she shook her head. "I've had years to think about it and I didn't know him. He was taller, blond and skinny with glasses. I remember he almost looked like he was laughing when he saw me."

Dove swallowed hard. The description loosely fit Peter Hayworth, but they could get a sketch done later, show Eden some photographs. Meanwhile, what the fuck was Alex doing with Hayworth? Her brother-in-law was being reformed in front of her eyes, mutating into someone entirely different.

"Mum'll hate me," Eden said quietly. "She's going to wish I hadn't come back."

A rush of protective love flooded Dove and she ached to pull her niece into her arms.

"Never, ever think that, Eden. *None* of this is your fault. The fact that you were betrayed by one of your parents doesn't mean that Ren will hate you. The opposite. She'll be so, so happy to have you back." An image of Ren lying in her hospital bed earlier flashed through Dove's mind. "Yes, this is going to be tough, but, my brave and beautiful girl, you are coming home to us. To me, to Ren, to Gaia . . ." She hesitated a second but forced herself to go on. "We love you so much and we are here waiting for you. We've been waiting four years for you to come home, my love." Her voice cracked, and Eden was crying properly again. She stretched a hand towards the screen, as though she could touch her aunt through the camera, as though there was no distance between them at all.

Dove touched her screen too and told Eden that she would get her home as soon as possible. She waited for the girl to end the call and then sat back, tears streaming down her cheeks, not caring who saw. Bloody hell. Alex. She wanted to go straight round and tear his limbs from his body.

Instead, she managed a quick debrief with her colleagues. As they walked back out into the corridor, she found DI Blackman's hand on her shoulder.

They faced each other, and she noticed again how tall he was. She had to tilt her head up to look him in the eyes. "Sorry, I didn't mean to lose it."

He smiled at her, all formality departing from his face and manner, leaving only concern. Just for that quiet moment, she saw who he really was, stripped back beneath his professional facade.

"You did well. That must be one of the hardest things to go through in our job, trying to work when you are personally involved."

"Well, I do keep trying to separate my life into compartments but it seems to get tangled," Dove said. The ring was now zipped inside her inside pocket, and she traced the outline through her jacket.

"It's hard, I know. Do you want some quiet time, or are you ready to do the briefing first?"

She lifted her chin. "Briefing first, boss."

He smiled, touching her arm again before walking on. It was warm and unthreatening, a gesture of comfort for a team player, that was all.

Dove took a minute to nip to the toilets and splash her face in cold water, then scraped her long hair off her face, tying it back. She smiled into the mirror.

Back at her desk, unable to settle, waiting for the briefing to begin, she soon found herself walking back into the DI's office. He was remote, formal and unreachable again, but she sat in the chair opposite.

"When Peter Hayworth was arrested, he confessed to Eden's murder," said Dove bitterly. "How did he and Alex even cross paths? I thought Hayworth was a loner. There was never any suggestion of a partner."

DI Blackman shook his head, his eyes holding hers. "Eden has managed to give a few more nuggets of information, but they are being careful not to press her. Everything has to come in her own time."

"I know." She paused. She understood that, of course she did. But she wanted answers, too. "So what else has she said?"

"According to Eden, the man who kept her prisoner for the last four years told her he, Hayworth and Alex were brothers, or perhaps half-brothers."

"But there wasn't . . . Alex comes from Truro and we know his family. They're lovely, normal people. He's got a younger sister, but no brothers. We would know!"

"It might not be true. We won't know until we start digging."

"I can't get my head around it . . . I just think . . . I wonder if Alex is responsible for the recent murders too. It does all centre around Hayworth, so perhaps Delta discovered something, he tried to keep her quiet with the murder, and it didn't work." She ran out of steam, aware she was babbling.

"Everything is possible at this stage. Alex is obviously a very smart and careful man, not to mention dangerous. I'll keep you posted, DC Milson. I know how hard it is to have a case go this personal." His expression froze, clear grey eyes like ice on a winter's day. "Yes, I *do* know."

She didn't ask and he didn't volunteer, but an understanding passed between them. Full of pain and regret, but also protection. Dove *did* trust him, even if she couldn't see a way out of her own personal hellhole. If Alex had done anything to Delta . . .

A sombre team gathered for the briefing.

"Eden Matthews, who was found this morning, has given a statement now." DI Blackman paused. "She says that when she was walking home from her friend's place, she saw her father, Alex Matthews, and another man abusing a young girl in the car park. There was a mix-up with pick-up times so she wasn't supposed to be there. Bad timing in the extreme. She says she tried to run, but was caught by the other man, whose description *could* fit that of Peter Hayworth." He paused, glancing round the room to silence the muttering that had broken out.

"Eden has given us the briefest details of the time following her abduction. She was kept in a holding house with other girls, and then stowed in a van all the way to Shetland, before being put on a boat to an island in the Vaila Sound. She's been there all this time. The man who kept her captive was identified as Philip Ashley. At this time, we don't know what connections Philip Ashley has to Alex Matthews or Peter Hayworth, but for the purposes of our timeline, it seems once Alex Matthews recognized his daughter, he arranged for her to be removed."

"He never came up as a contact of Hayworth's, did he?" DC Conrad asked.

"No. Perhaps Hayworth was told to say he had killed Eden. It is possible that the three men were connected and involved in larger scale sex trafficking. It was always understood that Hayworth worked alone, but if one of them, say Philip Ashley, was a player in the trafficking, Matthews could have asked him to make his daughter disappear."

"Hayworth never grassed anyone," Dove observed.

"No. Which suggests the three had some kind of mutual blackmail, or loyalty to each other in place. Did the other two know Hayworth was killing as well as abusing, or did they assume he was just one of the boys? We mustn't forget that Colin Creaver also hails from that neck of the woods," DI Blackman continued. "I'm bringing Alex Matthews in, obviously, and DS Allerton, I want you to be there as FLO. You can break the news about Eden's reappearance and abduction privately to the other family members, and we will deal with Alex. That way, we should be able to get him over here with minimal fuss. Please don't forget, any of you, that the press are hounding us, so the less time we spend giving them front page opportunities the better."

Officers were dispatched on various jobs, with three cars being organized to pick up Alex. Dove told them he was currently at home with his wife, this being his day off from the market. She listened again to his most recent voicemail and could detect nothing but concern for both Ren and Delta. The two-faced bastard. Could it really have been him?

Dove tried to pick up the reins of her own case, but it was impossible to concentrate when she spent the whole time wondering if her own brother-in-law was responsible. Steve had been sent straight out with DC Conrad to speak to the possible witness in Evie's case, but the DI had suggested she remain working at the station for the morning.

Various officers came over to her desk with words of encouragement and commiseration, as, despite good intentions, word had spread.

Lindsey plonked a cup of coffee next to her keyboard. "Don't sit here beating yourself up. You've got murders to solve, lady."

Dove gulped the hot drink. Her brain was still screaming *No, no, no!* Alex? Her solid, dependable brother-in-law? Ren's bloody husband, the girls' own father?

"Lindsey, how could I have not known it was Alex? I work for the fucking police and one of my family members has turned out to be . . . I don't even know *what* he is at the moment, but potentially a murderer, I suppose. Certainly someone cold-blooded enough to send his own daughter off to live in a bloody cellar, just to save his neck."

CHAPTER FORTY-FOUR

"Because he's clever, and hiding in plain sight. I saw he was questioned at the time of Eden's disappearance as part of the investigation, but it was routine and he never gave any cause for any follow-ups. I'll be honest, we checked him out again when his other daughter disappeared, but he is clean as fuck and his alibi checks out."

"Do you think he's taken Delta as well? Do you think she found out what happened to her sister?" Dove asked.

"Can't say at the moment, but I think you have to face up to the possibility. There is something in this Tough Justice link, I know it," Lindsey said. "Got to get going, but I'll keep you posted. Don't let the bastards get you down!"

She slapped Dove's shoulder and walked off, yelling for her current partner, DC Shipton, who rolled his eyes at her. "Right, Lindsey, I think the whole town heard my name. Let's get out of here!"

Steve appeared ten minutes later with the witness statement. She brought him up to speed on Eden's case.

"Fuck. Do you want to take time off? Be with your family?" he said, horrified by the turn of events.

"I'm not sure what's going to happen. After Eden's statement, it's possible, in fact entirely probable, that the DI will take me off the case," Dove said.

"Why? Do you think Agnes's and Evie's murders are down to Alex?"

"I don't know what to think. Just because he was involved in Eden's abduction, doesn't make him a killer. We don't even know for sure what his connection was, if any, with Hayworth at this stage."

Steve shrugged. "I really couldn't say, but before the boss makes any decisions, how about I distract you with that witness statement?"

She tried to smile, but ended up just nodding. "Hit me with it."

"This paddleboarder, Aiden Furley, reckons he saw a boat around five thirty in the morning."

"He was out early," Dove commented.

"Total fitness fanatic. He runs a gym, Active World."

"I know it."

"It was a small motorboat-type craft. He's not hot on makes and models so this is his description. He says it was close inshore and he noticed it because it was unusual. Lots of rocks around there and he wondered if the boat was in trouble. There was one man on board. Muscular, quite tall, he thinks, wearing a blue hoody with no logo. He's not sure but if he had to guess, he thinks the man might have been Caucasian with blond hair."

"Which, if he is correct, fits with both Alex Matthews and Colin Creaver," Dove said.

"The man fussed around, seeming to be unloading something in a wooden box. Our witness was on his way back to Petty's Cove where he left his car, but the last thing he saw was the man shifting this wooden box off the boat. He went away on holiday that day, to a fitness retreat in Ibiza, and just got back yesterday."

"Only now he puts two and two together." Dove was sceptical.

"Witness says no phones were allowed at the retreat, and when he got home, the latest appeal was all over social media and the TV. That's when he remembered this 'fisherman' as he thought and decided to call the Crimeline."

"What about the boat? Shall I check with the marina?"

"You could, but if he keeps the boat along the coast somewhere, and if it was our killer, we have to assume it would be really close to his Glass Doll factory due to ease of transportation."

"What do you think of this guy, as a witness, I mean?"

"Yeah, I think he's straight up. Very self-absorbed and can't complete a sentence without dropping in a fitness tip, but it fits."

"All right, let's see if he can ID Alex from a photo, but I want to wait until after Alex has been interviewed. The first thing to hit him with is Eden and Delta. Delta's still missing and that has to take priority," Dove said firmly. "You're going in with the DI, aren't you?"

"I am. How about a long lunch break, so you can call your family?"

"Thanks, Steve, I'd really appreciate that." She smiled at him. "Bacon roll for you?"

"With brown sauce!" He gave her the thumbs up and she went out into the car park with her mobile. The food van had a queue, so she braced herself and rang Gaia. Waiting for the call to connect, she noticed her colleagues arriving back from Ren's house. From across the concrete, hidden by a van, she watched a volatile Alex being brought in. She dug her nails into her palm, nausea rising in her stomach. Bad timing.

"You can't be serious?" Alex was shouting at the officers, and Dove caught her breath in horror at the situation. "I've been set up! You can't do this! My daughter is missing!"

"Dove! What the fuck is happening? Ren just called and said Alex has been taken off by the police, and Eden's alive." Gaia's clipped, furious tones blasted her sister's eardrums. "She's back home, by the way. The doctor gave her a referral to mental health. Again."

"Just let me speak, okay? I know how it looks to you and Ren, but you don't know the full story—"

"Ren says that Alex was involved with Eden's abduction?"

"Yes. Eden told me so, and with Delta still missing, we don't have time on our side."

"You're certain about this? I thought it might be Ren's medication talking . . ."

"Gaia, I spoke to her via video link. She is absolutely certain. You need to stay with Ren, if you can. Get her to focus on Eden coming home. She's got a little boy, too."

"Fuck me." Gaia let out a low whistle. "Did Alex kill those two girls from my club as well?"

"We don't know yet."

"And Delta?"

"Ditto. We are doing everything we can, but I'm not allowed to be part of the cases involving the family, so I'm focusing on the murders."

"And if they *were* down to Alex, they'll take you off the case?"

"I guess they'll have to," Dove said softly.

"I have so many questions."

"Me too, but I can't answer them now. Please look after Ren."

For once, Gaia didn't snap back at her. "I will. Will you come over here?"

"I'll try. I want to so much, you know that, but I can't do anything that might compromise the case."

"Well, find Delta, then, and nail Alex's fucking balls to the wall."

* * *

"I have a couple of things to say to you, DC Milson, some of which you will have expected." DI Blackman studied her face, but she made no comment. "Firstly, I can see how tough this, not being involved, yet being fully involved. Secondly, as you will no doubt have guessed, if we get any evidence that

Alex may be involved with the murders of Agnes and Evie, I will have to take you off the Glass Doll case."

She nodded, unable to speak.

"This is a bizarre situation, but I'm going to say that you can watch Alex's interview from the viewing box. I've never used this facility before, but if you can follow the interview with a professional head, you can share any insights with me afterwards."

Dove smiled at him now, relief pouring through her veins. It wasn't much, but if she could pick up on anything, knowing Alex so well, she would feel a contribution had been made. "Thank you."

He nodded. "If it gets too much, you can just leave at any point."

CHAPTER FORTY-FIVE

Dove watched from behind the tinted glass. There were only two interview rooms, with an extended narrow passageway between them and the main corridor, but she had full audio access. She was grateful to the DI that he had chosen to conduct the interview here. The slightly chemical smell of new carpet and paint told her she might have been the first person to use this facility.

Her brother-in-law was sitting with his solicitor, his blond hair falling across his face, his expression one of anger and sorrow. Perfectly pitched as a balance between a wrongfully arrested man and a desperate father.

She wanted to hit him, and carry on hitting him until he told her where Delta was. Instead, she gnawed on a battered thumbnail, her breath steaming the glass as she glared at him.

DI Blackman made the introductions and set the tape running.

"Your daughter, Eden Matthews, has made a statement, as you have been informed. Would you like to revise anything you have previously told the police regarding her disappearance?"

"No. I'm over the moon she's been found, and her mother and I can't understand why she can't come home, why we can't see her. What is going on?" He spread his hands in an apparent plea for understanding. "It breaks my heart to think of what she might have been going through all these years, and I understand she might now have mental health issues as a result . . . but to accuse me of being involved in her abduction . . ." Once again, Alex's expression and tone were pitched perfectly between the concerned father and the outraged victim.

His solicitor sat with her eyes on him, her bright red lips pursed. It was a nice touch to drop in early that Eden might be an unstable witness, but there was no way he was going to get away with this.

"Can you talk us through the night Eden went missing?" Steve asked.

"What? I've been through this all before. For God's sake . . . She was out at a friend's house for a party, and I was picking her up at eleven. She had a row with her boyfriend and walked out of the party early. She called but Delta didn't pass on the message. I had no idea she was walking the streets because I was at a Neighbourhood Watch meeting, before I went for a drink at the pub. You already confirmed this at the time!"

The DI consulted his notes. "Yes, and we will be talking to the witnesses again in light of this new evidence."

DI Blackman moved on to Eden's claim of familial connections between Philip Ashley, Alex and Peter Hayworth.

Alex laughed in his face. "You're joking, aren't you? Why would you try and pin this on me? She's my daughter. I thought she was dead. And now you're trying to accuse me of being part of her disappearance . . . You'll be saying next you think I'm the idiot behind these latest murders, or accusing me of doing something to Delta."

Blackman said nothing.

A shadow of fury crossed Alex's face. "You are, aren't you? No way." He turned and addressed his solicitor. "This is crazy, I'm being made a scapegoat because the police are too useless to investigate their own cases. You know what I think now? No comment."

225

After Alex had been led away, Dove went back upstairs. The interview had moved on to more questions about his second daughter's whereabouts, but Alex had fallen back on a scowling "No comment" to every question asked.

There was something niggling Dove about the three names, Philip, Alex, and Peter, but she couldn't place it. It was hearing them read out that had jogged her memory, and she muttered them to herself, changing the order, but it didn't feel quite right. She felt like she might have seen them written down somewhere, but despite dredging her memories, she couldn't quite make the link.

The evening briefing was short and straight to the point. They were gathering evidence on Alex, who was now the main suspect in both homicide cases and Delta's disappearance.

"Are we ruling Creaver out completely, then?" Lindsey asked.

DI Blackman frowned. "Not completely. Just because we've had to let him go doesn't mean something won't turn up. How did Alex get those girls to meet up with him before he killed them? It might be that Creaver is involved to a certain extent, but in answer to your question, our main focus is Alex Matthews. There is no link between the two men, and no evidence they knew or have known each other."

Dove was called into the DI's office for a private chat afterwards. She knew exactly what was going to happen.

"I'm really sorry, but we can't ignore the evidence now points towards your brother-in-law. His original alibi for Eden's abduction has fallen apart, as the fellow market trader he was supposed to have been drinking with admits he lied for Alex. Alex told him he was scared we would try to get him for his daughter's disappearance, and this witness had known him long enough, and trusted him enough to lie for him."

"What an idiot," Dove said. "We could have had him years ago."

"Possibly. It looks like his motive for Eden's abduction was simply that she caught him. Hayworth clearly lied for him, which suggests they had some sort of relationship. Perhaps Alex was able to blackmail him for some reason . . ." The DI looked thoughtful. "There are also plenty of vans down at the market where Alex works, so we need to check out all the owners and see if Alex has borrowed one recently. His own is red, so from the CCTV evidence, it can't have been the one used to transport Agnes."

"What about his alibis for Agnes's and Evie's murders? He couldn't have just vanished for twenty-four hours for each girl. Ren would have noticed!" She noticed her voice had raised, and relaxed her clenched fists.

"His work allows him quite a lot of freedom, and his wife has admitted although she thinks he was home renovating furniture into the early hours on the evenings both Glass Doll girls were abducted, she can't say for definite. The same for the evening when Delta went missing."

Dove propped her chin on her hand, thinking now. "He made a big fuss about building that workshop, and we always joke it was his man cave. Now I look back and think maybe there was a reason he wanted soundproofing, all the extra touches."

"We've been taking it apart all afternoon," DI Blackman told her.

"And?"

"Of course it isn't big enough to have housed the Glass Doll factory, and I doubt we'll find any DNA links from either murder victim. It would have been far too risky to take the girls back to his own home." He paused, and his expression told her there was more. "But he does have a basement that doesn't appear on the original planning permission, and we discovered another computer, several other phones. They're being looked at now."

"Shit. And Creaver?" The tiny flicker of hope was instantly closed down by his expression.

He shook his head. "Nothing new, so I'm afraid with this new evidence I've got no choice but to take you off the case. I'm sorry, DC Milson, because I feel like you've done some really good work."

"It's okay, I understand," Dove said, standing up. "I just can't take it all in at the moment, but in light of all this, I'm absolutely terrified for Delta."

He sighed. "You and me both."

CHAPTER FORTY-SIX

After work, Dove drove over to Gaia's flat. Her sister lived above the club, which was closed up, a placard on the main doors telling customers the business would reopen soon. Silver signs, with their sexy sheen, gleamed in the sunset, but the lights were off inside. No one was there, not even Janet the cleaner finishing up her work.

Dove pressed the intercom and was buzzed up to the flat. Gaia answered the door in her usual uniform of black leather trousers and a tight wrap-around top. She had discarded her stilettos and was barefoot on the carpet.

"Hey," Dove said, noting her sister's red eyes under the layer of make-up.

"Hey, copper. Ren's in the living room." Gaia swung the door open.

"I've been taken off the case," Dove said. "Hardly surprising, really."

Ren was huddled on the cream leather sofa, a blanket around her shoulders. Her amber eyes were wet, lashes spiked, and her long hair screwed up in a messy knot. There was a tiny moment as Dove approached her sister when she thought Ren was going to be angry, but then she saw the anger wasn't directed at her.

"Really? You aren't investigating the murders anymore, because . . . Shit, I know why, don't I? Oh, Dove, what's happening to us? I feel like I've been torn apart." Ren bit her lip and wiped her eyes with a crumpled tissue. "He was so worried about me at the hospital . . . so kind and just . . . Alex. Why did it have to be us?"

"I don't know. I'm so sorry." It seemed such an inadequate thing to say. Dove searched for something lighter to talk about. "Do you know when Eden's coming home yet?"

"Oh. Yes, I do. Lindsey says tomorrow evening, when the little boy is well enough. He had to be kept in because he was dehydrated." Ren's voice grew stronger as she spoke. "I did speak to her — Eden."

"I can't believe she's alive," Gaia said. She'd brought in a tray of tea and chocolate bars, and put it carefully on the glass-and-chrome coffee table. "I also can't believe what's she's been through to get to this point. She's a survivor, Ren."

"I know, and I'm so proud of her, and suddenly I'm a granny, which is so odd. But she's back and . . . Alex will be gone." She gulped the hot drink and reached for a bar of chocolate, ripping the foil, shoving a piece in her mouth. "I haven't taken any medication. Not since I left the hospital this morning. When Lindsey told me about Eden, about Alex, I wanted to feel raw and I wanted the pain. Does that sound weird?"

"No," Dove said. "It's a lot to take in. I couldn't believe it either."

"How did we not know who he really was?" Gaia snapped her fingers with a sharp click. "We're not stupid, and we've all been around, yet he has been getting away with this for years. When our parents came over last year, he even took them round his fucking workshop, showing them all the coving or some shit. He must have been pissing himself laughing, knowing that all the time he had this other life."

"He's clever," said Dove. "This isn't a blame game, and it wasn't us who committed any crimes. We trusted him, loved him and he never let us see the truth because we could

230

never see past the exterior he built up. He was never going to say to Ren, *'Hey, guess what happened the night Eden disappeared?'*

"But he had an alibi . . ." Ren sighed. "I've been thinking of all the times he went off in the van to look at furniture or did a house clearance in another county. I never questioned it, never went into the workshop when he was working late . . ."

"You couldn't have guessed," Dove assured her. "He never did anything that made us suspect, and he probably was travelling for legit business purposes. He made money from his stall, and from the trading online, didn't he?"

Ren shrugged. "He pays the mortgage and I pay the bills from the coffee shop earnings. Since my rates went up, he's even been covering some of the bills, too." She pushed her hair back from her face. "I was so grateful, and proud his business was doing well."

"What about Delta?" Gaia asked the question the others had avoided.

Dove winced. "We don't know yet."

"What about those two girls who were murdered? Do the police really think that was Alex?" Ren asked wearily. "Lindsey said there was no evidence at the moment and I can't see why he would suddenly go out and kill two girls from Gaia's club."

"Because he could?" Gaia suggested. "Perhaps something set him off recently?"

"Lindsey asked me if I knew anything about Peter Hayworth and Philip Ashley being friends of Alex's," Ren put in. "But he never mentioned Philip. Of course, we'd both talked about Peter Hayworth, since he supposedly killed our daughter." She was crying again now, wiping her eyes with her sleeve. "What am I going to tell Eden when she comes home and finds Delta missing too?"

The other two had no answers to give. Ren sighed and looked at Dove. "Where's your ring?"

Gaia's eyes widened, and a flash of surprise crossed her face. "You didn't?"

Dove shrugged. The timing felt awkward and inappropriate, but Ren was clearly looking for a distraction, so she slipped her engagement ring back on. It felt right. She needed to see Quinn so badly, but for now, her sisters needed her.

For the first time since they were teenagers, they huddled under the same blanket on the sofa, arms wrapped around each other, together safe from horror.

* * *

Dove stayed late but eventually left the other two sleeping in Gaia's bed and crept home, tears running down her cheeks. Once home, she pulled her own soft wool blanket onto her bed, and sat up watching an old movie. It was only as she was finally drifting off in the early morning that she remembered.

Three names crudely scratched in the rock. Out of reach of the tide, but weathered by the seasons. Eden and Delta shrieking with laughter as they ducked in and out of the caves, the sky a vivid blue backdrop to their picnic.

Cornwall, where Alex's parents lived. They had all been staying near Truro, in Feock, and enjoying the beauty of the coastline. Dove hadn't mentioned the names after she found them. She had merely traced the etchings with a curious fingertip before plunging back into the sea to give her nieces rides on her surfboard.

But now her memory brought the names back to her. It wasn't her investigation anymore, and she needed to be careful, but the link was so tenuous and fragile, it couldn't hurt to do a little digging herself. She told herself if she could confirm her memory, she could go to the DI and get him to check it out. But without further evidence, what were three names scratched on a rock on Loe Beach?

It was two in the morning. Isabel, Alex's mum, answered the phone. She sounded wary. "Dove, what's going on? I heard Alex had been arrested. Ren was quite hysterical when I spoke to her. It must be a mistake . . ."

"Isabel, this is going to sound weird, but I'm trying to get as much information as possible to rule things out. This isn't my case, because of the family connection, but something has come up that you might be able to help with."

"To help Alex?"

"It might rule certain things out," Dove said, hearing a noise in the background and Isabel explaining to her husband who was on the phone.

"Okay, shoot. What do you want to know?"

"Do the names Peter and Philip mean anything to you, in the context of being friends or relatives of Alex's?" She held her breath, hoping her voice sounded casual, ears alert to any change in Isabel's manner.

But there was no red flag, as the other woman thought for a bit, asked her husband, and then said, "I can't think of anyone. It's a long time since we all got together and we do have a big family, but I can't think of anyone with those names . . . Alex had a lot of friends at school, but I think the only ones he really kept in touch with were Kirk and Alan. I don't recall Philip and Peter. Sorry. Have you asked Ren? If it could be important, I can email the rest of the family?"

"Ren doesn't remember any connections, and I don't know at this stage, but yes, if you could ask around and let me know, that would be helpful. Don't talk to any press, will you?" she added quickly, wanting to protect them but knowing it was impossible for long.

Three names and two of them dead.

CHAPTER FORTY-SEVEN

Alex was the only one left, and she felt sure he knew exactly what Jon Blackman was talking about. It was the one moment in the whole interview where Alex had actually looked jumpy, instead of furious. She had seen his eyes change from angry to fearful. What was the connection? Hopefully, the lab would be able to trace the links via the phones and computers seized from the workshop basement, but could it do any harm to let her brain work on the puzzle?

Awake and dressed by five thirty, she phoned Quinn and told him the news.

"Jesus, this one just keeps kicking you back down, doesn't it?" He was shocked and tried to persuade her to come down to Cornwall with him. "Weather forecast is amazing and you can't do anything up there, can you, if you're off the case?"

"You're right. Fuck it, I might come down after all. It depends on what happens this morning. Ren says that Eden should be home tonight, and if so, I want to see her, of course, before I bugger off down the coast."

His enthusiastic response made her realize how much she needed them to be back together properly. To be sharing the same bed, making coffee in the kitchen on the rare occasions their shift patterns allowed, watching awful reality TV shows with popcorn on their laps.

"Let me know, babe, but just do what you need to, okay?" Quinn said before he rang off.

With a slightly lighter heart, she listened to a voicemail from Ren saying that Eden and her son would be home on Tuesday night now because the child was being kept in hospital longer than expected. It was nothing serious and she was trying to focus on one daughter returning home, while she waited for news of the other. She didn't mention her husband.

Dove, after a moment's thought, called Lindsey and warned her of the extent of Ren's fragility, telling her also that her sister had stopped taking her medication. Lindsey promised that she wouldn't be left alone, but added that, in her opinion, the news of Eden's return from the dead had given Ren something to focus on in the wake of Alex's arrest and Delta's disappearance. Talking to the daughter she had believed to be dead had been like a shot of sunshine straight in her veins.

Dove glanced at her board and gear, lying on the floor in the office. Would it be so bad just to take off for two days? She'd go crazy being so close and yet not being able to work on the investigation.

She answered a quick text from Adrik, trying to make her wording more formal than usual, preparing for the point when she would have to cut him loose. She was aware that she'd been quite short with him recently, which didn't suit his needy nature.

Adrik liked her to be reliable, to reassure him, and she could tell from his comments that he was in a strop with her. It was tough, but there was no future in this. Adrik knew that, and keen as he had been to help, he had known it was temporary, whatever Zak and Chris said.

* * *

Her phone buzzed again just as she was about to jump in the shower.

DI Blackman was sombre. "I'm really sorry, DC Milson, but we got the preliminary forensics back on the phones and computer from your brother-in-law's workshop."

She froze, naked and shivering, one foot in the shower, the other on the cold tiles. "Go on."

"It appears that Alex Matthews has been running an international paedophile ring. I've had to call in Child Protection because this is massive. We're going to be talking to at least three other agencies, not to mention all the different boroughs potentially involved."

"Bloody hell . . ." Dove felt like she'd been kicked in the chest. She hugged a towel around herself.

He continued speaking, telling her evidence was being gathered to charge Alex with for his involvement with Peter Hayworth's catalogue of child abuse, and with arranging his own daughter's abduction. His computer and phones had revealed a far wider scale of organized abuse, across three countries.

Dove pushed her nausea away, and told him she was planning on heading down the coast for the weekend with her partner.

The DI agreed she should take time out, and told her the witness in Evie's murder had picked out Alex in a photo ID parade.

It was him, she thought. *It was my own brother-in-law, all this time.*

"Take a complete break, won't you? If I need you, I know where to find you. And tell your co-handler to pick up the slack on your CHIS. This would be tough for anyone to deal with, but to have this degree of personal involvement in your first case is highly unusual," DI Blackman told her.

"I know — of all the people, of all the places, it had to be here and now," Dove said. "I'm not going far, just down to Cornwall for some surfing."

She put the phone down and called Zak, leaving a voicemail telling him she needed some time out, but that she would speak to Adrik and make sure he knew she was away for a few days.

"Hey, Kelly. What's up?"

"How's the family?"

"Good. You got problems?" His voice sharpened.

"A few, just a few. Listen, I'm going to be away for a couple of days, until Tuesday, but if you need a meet or you need anything, you can call Jack."

"You bailing on me again, girl?"

"No, I just need a bit of time out. Family problems, like I said." He was silent, and she could hear him breathing. How much did he already know? With Adrik, he could easily have put the full story together.

"All right. As long as you're coming back. Don't just disappear on me again, I mean it, I was so freaked out. I thought you might be lying dead on the street somewhere. You're my family too, Kelly."

"Thanks, Adrik, I appreciate that."

The drive down to Cornwall took five hours, but the sun was shining and although she was careful to turn the radio volume down every time there was a news bulletin, Dove made it through the traffic. First, she would hook up with Quinn, who was staying in Feock in their usual B & B, then she would get down the beach and see what she could find. She would decide what to do about Alex's parents later.

* * *

"I'm so glad you made it. Even two days is better than nothing, and I've been worried about you," Quinn said as they lay on the beach.

She brushed water from her eyes, twisted her hair, and felt the water run down her neck under her wetsuit. "Sometimes I think about giving it all up and just going to live in a beach hut somewhere."

"I know. Why are we doing this to ourselves?" Quinn smiled. His skin was tanning already, and his eyes were bright and alert. "Seriously, though, we're not getting any younger, although I know that's the wrong thing to say to a woman . . ."

"Why do people think that?" Dove asked him. "I've never got why it's such a compliment for people to say, 'Oh you look so much younger than you actually are,' because ageing is a gift, isn't it? I'd rather have scars and wrinkles than die early and stay beautiful."

He passed her a bottle of energy drink and she unscrewed the cap, still thinking, watching the blues of the sea merge with the sky. No wonder this place attracted artists.

This was the third beach of the day, and they would wander along the coast after a rest to check out a few more. She had been wrong about Loe, but that didn't mean she was wrong about the names.

"Do you really think they will still be here, scratched into the rock, just as you remember them?" Quinn said. She had confided in him as soon as she arrived, and he agreed they should take a look, saying he had always liked a treasure hunt.

"It would be between the B & B and that tiny ice-cream place, because we walked down to the beach, so it can't be much further along. It was only ten years ago, absolute max." Dove screwed up her eyes against the sun.

They lazed a little more, enjoying the peace, the clean, salty perfection of the air, and the sound of waves rolling onto the shoreline.

It was on the last beach, when her limbs ached from surfing, swimming and paddleboarding, that the memory clicked back with a shock.

The rocky cove, the shape of the cliffs against the pale wash of sky. Here. Quinn watched as she stepped across the green and slimy boulders, retracing her steps of ten years ago.

At head height, the scratchings were still there, half-hidden by other graffiti, other names, hearts and crude drawings.

Her bare foot scrunched on an empty coke can and she jerked backwards.

"You okay?" Quinn's voice echoed between the rocks.

With the stench of seaweed strong in her nostrils, she traced the rock with her fingertips, closed her eyes and remembered that sunny day. Before Eden was taken, before Delta vanished and before Alex betrayed his family.

CHAPTER FORTY-EIGHT

"Dove?"

"Sorry." She slipped out her phone from the waterproof case and snapped a quick photo of the names, before clambering back the way she had come, towards her boyfriend and the sunlight.

She blinked in the sun, taking in the houses on the clifftop, the caravan park to her right, and farm cottages to the east. "Got it."

He peered at the photo. "Jesus. But what does that prove? I know what your memory is like, but can you link the three men together down here?"

"Give me a chance," she retorted with a grin.

"If I didn't have a fairly healthy ego, I might think you'd come here to do your bloodhound bit, not to see your long-suffering boyfriend."

"Fiancé," she corrected. "Bloody hell, we're getting married."

He looked around. "You know, I always fancied a beach wedding . . ."

* * *

The sun dropped lower in the sky, turning the coast red and gold. Quinn was still in the water, and she was stretched out on the pebbles and rough sand, breathing deeply after a last swim, trying to enjoy the moment. But her mind was too busy now. When she left Quinn tomorrow night, she would have to drop in on Alex's parents.

Her other phone was also in her bag. Despite her promises, she couldn't sever the tie between her and Adrik yet, it would need to be done properly, when her mind wasn't cluttered with worry. She sent a text to Ren, reminding her to let her know what time Eden was due home on Tuesday, and sending her love.

Jess also sent a message, with a picture of a bottle of red wine and a question mark. Dove smiled — she would make a date to see her friend, have a proper chat. Jess would go crazy when she heard the engagement news.

Dove thought she might even invite everyone round to celebrate. Her mind skittered around, searching for the good things, trying to block out Alex and Delta for a few minutes. But it was no use. *Come on, Delta, come home, if you can. Tell us where you are, if you can't . . .*

The sheer mind-blowing awfulness of the situation had come to rest right there on the sunny Cornish beach. On one hand, Eden's homecoming would be everything she and her sisters had wished for since her disappearance. On the other, with Delta still missing and Alex arrested, the nightmare was only just beginning.

They ate at a little rustic pub, honouring the beach with large plates of fish and chips with mushy peas.

Quinn finished his pint. "It could have been anyone from years back, you know, scratching those names. Loads of tourists, plus all the weekenders and the locals."

"Or it could have been one of those three men, messing around on the beach as teenagers or younger kids, recording their names on the rock forever."

"Can't imagine what Hayworth was like as a kid. It creeps me out thinking that innocent kids playing around in this part of the world could grow up to become abusers or murderers." Quinn kept his voice low.

Dove was drawing patterns on the polished tabletop with the end of her fork. "Philip Ashley was from Devon originally, and so was Peter Hayworth. Hayworth was adopted when he was eleven. Could have been anywhere. It's just geography that brought them together."

"And Ashley?"

"His parents are dead, and it was only his dental records and a previous tenancy that tied him to this area, Plymouth to be precise, but he later worked in Cornwall." In a weird twist of fate, Colin Creaver was also from the area, but unless she heard otherwise, that was just a terrible coincidence.

"What does Alex's sister say? Louise, isn't it?"

"I haven't heard from her. His parents are lovely people and they are naturally devastated, but also — understandably — convinced there must be some mistake."

"Eden wouldn't be mistaken about her own father?" Quinn asked.

"No. She had a really good relationship with Alex before her abduction. Apart from the odd teenage spat, she was a real Daddy's girl. We didn't talk about it before I left, but I know Ren and Gaia were afraid it might come out he had been abusing his own daughters in some way, but there is no evidence of that so far, thank God." Dove bit her thumbnail and sighed.

"Yeah, he was just abusing other people's daughters," Quinn said.

"It's just vile, the whole thing. You know the beach hut and the island?"

"You want to pack it all in? Seriously?"

"Sometimes. I'm afraid of losing my shit again, Quinn, of not managing to keep my head above water." She smiled. "I spoke to my dad the other day and he told me to get over to their place for a month of meditation."

"Well, that sounds good. A month in California at this time of year. You could hit the beach when you aren't meditating," Quinn suggested.

"It would make a cool honeymoon," Dove said.

He smiled. "You've talked me into it."

"Then you'd have access to my parents in their natural habitat, and I'm not sure you're ready for the seventies throwback clothes, the incense sticks and the back-to-nature living."

"No tech?"

"None. We lived with six other families in the commune, and although we ran a bit wild with the other kids, they were strict about tech. No TV, no magazines, no plastic toys." Dove rarely spoke about her unconventional childhood. People usually got the wrong idea, conflating her experiences with those of cults or dodgy communes led by egomaniacs.

"Sounds kind of peaceful."

"It really was. Of course we rebelled as teenagers, which coincided with my dad being asked to host a retreat over here in the UK. My parents worked over here for twelve years before the farm was sold and they moved back home."

They got the bill and started walking back to the B & B, hand in hand, the mellow spring air deceptively warm in the fold of the hill.

"I can ask around a bit if you want, as I'm going to be here all week now," Quinn said. "About the names, about Alex . . ."

"Don't ask about Alex or they'll think you're a journalist or something. In fact, I know you want to help, but it would be better to just leave it to the police. I'll drop in and see Isabel and Joseph on my way back tomorrow, but they seemed pretty genuine when they said they didn't know anything."

* * *

Truro was only half an hour's drive, and a small detour on her way home. The cathedral city was bathed in shadows by the time she parked outside Alex's parents' house.

Dove pushed her way past tubs overflowing with spring flowers into the stone porch, ringing the bell with a shaky hand.

"Dove!" Isabel was wary, and rolled her eyes at Dove's explanation of having had a quick break to recharge her batteries. Dove had always liked Alex's parents, but now the horror she felt at her brother-law's involvement with Peter Hayworth, with the world of sexual abuse, stuck like tar in her throat. "Come in . . ."

Dove followed her into the living room, talking as she went, "Isabel, I'll be straight with you. I'm sure you're as shocked we are by Eden's statement, and Alex's arrest, but I was telling the truth when I said we're trying to rule things out."

The older woman swung round and stared at her, her hazel eyes half-hidden by wrinkles, curly grey hair wild around her shoulders.

"I just can't believe it. I think perhaps Eden was mistaken. It was dark, wasn't it? She could easily have been wrong . . ." Her voice, with its soft Cornish accent, trailed off again.

"I don't think she was mistaken. I said I'd be straight with you and that means untangling the past. At the moment, Alex is being investigated for involvement in Eden's disappearance and in Delta's, and the team are looking at the Peter Hayworth case again to see if it was possible Alex had any part in the original Glass Doll murders. It doesn't take a superbrain to work out if there is any evidence, we will link him to the current murders."

"But what if he isn't guilty?" Isabel was crying now. "I just can't believe this is happening. They were so happy, he and Ren and the girls. We didn't want him to marry Ren to start with. No offence, but you girls had an unusual upbringing and your dad didn't seem to like Alex at all."

"No offence taken, and you're right." Dove was thinking of Starr's most recent email. He would never have said *"told you so"*, but the implication was there. He always said Alex had an aura of evil about him. She had dismissed it as more of her dad's hippie rubbish, but he and Gaia had never liked Alex, it was true.

"I still don't see how I can help, Dove. The local police had been round, and I've had trouble from journalists. It's been worse than when Eden was . . . when Eden disappeared," Isabel corrected herself.

"Was Alex adopted?"

"What do you mean?"

"It's just a question I need answering. Was he?"

"I . . . Yes, he was. Didn't you know? We were told we could never have children, but then Louise finally came along, and we wanted another. This time it didn't work out, so we adopted Alex when he was ten."

"He obviously knew about his past, where he came from?" Dove probed, wondering why he had never told any of this to Ren. She realized she had covered her stomach with one hand and moved it to the arm of the upholstered chair instead.

"Of course. But he always said he was so happy with us, he never wanted to think of the past. His biological mother was a teenager when she had him, and an addict, we were told. Social services took him away for his own good." Her eyes clouded. "The care home he ended up in, Marston House, it wasn't the best place. There were allegations of . . ."

"Child abuse?"

"Yes," she whispered. "We were happy to take an older child and Alex was such a lovely little boy."

"He never told Ren about the adoption."

"No? Well, it was past history, wasn't it? I see what you're getting at. You think he may have suffered and grown up to make others suffer. But he never showed any indication of having any problems. Never. Louise loved him from the moment he arrived. Still does, and she will never believe he was in any way responsible for Eden's disappearance, or anything else. She came to idolize him, and I was happy. He was the charming, sociable one, but he always took Louise along with him, brought her out of her shell."

"Did Alex ever talk about his friends at the care home?"

"Never. Once he settled in with us, he went to the new primary school and was very popular. There was a constant stream of friends in through the front door from his first day, right through until he left home."

"I know I asked this already, but are you sure he never mentioned a Peter or a Philip that you can remember? Pete or Phil, maybe?"

She frowned, tanned brow creasing, and shook her head. "He may have done. I don't recall any one of those names, but as I say, he has always been popular."

The opposite of Peter, who had been a loner. What had happened to Philip, the dead man in the shack, Eden's captor and abuser? Had the boys somehow kept in touch? And were they really brothers, as Eden suggested, or was it just a figure of speech?

"Thanks, Isabel, and if you see Louise, maybe you can see if she remembers anything else that might help?"

"I don't think she'll talk to you, because she doesn't like the police," Isabel said.

On impulse, Dove scribbled down Quinn's number. "Well, I'm not part of the case anymore because of family involvement, so you can tell her that, if it helps. My boyfriend's down here for a week's holiday, so if you or Louise want to talk and can't get hold of me, you can pass a message through Quinn."

* * *

The coastline stretched before her, lights strung out along the towns, but the shadows of the moors were looming in darkness as the sun went down. It was a long way home, but she enjoyed driving, and spent most of the five hours back to Lymington-on-Sea trying to piece together Alex's past. It was like meeting a complete stranger.

To a certain extent, Dove too was a loner, but she was happy with a small circle of friends and her sisters. She could picture Alex as the Pied Piper at school, his cheeky face, tousled blond hair, and broad shoulders, combining with a charming personality.

What about Louise, his adoptive sister? She had never been friendly towards Dove and her sisters, keeping her own company, working as a potter in her studio out on the moors. She had never married, and although Alex would go off to meet up with her when they had stayed down in Cornwall, Dove could only remember meeting her once, at the wedding.

She had been a pretty but sour-faced woman, with the delicate features of her mother and her father's height. Louise had been barely polite to Ren, but she lit up whenever Alex spoke to her.

Just picturing Alex on his wedding day, seeing in her mind's eye the framed photograph Ren had hanging on the wall in the hallway of the happy couple sharing a kiss, made her eyes sting. What had gone wrong?

If there had been something going on behind that cheerful mask, Alex had hidden it so well that even those closest to him had never suspected the evil lurking beneath.

CHAPTER FORTY-NINE

On Tuesday morning, Dove surfaced after the long drive home to find a text from Ren saying Eden would be home by six. The rush of emotion made her sit back on her bed, blinking away tears.

Layla lay on the blanket at the end of the bed, her paws curled neatly underneath her chest. Her yellow eyes were calm and watchful. Eileen from next door had kindly popped over to feed and let her out, and the cat clearly bore no grudges against her owner for her break.

At a loss, Dove stroked the cat for a bit before she made coffee and wandered around her home. Exhausted but buzzing at the same time, she eventually settled down to unpack some more boxes, which were still stacked in her tiny spare room. She had never thought of herself as the type of person who would settle down properly, but she cared about her house to the extent of creating redecorating schemes and garden plots. And wedding dresses. A smile tugged at the corners of her mouth.

Now, in the first home she had ever owned, Dove caught herself wondering if the estate agent had told the truth when she suggested that maybe a genuine period Victorian fireplace hid behind that sixties monstrosity. Idly peeling off more slices of dangling wallpaper from the wall, she became distracted by a box stacked high with memorabilia — photographs, letters, drawings from both her nieces when they were younger, little homemade gifts they had shoved into her hands.

She sifted through the piles to find the most recent treasures. These were on memory sticks, containing photographs and school reports that Ren had proudly shared.

Dove found her laptop and inserted one USB, waiting for the screen to flicker on, before she scrolled through the most recent photographs of Delta.

Some were selfies taken by the girl and sent to her mother, and Dove recognized a few of her friends. She came to the most recent, frowned and enlarged the picture.

Delta was pulling a face next to a blond boy who was laughing at her. In the background was a tree branch, half covering a sign. The blond boy was David Bollington, but where were they?

She struggled with the picture quality. It looked like a primary school sign, but the tree branch was almost obscuring the boarded-up building.

Dove, after a brief search, found out that St Mary's Primary School, in Sonnington, had closed five years ago. A newspaper report showed a photograph of former pupils who'd gathered to mourn the closure on the village school. One of the pupils was David Bollington. Bollo, who had said Delta was safe, and then vanished himself.

Now what should she do? Sonnington was only about half an hour's drive away, and although Delta didn't have her driving license yet, Bollo probably would have. Had the school been searched?

She had time before Eden arrived. She was meeting up with Gaia first, but she had a few hours. Plenty of time to check out her theory. And as she was off the case, she wouldn't be breaking any protocol. Just a quick look . . .

Before she could talk herself out of it, Dove was in the car and turning onto the main road. She looped around

Abberley and Lymington-on-Sea, returning to the coast road further east.

The tiny hamlet of Sonnington was picturesque, with cobblestone cottages and spring flowers lining uncut verges. A little church sat in the middle of a cluster of houses, and opposite, someone was mowing the village green.

She checked the sat nav and parked at the end of the high street, trudging up a long lane covered in green moss and lichen. Overhanging trees made the lane darker, but soon she spotted a low wall topped with iron railings.

St Mary's was encrusted in last year's fallen leaves, the same moss and lichen as the lane, and the windows were boarded up with metal sheeting. Had she been crazy to come here? She glanced around, seeing nobody.

The gate was padlocked, but she swung with ease over the fence, landing with a light thump. She rubbed her grimy hands on her jeans. The school was constructed of the same cobblestones as the rest of the village. Years of disuse had allowed nature to take over. A huge vine grew from the old chimney pots down to a small toilet block and what must have been a sports shed was buried in ivy. A rabbit shot across the playground, making her jump.

"Delta?" she called.

Brambles, just beginning to grow into their spring spines, nipped at her jeans as she began a tour of the site.

"Delta?" Dove spun round as a figure appeared round the corner of the ivy-covered shed. "Hey!"

It was Bollo. She recognized him instantly, and he jumped, staring at her for a split second before he turned and ran.

Keyed up, she ran after him. "It's okay, Bollo, I'm Delta's aunt, and I'm a police officer." She caught up with the boy halfway along the weed-choked football field, grabbing his elbow, yanking him to a halt next to a rusty goal post. "Stop!"

"How did you know to come here?" he asked. He was panting, wide-eyed and afraid.

"You and Delta once took a selfie outside the gates. Where *is* Delta? Is she here?"

"You're Dove." He stared at her, and then nodded. "She was here. She's been hiding out all along, and I've been bringing her food and stuff."

"Why the fuck didn't you say anything?" Dove snapped. "Do you have any idea how worried we've been?"

He said nothing now, just scowled at her.

"All right, I'm sorry," she said. "Can you go and bring her out?"

"She's not here anymore."

"But you just said . . ."

"You get in over here." Bollo led the way around the back. After a moment's hesitation, Dove followed him, past the crumbling toilet block and an ivy-clad shed. One of the tall windows facing the woods had a slight crack in the metal sheet used to keep them safe from intruders.

Bollo gave the sheet a shove and it fell inwards, clanging on the concrete floor. "This is where she was staying, where we both stayed, but when I went out to get some food and water this morning, she'd gone."

Dove glanced out into the woods, which led uphill. "I assume you told her about Alex?" It had been headline news, along with Eden's rescue.

He nodded. "I told her what was happening, and bought some papers back for her to read. I thought she'd go home, now it was safe, now it wasn't all down to her. Eden already told everyone, didn't she?" Bollo glanced up into the woods, and then back towards the leafy lane. "I used to live in this place, went to school here, so I knew she'd be able to stay here."

"But she's left. Something's made her leave again. How did she seem when you talked about Alex, and Eden?" Dove said.

"Shocked, of course. We couldn't believe it about Eden. She already knew about her dad, didn't she? But it was still freaky. She cried a lot. I was trying to persuade her to let me take her home. But she said she needed one more night to get her head around it."

His eyes were wide with worry, and Dove smiled. "I'm sure she won't have gone far. I need to call my boss, though, so we can get a proper search organized."

Bollo nodded, and pulled out a packet of cigarettes, offering one to Dove as she made the call. She shook her head, and he stepped away to light his.

Afterwards, they sat on the fence side by side, and she kept her tone light, trying to get him chatting normally. "How do you know Delta?"

"We both work for Taj. I've known him for years, but Delta's only been with us for a few months. We go to the same college, too, but I'm leaving soon."

"Do you know why she ran away in the first place, Bollo?"

He glanced down at his scuffed trainers and torn jeans, bit his lip and then met her gaze.

"Her mum has been so worried about her, we all have." Dove kept her tone gentle, noting the restless fingers, the way he chewed his lip and glanced sideways at her.

"I know . . . But she made me promise not to say anything."

"Can you tell me what happened before she left home?"

"Okay . . . She went on a meet, with this bloke off one of the chat sites. It was totally normal. Two blokes in a car, which we didn't expect, but we're used to that kind of thing, so we blew them off. Elijah, he works with us but he doesn't do police, said she went all weird afterwards. Next day I saw her and she told me . . ."

Dove waited for him to speak, anticipating the words.

"One of the blokes in the car at the meet was her dad. She said that's why she was doing the whole thing with Tough Justice, to sort of make up for her sister being killed by Peter Hayworth, not to catch her bloody dad, obviously. She felt like she couldn't tell the police, because of her mum losing it again, but she knew she had to . . . She kept saying it was her fault about Eden, and now it would be her fault when she told on her dad . . . She was going to do it, she just needed to get her head round it."

"What about Taj? Did he know what happened, that Delta was safe?"

"Yeah, I had to tell him, but he doesn't trust police, he likes to do things on his own. I've been working for Taj for two years, now. He's a good bloke, and to be honest I enjoy the feeling of getting something on these sick bastards. I do a lot of the hacking for him, getting into locked forums and creating fake profiles for the rest of us."

"But then you caught Alex," Dove said.

"Yeah. I couldn't believe it, and I even said to Delta that maybe she'd made a mistake. But she knew it was him. She was a mess."

"I'm not surprised. It's a horrific thing to discover. But you must also realize you lot are playing with fire. These people you catch and string up on YouTube have everything to lose, and what happens if you get the wrong person?"

"We don't, and it's worth it," he told her. "Taj is smart."

DI Blackman, Lindsey and Steve arrived within half an hour, and Dove introduced Bollo.

"So she's been here all this time?" DI Blackman asked the boy, who nodded.

"At least we know she's probably okay," Lindsey added.

A search team fanned out across the woods, calling Delta's name. After an hour, the clouds had banked up over the hill and a chill wind was blowing. Dove was shivering, constantly checking her phone, listening to the radios, but so far, there was no sign of Delta. The abandoned school had become a thing of menace, and the flashing lights of the vehicles lit up the village in eerie blue and white.

Bystanders were gathering outside the church further down the hill, prevented from approaching by the fluttering police tape and several uniformed officers.

Common sense told her that Delta was fine. She had been safe all along, but that thread of fear still held on to her, wrapping its way around her throat. What if one of Alex's contacts had been sent to find her?

If she believed, she would have prayed, but instead she held onto her own faith, taught from childhood. That the ebb and flow of the world meant that sometimes the lost became the found. Her dad's words came back to her, his gentle arm across her shoulders, sitting in the darkness under a thousand stars as he talked about energy and light.

Ren would be stretched out on a blanket in the sand, taking it all in, wide-eyed and awed at her father's wisdom. Gaia would be cross-legged and carving a piece of wood, furiously slicing and dicing until a beautiful animal form appeared. At eleven, Dove had already begun to rebel against their unconventional lifestyle, and she would be sewing a cropped top and miniskirt out of the recycled items in the clothing box.

A shout came down the hill and Dove stepped forward, straining her eyes. The crackle of radios and the ambulance moving forward confirmed her worst fears.

CHAPTER FIFTY

Delta's name rang out across the darkening woods. Dove shivered, pulling her jacket close around her shoulders.

Lindsey listened intently to her radio and then grabbed Dove's arm. "She's safe, Dove. She's bloody alive!"

The two women faced each other, mirroring the relief and triumph the other felt.

"What happened?"

"The terrain is pretty rough out in this area, and with thirty square miles of forest, no wonder we couldn't find her. No phone signal either. She says she was trying to go home, but made a wrong turning, and has been wandering around lost . . ." Lindsey raised an eyebrow.

"Pretty big wrong turning," Dove agreed, but her heart filled with elation. Both girls were safe. She checked her watch. An hour and a half until Eden arrived home. Once again, tears threatened, but she managed to hold it together, and called the boy over to tell him the good news.

"Fuck, if she was all the way up there, the track only leads to the clifftop," Bollo said. His face was lit up with relief. "Thank Christ for that."

"Quite," Dove said. Her own body fizzed with relief and excitement at the thought of reuniting Ren with her two girls.

It was a while before the procession of medics and search team members appeared from the densely packed trees. Delta looked tiny, bundled up in blankets and foil, as she limped along beside them. Her face was pale, and there was a cut on her right cheek.

Dove's voice broke with emotion as she touched her niece's face. "Delta, I'm so, so glad you're safe. Don't worry about anything, okay? We'll sort all this out. Bollo told me what happened."

Bollo leaned over too. "Glad you're okay, you freaked me out running out on me like that." He grinned at her.

She smiled at them both, but tears were running down her face, smearing the mud. "Eden's alive, isn't she?"

"Yes." Dove forced herself to hit it head on, if only to reassure the girl. "And Alex is down at the police station."

"In prison?" she whispered.

"Not yet, but he will be. Now you just get better, and I'll ring your mum. Delta, Eden's coming home tonight, so you'd better make a quick recovery."

"Oh, shit! Really?" Delta wriggled her hands free of her blanket cocoon and snagged Bollo's sleeve with one hand, Dove's with the other. "Thank you."

Bollo winked at her, then turned away, apparently trying to hide any emotion.

Ren was crying down the phone, Dove almost in tears herself at being able to give good news. All the time that Eden had been missing, before they were told she was dead, she had dreamed of making this call, of telling her sister that her daughter was safe. Now she savoured the moment.

There would be time later for Delta to come to terms with Alex's betrayal, but for now, physical safety was enough. Dove thought of Ren's relief when she heard the news, of Eden reunited with her family, and just for a second, almost felt that energy and love that Starr had talked about so long ago, deep in the deserts of California.

It was only when driving home that she remembered she had left her other phone on the counter in her kitchen.

It had never happened in all her years as a handler. But Adrik knew she had only got back last night, and if he needed to call, there was Zak on the other end of the line.

The shock of the day, coupled with the realization of her neglect of her co-handling duty, made her suddenly exhausted.

Back at the house, Layla was now asleep on the sofa, and the phone was where she had left it on the countertop. She checked and was horrified to see a missed call.

No voicemail, and the call had been two hours ago, probably right after she set off for St Mary's. She quickly rang Zak, who didn't pick up, then tried Adrik, but his phone was switched off. What was going on?

"Am I being paranoid, Layla?" she asked the purring cat. "Eden and Delta are safe and Alex is locked up. In another six months or so, he'll be locked up for good, so why am I freaking out?"

Her fingers made trails in the cat's soft silver fur as she sat staring her phones. When her personal phone finally rang, she jumped, knocking her hand on the corner of the coffee table in her haste to answer it.

It was Quinn. "I saw on Twitter that Delta's been found. One of the news channels is doing live updates from St Mary's."

"Jesus, how do they get this stuff so quickly? I've only just got home." She told him about the selfie leading her to Delta's hideout.

"Smart. I thought you were off the case on unofficial leave, though? Bet your boss was thrilled to hear you were still knee-deep in everything." There was laughter in his voice.

"He doesn't know me very well yet, but he was fine about it. He's a good bloke, better than Chris ever was."

"Chris was a tosser. But anyway, I've got some news for you, but you probably don't need it now. I've been doing some detective work of my own, in between drinking beer and hitting the surf."

"Bloody hell, you're in the wrong emergency service. Go on."

"Funny. Anyway, I was talking to this old bloke. He's a potter, knows Louise, the sister, a bit, and he's been here years. He reckons that the kids from the care home used to go down that bit of beach and play."

"The care home?"

"He said it was a kind of orphanage that the local social services used for kids waiting to be adopted, so it became a care home. Marston Place."

"Marston Place? Yes, Isabel mentioned it."

"This bloke remembers that there was a kid from the care home who used to cause a bit of trouble locally, small fires and thieving. His name was Philip." His voice was quick with interest.

"Would this old bloke talk to the police?"

"Yeah, he said he would. I've got his number for you to pass on. I wasn't even really digging, it just happened to come up in conversation when we were at the bar."

Dove updated DI Blackman, who said he would get local police to visit the man, and reminded her she was on leave.

"Oh, and just to keep you informed, we already have an ongoing investigation down in Cornwall, as officers paid a visit to both the parents and the sister yesterday."

"Oh?"

"Yes. It seems Louise Matthews was involved with Philip Ashley until his move up north with Eden. She also seems to have played an active part in the paedophile ring, collating information and so on. She has admitted it, but claims it was all down to Philip and Peter, that she and Alex were drawn in simply because they had all been friends."

"Pathetic," Dove said. "With friends like that, who'd need enemies?"

"Yes. It's all finally coming together. I don't mind telling you I could do with a break myself after this. Perhaps I should take up surfing?"

She ended the call to her boss, imagining Eden travelling back home with her baby. Dove smiled at a text from Ren.

Both my baby girls are coming home. You and Gaia are welcome to come see us as planned xx

Still nothing from Zak or Adrik. She tried both again, and dithered over ringing Chris. No, she was reading too much into this. Instead, Dove switched on her computer. There were records of three care homes in the area during the seventies and eighties. All three were now closed down. Reports supported what Isabel had said about Marston Place suffering apparently unproven allegations of child abuse.

Was Alex really also responsible for the current Glass Doll murders? Certainly, no more had been committed since his arrest. Philip was dead, Peter was dead. Was there another member of the gang?

Louise, of course. Louise, who had actively protected all three men, who had by proxy involved herself in a web of lies and abuse. The Alex worshipper who might well have been swayed by anyone who said they were helping the trio, or who had similar tendencies. She must have got in deeper, met other members of the group online, and done it to impress Alex.

Louise, although tall and athletic, surely wouldn't be strong enough to haul the glass coffins around . . . Shit! Could she have come up and helped with the murders? As Dove scrolled through Louise's pottery website, she saw the page of links to affiliated businesses. The very first one was to a glassmaker in Lymington-on-Sea.

CHAPTER FIFTY-ONE

Dove emailed the links to Steve and shut down the computer. Her fiancé would be on his way home soon, and her first case with MCT was done. So what now?

In the end, she had chosen her family over work, had even managed to choose herself over work with the weekend in Cornwall. The two things that she'd consistently failed to do, and exactly what she was trying to achieve now — the elusive balance between work and life.

The all-consuming immersion of being a source handler, of constantly splitting her personality between three separate identities, had caused her to shut out everything but her job. Previously, when her work phone rang, she'd answered it, not caring if it was Christmas Day, or her sister's birthday, or if she was out with Quinn. To gain the absolute trust of her CHIS, she'd devoted her life to living in their worlds. But her fierce and passionate approach to work had cost her her mental health.

The sleepless nights, the highs and triumphs as she saw cases solved, knowing she and her CHIS had provided that vital evidence or that all-important tip-off, had tipped the balance until she was a hybrid half-creature. She had lost her true self in all the legends and identities. Her therapist had asked her many times, *"Who is Dove Milson?"*

Terrifyingly, to begin with she'd had no idea, but now she felt she was grounded. It was now a case of keeping her soul anchored in reality, and letting work stay at work. Simple. She almost laughed. It would be a constant fight, if she stayed in the police force.

"But do you know what, Layla? Even if I am turning into a mad cat lady, I think we're winning. And my surname won't be Milson for much longer. How funny is that?"

Layla purred approval, washing her whiskers with an immaculate paw, as Zak finally called back.

"Sorry, I was tied up with one of my other CHIS. Good result, though."

"Did Adrik call you?"

"He did. He said he'd tried you but you weren't picking up. He went off on one about that, so I told him to deal with it, as soon you wouldn't be there at all, it would be me one hundred per cent of the time."

"Zak! For fuck's sake, I thought we talked about this. I was going to wean him off gently, not cast him aside like a bit of unwanted rubbish."

"Calm down, he was fine about it. Said you'd been straight with him from the beginning and this was what he'd expected. Chris and I discussed this when you were off chilling on the beach, that the cut needed to come soon, and it seemed like perfect timing."

She was seething. "But I needed to do the cutting, that's all I'm saying. What did he want, anyway?"

There was a pause. "He said he was just checking in, and I know you mentioned he was one of those that liked a bit of a chat to touch base. See? No issues, so I don't know why you're so fired up."

"As long as he's okay with that," Dove said. She ended the call. Was she just being a dog in the manger, wanting to hold on to part of her old life, propping herself up, enjoying the feeling of being needed by someone like Adrik? Did she have deeper feelings for him?

Horrified at the thought, she decided it was none of those things. She simply wanted to make peace with her past. Surely there was no crime in that.

CHAPTER FIFTY-TWO

Dove watched as a slight figure slid awkwardly out of the car. Ren and Delta, who was balanced awkwardly on a pair of crutches, engulfed her in a hug that seemed to last forever. The girl who had been Eden was gone, but the woman who stood in her place held her head high. Her long hair streamed down her back and her chin was up in a gesture of defiance.

This wasn't a beaten, cowed person, but someone who, against the odds, had made it through years of suffering and had emerged triumphant. Eden turned back to the car, lifting her son from the seat.

His black hair also lifted in the spring breeze, mingling with his mother's.

Gaia smiled, her eyes wet. "Shall we go down and say hallo?"

The two women were sitting on the bonnet of Dove's car, a little way up the road, hidden from view, having agreed that the first reunion should be between mother and daughters.

"Let's give them a bit longer . . . Why don't we grab that coffee? We can go across the park, and then we're only five minutes away." Dove rubbed her own eyes on her sleeve, feeling her own grin plastered across her face.

"Sure. So have you heard any more about Alex?"

Dove shrugged as they walked in the evening sunshine. "It'll be ages until it goes to court. Now the CPS have agreed to take it forward, we'll spend a few months gathering evidence and getting it all organized. It feels odd not being involved, but anything I do could be used to try and discredit our case by his legal team. There's no more to it."

"Fucking bastard. I *still* can't get over it. He was family, and we're not stupid, are we?"

"He was family, so we never considered him as anything but our brother-in-law. Don't forget he was interviewed when Eden went missing, and that turned up fuck-all. He had alibis, and it looks like he's been playing this game for a long time. Alex was clever, very clever, but it's over now."

They stopped at the kiosk to buy drinks, wandering along the loop that took them around the edge of the park, passing the church and the grocery store with its lush display of fruit and vegetables.

"But he won't admit to being part of Peter Hayworth's murders?"

"No. It makes sense that he would at least know who is responsible for Agnes's and Evie's deaths, but at the moment he's not talking. The only thing we can do is link him, via Eden's statement, to Hayworth. But as Hayworth is dead, we'll never know the extent of Alex's involvement, anyway. The best evidence is from Louise, Alex's sister, because she knew all three men. But as two are now dead, I'm sure Alex will be trying to pin as much on them as he possibly can." Dove ran a hand through her ponytail, shaking out the tangled strands of hair. "It's so bloody frustrating because I want him nailed for the recent murders, if he did them."

"If he did them? You're starting to doubt what's right in front of you."

Dove ignored this, "What about you? What will happen with the club?"

"I've reopened now. I'm keeping the extra security, but I've been reassuring the staff that Alex has been arrested and now we should be safe. Takings will be down for a bit, but people like Uri will also prop me up." She grinned at her sister, a spice of mischief in her voice. "Don't look like that, he isn't a drugs baron, he's a broker. I did him a favour once, stood up for him, and he got his daughter back in a custody case. He takes these things seriously, and sees himself in my debt."

"And there was me thinking you were hard as nails, when really it's just an act," Dove laughed at her.

In her bag, Dove's CHIS phone buzzed with a call and she glanced at Gaia, who nodded. "Adrik?"

"Yeah."

"How's it going? Sorry I missed your call."

"Yeah."

"Adrik? Talk to me."

There was silence for a moment, and then his voice came back, taut and angry. "Tommy's dead."

"Fuck. How? When?" She caught Gaia's sharp glance, and bit her lip.

"Early this morning. I found his body. He went over and picked a fight with one of my uncles, they rowed, and he stabbed him. Don't think he meant to kill him, but he's always been trouble, hasn't he?"

"I'm so sorry." Dove knew that was totally inadequate, but what else could she say? She knew how hard Adrik had tried to keep his younger brother's temper in check, how much his family meant to him.

"He's got a kid too, and his girl is with Aleesha crying her eyes out."

"If I can do anything . . ."

"You can't, I just wanted to let you know. Anyway, what do you care? According to Jack, you're cutting me loose."

Cursing her co-handler, Dove tried to reassure him. "We knew that co-handling wouldn't work in the long-term, but no, I'm not going to suddenly stop taking your calls, especially not at a time like this, okay?"

"All right. Got to go, Kelly."

She waited for him to end the call, and then turned to Gaia. "Fuck! Ever felt like you've just screwed up?"

"All the time. What's happened?"

She was so upset that she told her the whole story, which took them almost back to the park gates again. Zak thought he could do the job better than her, but she knew how stubborn Adrik was, and how hurt he would be by this latest bereavement. He had taken so much shit during his life. Now he finally seemed happy with Aleesha and baby Josiah, this had to happen.

"So this guy, Adrik, he's like a long-time contact, a friend almost?"

"Yes, I knew that once this was over, I was going to have to tell him to let go, to move over to Zak and not contact me anymore. It's not like we can be proper mates. There is no crossover for an ex-handler and a CHIS, it just doesn't happen."

"Sounds like some of my business contacts from before," Gaia commented. "You can't make the two worlds gel, because I tried and got burned. It's got to be: you're in his world, or he's in yours, and from what you say, he's not going to be able to get out, go straight."

"No, it wouldn't work. I really just wanted to tie it up properly this time," Dove explained.

"Happy endings all round? That's a myth, girl, and you know it. But it's good that you care, good that you don't just see these people the way your colleague does. It's not a bad thing to care. It just depends how much, because it sounds to me like you are going to have to end this sooner than maybe you thought." Gaia peered at her sister.

"Let's go round to Ren's," Dove said. She scrunched her coffee cup and chucked it in the bin. It fell with a hollow clang. She marched ahead, striding out the gate, trying to process her feelings.

Frustration, so familiar it made her heart pound faster, clenched at her gut. She'd been there before, had become so involved in the legends she created that she had forgotten

266

real life. The stonemason abduction had been the last in a line of near misses, and her mind had imploded out of sheer instinct to survive.

Now she was in danger of tearing apart the reconnections she had made, the first green shoots of a normal life. Being distraught at not answering *that* phone was the start of a slippery slope.

Again. It was happening again.

She sighed and picked up the phone again.

"Dove, what can I do for you?" Zak sounded harassed.

She filled him in and he tutted with annoyance. "Fucking unreliable CHIS. I'm not being funny, but who cares if his brother is dead? I wonder how much you are enjoying the fact he prefers talking to you . . ."

"It's not a competition, you dick. He is just more used to me. This is major. His brother is dead."

"You're just going to use it as another excuse to keep hanging on. I'm going to have to go to Chris with this, because you really can't seem to let go."

She bit back her angry reply, and killed the call. Adrik was right, Zak was a wanker. But there was often a bit of attitude between fellow officers, everyone doing things their own way. Some, despite the way things had progressed, still didn't like a woman being successful or in charge of anything important.

One former colleague had expressed the opinion that women handlers usually used sex, or the promise of it, as a trade-off for the information. Dove felt that officer had deserved a kick in the balls, and she was beginning to feel the same way about Zak.

CHAPTER FIFTY-THREE

Ren opened the door slowly, cautiously, but beamed when she saw her sisters. "Sorry, I've had trouble with the press all day. They're driving me mad. You didn't have to leave us. You know you would have been welcome when they arrived."

The normally clean and tidy house was strewn with boxes, shopping bags and the washing up was still in the sink. But in the living room, with the curtains tightly shut, the two girls sat curled together under a blanket, arms looped around each other. A tray of biscuits and tea sat on the coffee table, and the TV was showing some reality programme with the sound turned down low.

"We won't stay long, because it must be so weird and wonderful for you, but we just wanted to say how glad we are that you're both safe and well," Dove told the pair.

Ren was sniffing again, smiling though her tears. "I still can't believe they're okay. I feel like I'm going to wake up at any moment."

"Sorry, Mum," Delta muttered. She had a bruise on her face, and looked pale and exhausted.

"Darling, it's okay. I understand why you ran away, but he's gone now." Ren's face tightened, and her mouth trembled. "He'll never be able to hurt anyone again."

Eden smiled at her aunts. "It feels like it isn't real, some-how. I keep having to check on Elan to make sure he's still there, and he wasn't a dream as well."

Dove smiled at the little boy sprawled under a blanket on the end of the sofa. "You are amazing, both of you, and I can't wait to meet Elan when he wakes up. Don't disturb him now, though."

"You look just the same, you know, Eden. Just stronger," Gaia told her niece fiercely, and the girl nodded, her dark blue eyes enormous in her thin face, dark hair limp and strag-gling on her skinny shoulders.

"All the time, I wanted to die, was looking for ways to kill myself, but there was some part of me that wouldn't give in. Then I had Elan and I knew I'd never give in. It happened on my birthday, did I tell you? My birthday miracle was that I got out of hell."

Dove felt her own eyes smarting with tears, and wiped them with the back of her hand. Ren was watching her daughter with pride, cheeks wet, smile wide. There could be no doubt that the abuse she had suffered would have taken its toll, but it was encouraging that Eden could talk about it, was finding little positives within herself.

Delta was subdued, clinging to Eden's hand, her own dark hair tied back in a plait, making her look younger than her eighteen years. "Did you have more news on Da . . . on Alex?"

"Nothing new, but he will be charged for the offences we have evidence for," Dove said. Now was not the time to reveal just how long that list of offences was likely to be.

"Did you find out what happened to the other girls? The ones who were taken with me?" Eden asked.

Dove was aware of all eyes on her. She was unable to tell them that there had been so many girls, so many missing teenagers who had just vanished, that they had so far been unable to trace the girls from the industrial site.

"I'm not allowed to be part of the case anymore. I know my boss is trying to find out what happened to them, but it will take time to collate all the data. I promise I'll let you know when I hear anything."

Eden nodded, apparently satisfied, but her eyes held a faraway look, as though she was lost in her memories. One hand gently stroked the little boy's downy hair.

The sisters parted, with Gaia heading back to the club to get her paperwork done and Dove home for dinner.

Quinn sent a text saying he was looking forward to seeing her when he got back, and Dove smiled, twisting her ring around her finger. She wandered into her living room, imagining Quinn living with her in the house, his processions scattered around. It felt good.

Her phone pinged with a photo from Ren. Both girls fast asleep on the sofa, the baby cradled between them. All the pretty girls. Safe. Back in the kitchen, she turned on her tablet and switched to the local news station, propping the device against the kettle. The name caught her attention as she emptied a can of soup into a bowl, ready for the microwave.

"We're getting reports of a building fire at California Dreams on Denne Road. First responders are on the scene and police are advising drivers to avoid the area. Several local residents and businesses are being evacuated . . ."

There was no answer from Gaia's phone and she couldn't call Ren, not to deliver more bad news. Would Gaia have finished her paperwork and left by now? Upstairs in the flat, though, wasn't that worse?

Her phone rang and she grabbed it. "Steve?"

"Your sister's club is on fire. I don't know the details, but I wanted to make sure you knew. Is she at home?" His voice was sharp but steady.

"Her flat is above the club, and I think she should be at home. I'm coming down . . ."

By five to ten, Dove was outside Gaia's club, choking on the gusts of thick black smoke, staring at the towering inferno, the snakes of hissing fire that lashed at the building.

If Gaia was in there, she was dead. Had they been wrong about Alex? Was there someone else involved, targeting Gaia?

Her phone rang and she almost sobbed with relief as Gaia's number flashed up on the screen. "Where are you?"

"Outside my club, at the south end of Denne Road — I'm fine."

"Thank God for that! I'm at the north end. Shit, Gaia, I saw it on the news and then you didn't answer your phone, so I just came straight over. Are you all right?"

Her sister assured her she was. "I had just been locking up when the club exploded into flames. I've got a few cuts and bruises, because the force of the explosion knocked me right over, and they tried to make me sit in the ambulance for a bit."

"Oh, Gaia! Wait where you are and I'll get out of this crowd and go round the long way and meet you."

Dove started to inch her way out of the crowd. She was jostled and shoved as people shouted information to those further back, or held their phones up to snap pictures of the desolate scene. Her car was right at the end of the road, behind the police tape, also surrounded by people. The fire service appeared to be winning, as the bright orange and yellow began to dull to sullen black. The smell of smoke and burning drifted in the breeze.

Dove dodged into an alleyway to get past a group of gawping lads, and ran straight into a man. A familiar man.

"Sorry . . . Adrik? What the fuck are you doing here? Are you all right?"

His eyes were bloodshot, and his usual swagger was missing.

He shrugged. "I heard about the fire, and came for a walk."

"Really?" Dove said. Her T-shirt was sticking to her back with sweat, partly from exertion, partly from the stress of the evening. "Bit of a long walk, all the way down here. If you wanted to meet, you only had to say."

"I've been staying with a friend down this way. Couldn't go home because half my family keeps coming round asking why I couldn't keep the kid out of trouble."

"Tommy was your brother, not your son," Dove said. She suddenly hoped Adrik hadn't set fire to the club. His expression was distant and he seemed to sway a little as he stood in front of her. "What about Aleesha and Josiah?"

"They're fine. They're with Aleesha's sister."

The crowd had swelled and the noise meant nobody was listening to their conversation, or even noticed them on the outskirts of the main group. Hungry for action, their focus was on the fire.

"Come on, I'll drive you back to your friend's place. Where is it?" Dove asked. "Adrik?"

"Sorry. Yeah, that would be good. He lives up near the antiques market in the square." He dropped his sports bag on the ground, where it landed with a thump against some blue recycling bins, and started rummaging for something. "I've got the address on my phone, hang on . . ."

"Let's go then, you can find it in the car. And, Adrik, I'm sorry about what Jack said to you. More for the way he said it. I'm not going to just ditch you, we'll work something out."

"No problem, I overreacted. You got a life too, right? I really do care about you, though." He straightened up, phone in hand, his dark eyes intense and gleaming like glass.

Unnerved, Dove turned away. "I know. Come on, let's get out of here."

The burst of flames from the recycling bin made her spin around. "What the fuck?"

The whole line of bins was on fire, flames stretching up the walls of the business opposite. The crowd screamed and the surge of panic swept people along the road, some falling as they scrambled away from the alleyway.

She turned to run, to join the tide of people, pulling Adrik with her to safety.

Focused on the immediate danger, she hardly felt the needle plunge into her arm, until she felt herself falling. She

272

was aware, but could do nothing to save herself as he lifted her through the crowd, reassuring others that she would be okay. He carried her along the road to her car, as the fire crews began to arrive at the new scene in the alleyway.

The flash of blue lights, the screams and shoves of the crowd all registered, but she couldn't call out, couldn't move. Only her eyes moved, terrified, as he lifted her into the back of her car. Paralysed, within shouting distance of her colleagues, she could do nothing. Every word she tried to utter came out as jumbled nonsense. Her breath was ragged with terror. She gasped for air, trying to draw in as much as she could, certain he had given her an overdose of crack or something.

Adrik covered her with a blanket, fussing over her, blending with the thronging masses. Mistaking her for a casualty of the crowd, a woman asked if she needed help. Dove could hear his voice, steady and reassuring, as he explained that his girlfriend was fine, had just felt a bit faint . . . He would take her home and she would be okay, he said.

CHAPTER FIFTY-FOUR

Her eyes flickered, mouth twitching as she woke. Nightmares of fire and darkness still spun around her brain. Fully conscious now, a jolt of recognition slammed through her body. It was real. Adrik had abducted her.

She was lying on her back in the semi-darkness. The room seemed to be a basement of some kind, with steps leading upwards to a shut door. Grilled windows stretched along one side, showing only blackness, so she assumed it was still night.

"Adrik? Is anyone there?" Her mind rattled through the evening. She had heard about the fire from Steve. He would have known she was likely to get over there. CCTV would catch the moment Adrik drugged her. She rubbed her arm thoughtfully, trying to process events in a logical fashion, to drive out the terror that threatened to engulf her.

Gaia! Thank God her sister was safe. With her common-sense attitude to everything, she would have installed a top-of-the-line sprinkler system and fire alarms beyond whatever regulations called for. She was safe and the fire had been a front. When Adrik bent down to rummage in his bag, he must have inserted an explosive device under the bins, sending them all up in flames, which meant he would have had no trouble setting fire to Gaia's club. But why?

She wriggled upright. No ropes or ties restrained her, but her body still felt weak from the drugs hit. She was so thirsty. Her phone was gone, and her wallet, but she was still fully clothed.

The door at the top of the stairs was locked. The room had an airless feel about it, despite a spinning ceiling fan and a couple of vents. It was cool but not cold.

There was a simple bed, a basic washroom with toilet and a large table bang in the middle of the room. Too large. It was covered with scratches and stains. Dove shivered as she trailed her fingertips across the rough wood. The sense of evil and foreboding increased in the cell-like, claustrophobic room.

The window was useless but she tried anyway, shaking at the rusting bars, yelling until her voice grew cracked and hoarse. She thought she might be able to hear waves from the sea, and the taste of salt in the air struggling into the room through the bars of two small ventilation grills.

By the time morning slipped pale fingers through those same bars, she was lying exhausted on the narrow bed. Eager to see if she could catch a glimpse of where she might be being held, she rolled off the bed and peered out.

Shit! She could just make out the chalky edge of a cliff. Below she could hear the sea pounding onto towering ramparts. She must be much further along the coast — this kind of coastal spectacle didn't start until you got past Beddingham. Dove searched her mind for the area, but she wasn't familiar enough with the west side of the county. Not a house, unless it was a mansion, but perhaps somewhere industrial . . . She searched the room again for clues, but found nothing. It had been intentionally scoured clean of any history. This in itself made her skin crawl. Who else had been held down here?

She heard a footstep at the door and tensed. Should she call out? Was it Adrik? If she shouted, it would alert her captor to the fact she was awake. But in her weakened state, she wasn't sure she could rely on her usual physical strength to fight her way out. Adrik was well built and muscular. Even at full fitness she wouldn't stand a chance.

"Hallo?"

There was no answer, but she had a sense of someone standing, listening. Then there was a clicking sound, and another, like a plastic box being closed.

Dove inched up the stairs. "Hallo? Adrik, is that you?"

He was still there, but she was starting to feel dizzy, woozy. There was a sweet smell to the salty air now, and she inhaled deeply without thinking. She sank to sit on the stone steps, smiling stupidly at the door. She felt drunk, relaxed and dreamy.

The tiny spark of terror that fired up deep inside wasn't enough to keep her awake, and when the door opened, she smiled at the figure who descended the steps.

He smiled back, and lifted her into his arms.

Dove opened her mouth to speak but the words fell uselessly, like a scattering of pebbles, bouncing away across the concrete floor. It was like being present and awake while under anaesthetic. Dove had once woken up too soon after an op, feeling numb and bruised, horrified to see the surgeon still stitching her up.

Adrik spoke reassuringly, his voice a soft drone buzzing in her ears. He carried her down a long corridor, passing disused wards. Hospital paraphernalia lay abandoned in side rooms. Wheelchairs, beds with rusting bars, operating apparatus, monitors and wires were covered in dust and grime.

A huge spider's web drifted high up on the corniced ceiling. The dust-covered building looked utterly at odds with its previous medical function. He laid her on a table. His hands moved over her, then the sound of something boiling and the smell of glue filled her ears and nostrils. The sharp sting of a needle sent her under again.

She woke back in the cell-like room, sprawled on the bed face up, like an abandoned doll. This time the after-effects of the drug made her vomit, and she didn't make the toilet before she heaved.

Shivering and sweating, she crouched on the floor, trying to steady her breathing. What happened? What did she remember? But her brain was fogged and her limbs unresponsive. Her clothes! They were gone. Instead she was wearing a nightie . . . Her fingers tentatively explored her body. The garment tied at the neck, and she blinked at the rough fabric, trying to focus. Not a nightie, but a hospital gown.

Adrik had fooled her. After all her years of experience, all the training and her own caution, she had been blindsided not only by her own brother-in-law, but now by someone else she had allowed to get a bit too close.

Think, Dove, think . . . You need to get out of here.

There was nothing she could use as a weapon. The room had been carefully prepared. Her legs still felt like they didn't belong to her, so she stayed crouched, taking deep, calming breaths until she felt steadier. The only way out was when Adrik opened the door. The only time he'd open the door would be to take her to her death.

A soft step outside provided her with the notice she needed. She jumped back on the bed before the door opened, feigning weakness and confusion. He walked down the steps, each tread measured and confident.

"Time for you to come with me, Kelly." He was savouring each syllable, his breath quickening as he spoke. "Don't try anything stupid, either. Because we know each other so well, I'm totally up for a bit of play before you die."

She rolled over, blinking at him, trying to control her shivering as adrenalin raced through her bloodstream. The first chance she got would be her last — she would need to take it with everything she had.

"Adrik? What the fuck are you doing?" It came out well — slightly aggressive, confused and very much in character for Kelly. "How could you do this? What about Aleesha and Josiah?"

He might know who she was, but he really only knew Kelly and the legend she had created for him. Names were nothing, not when you considered the personality behind them. Adrik knew Kelly, and therefore she would push him with the bond they had shared, the one he'd kept on and on about, to the extent of guilt-tripping her into not leaving him to Zak after that first meeting. The DC Milson who worked on the MCT was alien to him, and she could use that.

"They're staying with Aleesha's sister, and when this is over, we're going. It's all organized. That last payment from you was enough to get us out of the country. You know what I'm doing, Kelly, you can see for yourself."

"I can't. I've got no clue why you'd do this to me!"

He scowled at her. "Surely you can't be that stupid. You fucked up. Twice, now. This was your last chance, and you blew it. Before, I could see that all that shit freaked you out, so you had to leave the IU, but this time, I thought we'd got something back . . . something strong. Then when I called you about Tommy, you never fucking picked up. You ghosted me!"

Dove pushed herself up onto her elbows and tried to stop her body from shaking, tensing her muscles as she swung her legs around to sit on the edge of the bed. The drugs were making her stomach twist with nausea.

"Adrik, you're reading this all wrong, mate. You know I had my own family stuff going on. I never ghosted you, and I still see us as strong. It's just a misunderstanding."

He shook his head, rubbing his hand over his hair. "You still don't get it, do you?"

"You're right, I don't get it. I've done nothing wrong."

"I know you're trying to jump. That wanker Jack said as much. You aren't with me for the long haul." He smiled grimly. "You're the last doll, and it's going to be perfect. I'll make sure everyone sees you now. The real you." An edge returned to his voice. "I just wanted you back to your proper job, so we could carry on as normal. I knew about Eden, didn't I? I knew how you'd react if there was another Glass Doll murder. It was the best way to get your attention. The best way to get you back with me."

She stared at him, her heart hammering, unable to comprehend what he had just said.

Adrik walked over to her, reached down and touched her face, as she sat frozen. "But now it seems like a good way to go. This is the end of our story, Kelly."

"You killed those girls?"

"Those girls were just sluts from the club. Girls that strip for a living don't count as anything. It was so easy to hook up with them, arrange a date. Once they were in the car, I drugged them up, just like I did you."

"How did you make the glass cases?"

"Easy. Amazing what you can find on the internet these days. I had to do it a few times before I got it right, but this place is perfect — derelict, with lots of space for the materials. I've got a van, and a trolley . . ." He sighed. "I almost enjoyed it, having a plan. You think you know me, but you don't. I'm way smarter than you, and I'll do anything to get what I want. You can't do that, but I can do what I like."

Dove bit her lip, trying to keep up the deep slow breaths, frantically hoping to clear her system of the drugs, to at least give herself a fighting chance. She'd taken her eye off the ball, had been distracted by her personal life.

Adrik was the second Glass Doll murderer and he'd done it to keep her attention. She would never have restarted as co-handler if he hadn't offered her information on Agnes, and would never have continued without him playing the family card, stressing how much he depended on her. Those two young women had lost their lives because of an obsession. It was hard not to beat herself up about this, but she knew that the guilt would come later. *If she survived.*

CHAPTER FIFTY-FIVE

"You don't need to kill me, Adrik. We can work something out. I trusted you . . ."

"That was stupid. You were so smart at times, but then you let stuff get to you. You were too open, and you let me in."

"Fuck that." She let genuine anger break through.

He continued as though she hadn't spoken. "You would never have made contact again just for some fight or a bit of coke. It had to be big and it had to hit you hard in the heart." He thumped his chest. "But I realized after Tommy died, I had been wrong in thinking you were different, that you cared about more than just your job. You're the same as the others. Not worth any more than those club girls or any other copper."

She met his eyes, fighting to re-establish the thread that linked them.

"I'm sorry, so sorry about your brother. You are important to me, but I'm also loyal to my family. Blood ties, you know? And I wasn't ghosting you, I was trying to save my family from being torn apart. The day I didn't answer the phone, I was looking for my niece. I thought she might be in trouble . . ."

For a moment she thought she had him, but then his face clouded with anger again, and he yanked her to her feet.

"Don't talk to me about shit like that. It was a test. You chose them over me."

"My sisters. I had to support my sisters and my niece," she insisted. Her nakedness under the gown was terrifying. As her gaze swept his face, she clocked the open door at the top of the stairs. Not yet.

"You didn't have to do anything. That's what we used to talk about, didn't we? That you don't have to do what people expect, that you can do what you think is right?"

"Adrik, I do care about you, but you know what happened. The one time I didn't answer my phone to you. I've never missed another call, ever, have I?" She was clawing for a mental foothold, shocked that Adrik, who had always seemed so rational, couldn't understand about Delta, about Eden. But then his pain was evident, and his brother — another brother to lose his life in a stabbing — had been his best friend. She had let him down and, in his mind, nothing else mattered.

"Shit happens all the time. I wanted to help you, get you back where you belonged, back to working with me again. But you ruined it. When I *needed* you, you weren't there. I needed to tell you about Tommy, and you didn't want to know. Just another kid getting stabbed, whatever."

He was getting more and more pumped and she didn't want to end it here, so she staggered against him, limp and fainting, jumbling her words.

His physical reactions, as ever, were lightning-fast, and he swept her into his arms. She hung like a rag doll, limbs floppy, head lolling into the crook of his shoulder.

"Kelly? *Dove?*"

Yes, there was definitely a flicker of uncertainty. She stayed limp, feeling the heat of his body warming her muscles, keeping her eyes shut as he carried her across the room and up the stairs.

Daylight flooded the passageway. She could feel it on the backs of her eyelids, remembering the big window at the far end, the stained-glass patterns on the wall . . .

He was muttering to her now. "I don't know if you're faking this, but I'm not going to stop. This is how it's meant to end for you and me . . ."

Now!

She drove a fist up into his jaw, flinging her body into a roll and going down hard on the window side of the passage. Adrik grabbed at her wrists, but Dove seized a chair from the toppling stack and smashed it towards him, separating them.

"Fucking sly bitch! You're ruining it!" He was tossing chairs aside with ease, but she was running, forcing her legs to sprint down the corridor towards the light.

The sun, pouring in through the coloured glass, blinded her, but she snatched up another chair and smashed the window with desperate blows. Glass rained down, and she threw the chair behind her, jumping wildly in the direction of the hole she had made.

Adrik snatched at her, grabbed her right arm, but she was torn from his grasp by the force of her leap. He seized the gown from her body, but she was free. The burst of sea air, the exhilaration of escape lasted only seconds before she realized she was in trouble.

The window led not to gardens or a car park, but straight out to the cliffs. It was a sheer drop of some six metres into the waves below. Dove had no chance to prepare, and fell, trying to swivel her feet down first. The pain of the impact ripped through her side as she hit the water, plunging down into the salty depths.

CHAPTER FIFTY-SIX

Her first instinct was to panic, to flail wildly, to force her way to the surface, but survival training took over.

That cool, calm voice in her head that was at the back of all her training — all the legends she had created, had woven, were essentially her. And she was going to fucking live.

Dove surfaced, gasping for breath, and floated, allowing the waves to carry her further away from her escape route. The sun was in her eyes and the icy water encompassed her naked body, shielding her from further attacks.

Sanity returned, and she scanned the coastline. Unfamiliar, rugged inlets sat between jagged white cliffs. There was a cluster of buildings to her right, including the concrete monstrosity she assumed had been her prison. She eyed it as she floated. It was perched on the side of the cliff, with a scattering of other similarly ugly buildings dotted along the skyline. A huge industrial chimney stack thrust high into the washed-out sky.

The water began to numb her limbs. Dove needed to swim. She started a slow, weary front crawl. Every stroke sent daggers of pain stabbing into her right shoulder. The shock immersion into the sea seemed to have cleansed her of the last after-effects of the drugs, but there was a real danger of hypothermia now.

She swam at an angle to the shore, checking every few minutes that she was on course. The tide seemed to be coming in, which allowed her to take advantage of the ebb and flow of the waves.

Soon, her world was reduced to the taste of salt, the sting of her fresh wounds and her icy, clumsy body. But she kept going with the slow front crawl. One arm after the other, each stroke bringing her closer to land.

She beached onto a stony cove, dragging herself up out of the water, past banks of seaweed, to the sunny shelter of a vast boulder. Her long, shuddering breaths grew quiet and even as the sun heated her freezing body. *I will live.* Dove raised her head, searching the buttresses for a way up. There didn't seem to be any way out, so she slumped, naked and exhausted, on the warm stones, waiting for her body to recover.

With no signs of help, she struggled up onto wobbly legs, exploring this new prison, forcing herself to be alert. She could clamber across the rocks on to the next cove, if she did it quickly. The tide was rising fast, already lapping at the shingle bank where she had collapsed.

The rocks were sharp on her bare feet, but she gathered reserves of strength, thinking about Eden, how she had survived for years, holding on to a tiny thread of sanity, waiting for a chance that might never have come.

The next cove had a steep, winding path that led up between the cliffs. One foot after the other, she hauled her weary body upwards, until she could see a patch of grass. Her leg muscles were agony, and she was on her hands and knees crawling, trying to ignore the shooting pains in her right shoulder.

She emerged at the top, aware she had no idea what had happened to Adrik. Caution, always caution, even though common sense said there was no chance he could have followed her, could not be waiting at the top of the cliff, toying with her, like a spider with a fly.

The grass was a wide, sheep-nibbled stretch of field, giving out onto a road. Dove made her way towards it. Her feet were bleeding and her numerous glass cuts stung and itched as the wind dried the salt on her skin. But part of her revelled in the freedom, the escape. She was alive, and that was what mattered.

In the distance, she could see flashing lights, hear the wail of sirens. She waited, clinging to a footpath sign, fingers clenched on the rough wood, leaning her head against the post.

The first car was followed by another, and further back an ambulance pulled in and waited, blue lights dazzling in the sunshine.

Car doors slammed and she could hear exclamations, sharp conversation and the crackle of radios. A helicopter appeared over the hills.

A man was approaching with a blanket, and she blinked at him, trying to focus, suddenly painfully aware of her naked body.

"Hallo, boss."

EPILOGUE

Dove spent two days in hospital, but miraculously had managed to dodge any major injuries. The glass cuts were superficial, and only a couple needed stitches. Her shoulder muscles were pulled, but the physio assured her that in a couple of months, they would be healed just fine.

Adrik was dead. He had hurled himself after Dove, but had not been so lucky in his landing. He had fallen straight onto a treacherous line of jagged rocks, and had suffered fatal injuries.

"I thought you were dead when I looked at the CCTV and saw him carrying you away," Gaia told her as they sat watching the waves and swooping gulls, their surfboards beside them.

Ren was lighting a fire for the barbecue in a sheltered corner. Eden was standing knee-deep in the water, holding Elan so that the waves tickled his bare toes. They were both laughing. Eden's long black hair was tangled in the breeze, falling over her bare, tanned shoulders.

"Maybe she's got nine lives, like a cat," Delta suggested. She was skewering prawns and mango, shaking flakes of salt and chilli over her dish. "She also goes and does all the really dangerous stuff, but she comes out of it okay."

"Look who's talking. It must be a family trait." Dove shook her head, smiling. "It was a bit of luck and my own bloody-mindedness. I kept thinking about all of you, and how much all of us have suffered in different ways, but we're all still here. No way I was letting the side down." She grinned.

"I'm surprised Quinn didn't come down today."

"He thought we needed some time by ourselves," Dove told her. "Besides, he's busy . . . moving his stuff into my house."

"I'm so happy for you." Ren, coming back with a smudge of charcoal on her cheek, bent down and hugged her.

"It's lucky your boss managed to track you down. As I heard it, they were all going to storm in and rescue you, after that speed camera picked up your car on the A27. The only place you could be was the old hospital. Sounds easy, but you lot had been looking for the place these girls were murdered for ages now," Gaia, said, with a trace of anger. "Poor Agnes and Evie. It pisses me off to think those poor kids were just used to get attention. Such a waste . . ."

"Hiding in plain sight," Dove muttered.

"Were Alex and the rest really brothers?" Delta asked.

Dove sighed. "They weren't blood relatives, but they were together at the care home for four years. The investigation into the alleged abuse didn't reach a satisfactory conclusion but it is possible that any of them may have suffered. That doesn't excuse what they became. I've met so many people who have had the most horrific things happen to them as children and they turn out to be the most generous, bravest, amazing human beings ever."

Eden was back from the sea, her pretty face serious as she gathered her son into a towel, rubbing his hair as he played with a handful of shells.

"How did they stay in touch?"

"Philip met Alex on a school trip, and together they tracked down Peter as they got older. None of them ended up a million miles from each other after adoption. Philip was the oldest by five years, but Alex and Peter were the same age."

"It feels so weird to hear you talking about him like he's a stranger," Delta said.

"He is a stranger," Ren said, her eyes bright. "The other men are dead, so we only have Alex's word that they pressured him into helping them. Well, his and Louise's. He put his family in danger, took Eden from us, and was part of a group who were doing horrendous things. At any time he could have got out, could have told the police what was happening, and he chose not to."

"Maybe he was scared," Eden said. "I can't ever forgive him for what he did to me, and even if he wasn't part of the . . . abuse himself, it doesn't mean it's okay to help others do it."

Dove was thinking of three boys on a windswept beach, swearing eternal friendship as children do, scratching their names on the rock, swimming in the sea. Then returning to Marston House and the footsteps in the night. In a twisted way, perhaps Alex had been convinced he was protecting Eden by sending her away with Philip, and not allowing Peter to kill her. But he could have got out, got away from his "blood brothers" and broken that evil bond.

Unlike the other two, he had looks, charm and a family, but he was weak, and had kept a foot on each side, unable to make the final decision that might have saved so many children from abuse.

The strangest coincidence was that both his daughters had glimpsed the other side of him, had caught him out when he was playing in the darkness. He had nearly destroyed both their lives — and Ren's life too —but Dove knew they would all be okay. They had the strength he lacked, and they also had something she herself lacked — they knew when to ask for help and who to ask.

"Dove! Your phone's ringing!" Ren called. "If it's work, make sure you don't answer it."

She dodged a poke with the salad fork, and fished around inside her rucksack, grabbing the phone just in time. It was a number she recognized, and she didn't hesitate to answer, moving away from the other women, her heart speeding up.

"DC Milson?"

"Hi, Chris. You're not normally so formal."

"I hear you're on leave."

"I am." Her heart was thudding so loudly, it seemed to echo the waves on the beach.

"Listen, I've been thinking that maybe if you get bored on the MCT, you might like to come back to us."

She felt her mouth drop open in surprise. Just when you thought you had things sussed. She cleared her throat. "Chris, you know why I left, and this fuck-up with Adrik must have convinced you I don't belong with the unit."

"It wasn't your fault. If anything, Zak didn't pull his weight, and you could never have predicted what happened. You handled it. You may have bent the rules slightly, but you managed not to break them, despite the intense situation. We've got a new unit opening up in West Hoathly. That's not much further along the coast than you already are, is it?"

"You got funding for a new unit?"

"Yeah. Anyway, I thought you might like to make another move and come back to us, as it were. A few of the Nantich Valley team are moving over."

"Including you?"

"Including me. How do you fancy making a fresh start, Dove?"

Her eyes were on her family. One finger traced the stones of her engagement ring.

She didn't hesitate. "No thanks, Chris, I already did that. And actually, I'm pretty happy just where I am."

THE END

ALSO BY D.E WHITE

RUBY BAKER MYSTERIES
(as Daisy White)

BOOK 1: BEFORE I LEFT
BOOK 2: BEFORE I FOUND YOU
BOOK 3: BEFORE I TRUST YOU

Don't miss the latest D.E. White release,
join our mailing list:
www.joffebooks.com

FREE KINDLE BOOKS

Do you love mysteries, crime fiction and thrillers?

Join 1,000s of readers enjoying great books through our mailing list. You'll get new releases and great deals every week from one of the UK's leading independent publishers.

Join today, and you'll get your first bargain book this month! www.joffebooks.com

Follow us on Facebook, Twitter and Instagram @ joffebooks

Thank you for reading this book. If you enjoyed it please leave feedback on Amazon or Goodreads, and if there is anything we missed or you have a question about, then please get in touch. The author and publishing team appreciate your feedback and time reading this book.

We're very grateful to eagle-eyed readers who take the time to contact us. Please send any errors you find to corrections@joffebooks.com

Printed in Great Britain
by Amazon

39862127R00177